winner of the Miguel Mármol Prize for
a first book-length work of fiction in English
by a Latina/o writer

/ SOY LA AVON LADY
and Other Stories /

by

Lorraine M. López

CURBSTONE PRESS

Printed in the U.S. on acid-free paper by Bang Printing

Cover design: Susan Shapiro
Cover art: Elena Climent, *Corner Cabinet with Objects and Flowers*;
courtesy of Mary-Anne Martin/Fine Art, New York.

This book was published with the support of the
Connecticut Commission on the Arts, the State of
Connecticut Office of Policy and Management, and
donations from many individuals. We offer special
thanks to Rep. David Pudlin and Rep. Walter
Pawelkiewicz.

The publishers are very grateful to Sandra Cisneros for
serving as the judge for the first Miguel Mármol Prize,
and also to Jane Blanshard and Jantje Tielken for their
help in editing and proofing this book.

Library of Congress Cataloging-in-Publication Data

   López, Lorraine, 1956-
   Soy la Avon lady and other stories / by Lorraine López.
   — 1st ed.
    p. cm.
   ISBN 1-880684-86-1 (pbk.)
   1. Mexican Americans—Fiction. I. Title.
   PS3612.O64 S69 2002
   813'.6—dc21   2001007704

Published by
CURBSTONE PRESS
321 Jackson Street • Willimantic, CT 06226
info@curbstone.org • www.curbstone.org

ACKNOWLEDGMENTS

This book could not have been written without the guidance and encouragement of the everchanging—shrinking, expanding, and shrinking again—group of women writers who have read, re-read, and commented kindly and helpfully on these stories through the half dozen years it took to collect them. This group includes Karen McElmurray, Sarah Baker, Courtney Denney, Sheri Joseph, Melissa Crowe, Lauren Cobb, and my dearest friend, Kathryn Locey. Additionally, I extend my heartfelt thanks to James Kilgo, who has been able to read my work and tell me what it is about before I know what I am doing. His interpretations, suggestions, and insights have shaped this work and shaped me as a writer.

Furthermore, this book would not be published if not for the persistent efforts of my mentor Judith Ortiz Cofer, who keeps me apprised of opportunities and suggested I submit the manuscript to Curbstone.

I am also grateful to Sandra Cisneros who selected my manuscript for publication. I have been a great admirer of her work for many, many years, so the fact that she chose my work is a profound honor to me.

And I would like to acknowledge the inspiration provided by my sisters, Debra López, Frances López Whyte, and Sylvia López, and my brother Kenneth López.

Finally, I must thank Louis Siegel, who makes possible that which is wonderful in my life.

I dedicate these stories to the memory of my mother, Diana S. López, who showed me through the example of her life that beauty in a woman consists in equal parts of compassion, intelligence, and strength.

And I dedicate this work to my father, Espiridión López, con respeto y amor.

Contents

Soy la Avon Lady and Other Stories

Sophia

If you are anything like me (and most likely you've had some luck, some mercy shown somewhere and you're not one bit like me—unless, of course, you travel with the circus or are on display in some laboratory) but if you happen to be anything like me, anything at all, you wake up every morning with the same prayer stamped in your heart that is burning on your lips: *Dear Virgin* (because you don't believe in God, never have really, but you don't dare ignore *la virgen*), *Make me skinny! Please, oh, please! And while you're at it, fix this blasted eye!*

So you have two prayers, really. But you try to collapse them into one so you won't seem so greedy, the way you were last night, stealing the last two tortillas out of the bread basket, drizzling them with butter and smuggling them into bed to wolf under the sheets, so your older sister Rita wouldn't see, so Rita wouldn't say something like what about that diet you're supposed to be on, huh? Now, if you're at all like me, you've got these shiny yellow spots of grease all over your pillowcase, which will probably never come out, which will always remind you of your greed, your piggishness. So you throw in an extra part to the usual prayer: *And, Virgin, try to get these grease spots to wash out of the pillowcase, if you can. But, most of all, help me lose some weight and do something about this goddamn eye, Blessed Mother. I beg your intercession!*

Then, being like me, you roll out of bed, rolling a little more literally than you'd like to, and you fumble around on the night stand for your eyepatch and your glasses. The eyepatch, a beige-colored adhesive job cut the size and shape

1

of a campaign button, is a real fashion statement. It's meant to look natural, like a flap of skin that just casually happened to grow over your eye, but it goes with your shock-white face about as well as a splash of cocoa goes on snowy linen. It's about as unnoticeable as an I AM DEFORMED! sticker pasted on your forehead. The only thing worse than wearing the patch is having that wild eye show. Lazy eye, the optometrist, with excessively hairy nostrils, told your father. But you know the truth, that eye is about as lazy as a hummingbird on benzedrine. In fact, the way it jumps, starts and flinches, it feels ready to leap out of its socket and make its way, bouncing like a superball, for the Mexican border. It's the only part of your enormous, slothful body that isn't lazy! It's not a lazy eye; it's a crazy eye. *Dear Virgin, will you please control that eye!* So you pull the plastic backing off the adhesive and stick the patch over the wild eye, then you slip on your glasses.

Now you have begged the Virgin (and your father) for the newer, more attractive "granny-style" wire frames that every self-respecting glasses-wearer owns. After all, this is the seventies, and people—especially fifteen-year-old girls—don't want to look that much like Walter Cronkite any more. But the optometrist with hairy nostrils has vetoed this option, saying your lens is too thick to be supported by delicate, decent-looking frames. While your exposed eye is neither lazy nor insane, it is quite calmly, peaceably, and even legally blind. Requiring glasses as thick as a slice of Texas toast. About the only frames that can hold the lens are a mannish tortoise shell or an industrial strength pink plastic deal studded with rhinestones. The pinks are probably safe for welding in. The horn rims are in the style worn by Clark Kent, the glasses he always tears off his face when it becomes necessary for him to turn into Superman. The very act of ripping those hideous glasses off his face signals his transformation from a worthless frankfurter into the man of steel. You decided you don't especially want to look like Clark

Kent, the wiener, so you've picked the pink plastic, which, with the patch, give you the look of a maniacal secretary for Long John Silver.

"Yo-ho-ho!" your seventeen-year-old brother Cary hails you when you finally force him out of the bathroom. He doesn't dare tease you about your weight because, truth be told, he is even fatter than you are, and though you're two years younger, you can fling weight insults with greater zest than he could ever muster. But, if you're like me, you don't really want to slit open that particular vein of discussion.

So you say, "What do you *do* in there?" You're brother spends half his life in the can, and though you've applied some thought to this mystery, you can't figure out what he's doing the whole time. He doesn't flush, run water, creak the medicine chest open, turn pages of comic books or even pass gas—you know because you've knelt with your ear pressed to the keyhole, and you can hear nothing. "What do you *do* in there anyway?"

Of course, Cary doesn't answer, he just starts singing, "Yo-ho-ho, and a bottle of rum..." Since these are the only words he knows to the pirate ditty, he simply sings them over and over and over. "Yo-ho- ho, and a bottle of rum!"

But you put this out of your head and you try to enjoy your bath, ignoring your older sister who has begun to pound intermittently on the door. If it's urgent enough, she'll bust the door open with a shoulder block and come in to piss while you shave your legs. But when your dad starts yelling, "*Por dios*, hurry up in there," you figure it's time to grab for the baldest, stiffest, and scratchiest towels on earth which your family happens to collect much like other families collect pewter or valuable stamps. You wind yourself in the best and biggest of the lot.

"Sophia!" your dad is screaming, "Sophia Loren, please, *hita*, I gotta go!" And you think what a sour joke it is for your mother to have named you for one of the most gorgeous women to grace the planet. She died (your mother, not Sophia

3

Loren) before you were one, so you never knew her, and you don't miss her. You can't even cry for her, especially not with this patch threatening to curl off with any trace of moisture. But you've always wanted to meet your mother to trade a few words on this subject. Somehow, it's not so bad for your older sisters to be named Bette Davis, Loretta Young, and Rita Hayworth Chacon. Even your brother being called Cary Grant doesn't seem too jarring. But when people hear your name is Sophia Loren, they just have to laugh. You are resolved to change your name to Ethel Bland as soon as you are an adult.

Though the mirror is foggier than ever, you can see that your *huevon* eyepatch is getting limp from the steam of the bath. You press it back in place, but it wilts away from your damp skin, and you know you will need another one before school. You hate wasting them, but it's worse to have Cary or your dad see the eye and look away sharply, pretending not to have seen it at all.

"*Hijolé, muchacha,* I thought you was never coming out," says your father, taking in your towel, your piglet skin, the electrified look of your toweled hair and your rebel eyepatch. He suppresses a smile, but gives in to a snort—a single honk of laughter.

"What's so funny?" you say, imitating Minnie Mouse, so he will have something legitimate, something other than your frightful appearance, to laugh at. "You think I'm funny or just funny-looking?"

Here he laughs long and hard, pushing you out of the way to get in the can.

You roll your eyes, heading for his room, for the small cabbage of bills he leaves on top of his chest of drawers with his penknife, the twelve trillion keys and assorted wads of lint, pencil stubs and crumpled scraps of paper from his pants pockets. You are careful to pluck only one dollar bill from this nest for your lunch, just in case you get hungry at school. You have made up your mind to fast all day, but you never know what they'll serve in the cafeteria. If it's taquitos with guacamole, you're a goner, even though the guacamole is as thin as water and a shade of green not usually found in nature.

On the way to the kitchen, you stop in the laundry room and flick on the iron. You wash your uniform blouse and skirt every night and iron them every morning. Always. You are the neatest, best groomed freak in the world even though you're not sure why you bother. Maybe you're hoping people will be so taken with the razor pleats of your hounds tooth skirt, the glowing whiteness of your blouse that they will completely miss your hideous eyepatch and the several pounds you need to shed. *Are you listening, Virgencita?* That Sophia, some kind of ironer. Wonder what bleach she uses?

But wait, what's that rich buttery smell curling suggestively from the kitchen? Can it be? Yes, Loretta is diabolically and delicately sizzling french toast in a skillet, your favorite food in the world, especially the way she makes it with finely grated orange peel, cinnamon, nutmeg and cream beaten into the egg. Loretta and her cooking are your body's worst enemies. At least with Bette, and her habit of preparing dried-out, unidentifiable meats with blackened potatoes served cold night after night, you had half a chance. Not so with Loretta at the stove. Clearly, you'll have to begin your fast tomorrow.

"You're gonna eat in that?" Cary asks, not very nicely, jutting a thumb at you.

"I'll take it off, baby, if that's what you want. I'll take it all off!" And you begin to hum the striptease song while plucking at the knot of towel between your breasts. Ta-da-da-DUM, ta-da-DA-DUM, DUM, DUM, DUM-DA-dum-dum-dum!

Loretta thinks this is funny as hell. Somehow, she knows how to laugh without smiling. Her pretty mouth just opens and the laughter streams out like a musical ribbon. Cary, of course, fixes his eyes on his plate, turning blister-red clear up to his scalp. "Ta-da-da-DUM, ta-da-DA-DUM, DUM,

DUM, DUM-DA-dum-dum-dum!" You stand, dropping the towel in a puddle at your ankles, and you start shaking and gyrating, wiggling your boobs like a tassel twirler having a seizure. You grab the towel and start swinging it over your head. You think you might hop on the table, but you're not sure it would take your weight, when the towel catches on the light fixture overhead. You interrupt your performance for a brief tug of war with the fixture, which you win when the glass globe comes loose and shatters on the kitchen floor, just missing your head.

"WHAT ARE YOU DOING?" screams your aunt Nilda just opening the back door into the kitchen. Her brown face is bleached with shock. "*VÁLGAME, DIOS,* YOU'RE NAKED AND YOU'RE BREAKING THE LIGHTS! ARE YOU INSANE?"

Now, you and Nilda have a lot in common when it comes to praying. She talks to God at least as often as you call on the Virgin, but she never asks for anything. She just shares her insights on how all the people around her are out of their minds and a real pain in the ass to deal with, then she tells God to value her. *Válgame, dios* is her favorite saying, and literally it's "value me, God," meaning you got to notice I'm surrounded by nuts and *that*, God, has to count for something. But just because you and Nilda are both prayerful people doesn't mean you get along too great. You wrap yourself back in the towel remembering what Bette says about you and Nilda, and that is that Nilda just doesn't "get it" about you. Usually everyone else laughs their head off whenever you open your mouth or just walk into a room—which can be disturbing—but Nilda is almost always immune to your kidding and funny faces.

Never in a million years could you satisfactorily explain to Nilda why you were caught naked breaking the light fixture with a towel. Truth be told, you're not quite sure yourself, but it's not something that upsets you, the way it seems to upset Nilda. But she's calmer now, after a drink of

water and then a plate of french toast—your breakfast—
which she ate while Loretta swept up the mess and you ironed
and put on your uniform, hoping to erase the earlier im-
pression with your superior laundry habits. Nilda sadly takes
your hand and looks into your good eye, which is also a bad
eye. "I guess I'm just in time with this," she says softly,
handing you a flat package you didn't notice when she walked
in.

"What's this?" you ask, thinking it's to do with dieting.
Nilda's a great one for telling you just how fat and terrible
looking you are. Her favorite greeting to you is: "My God,
you're so fat!" She was probably horrified when she saw you
in the raw.

"*Pues*, it's a record, one of those record albums. Go on,
open it up."

You pull off the bag and hold an album with a big-headed
bald priest smiling at a bunch of zombie-like teenagers on
the album cover, which reads: *Father Cochran: The Straight
Dope on the Birds and the Bees*. Great waves of laughter roll
to your throat, but you swallow them back because Nilda is
so wholly and seriously embarrassed.

"It's about the you-know," she whispers, "the facts of
life."

The title alone makes your eyes sting with merry tears.

"Thanks, Tía," you say, humbly, while biting the soft skin
inside of your cheek hard, very hard, so you don't giggle.
"You want to listen to it with me?"

"Oh, no, no, no, no." Nilda shakes her head several times,
saying, "absolutely not. You and la Rita listen together. You
can get some good information, you know what I'm saying?
Good information for teenage girls. You'll find out why a
girl shouldn't fool around naked in the kitchen breaking the
lights, *válgame, dios*."

"Really?" You turn the record around to read the back,
curious to see if there is a relevant track. Disappointed the
tracks aren't listed, you tuck the album under your arm. "I'll

listen to it after school," you promise Nilda, wondering if your friends Rosa and Aracely will be free in the afternoon to come over for a few laughs.

"You listen to it good, and you mind what it says, muchacha," Nilda advises.

Cary laps up the last of the syrup on his plate. "Maybe I oughta listen to it too," he says, reaching with smelly fingers to grab the record.

"No, no," says Nilda, "this is not for boys. This will only give them ideas."

"But I need ideas!" protests Cary, and you can't help thinking, boy, does he ever. He makes a lunge for the album, but Nilda smacks his paws with her sharp little hands. "Yow!" cries Cary, pulling back.

* * *

Now, if you're like me, it's not sufficient for you to have a freakish appearance, but you must also have freakish friends as well. And owing to their grotesque appearances, it doesn't take you two seconds to spot Rosa and Aracely in the crowded schoolyard before first bell. Loretta once mentioned that it was like seeing a Watusi walking with a Pygmy whenever Rosa and Aracely came over to the house. Rosa is at least six feet tall in flats, slightly taller in her uniform regulation saddle oxfords, and Aracely's lucky if she reaches four foot ten in hers. And it's not just size that makes these girls odd. Rosa looks like she could be Frankenstein's sister, not his bride, because her lank black hair hangs flat, like a dull horse's tail. But she could easily be his sister with her greenish olive skin pocked by deep acne scars, pits and blips and boils. If you come upon her suddenly, she could give you a fright, until she opens her mouth, that is, and the whining starts. She's Frankenstein's whiny sister, the one who never made it out of the laboratory because she was so busy complaining about everything. Then there's Aracely, a brown terrier of a girl, who gets so worked up running around and shooting her mouth a mile a minute that she actually does pant with the tip of her pink tongue showing. *A-huh-a-huh-a-huh.*

You know these are not easy friends to be branded with, but with your weight and the eye thing, what can you expect? The three of you blend in with the crowd in the school yard about as well as a trio of circus clowns in a Junior Miss Pageant. *Mother Mary, how about some new friends? Some normal looking people to hang around with? Would that be too much trouble?* This morning, you see Aracely has a new hairstyle or maybe she had some bad luck with her crème rinse. Her short blue-black hair rises shock straight up from her scalp, giving her the look of a startled hedgehog. And Rosa has forgotten to wash her face; yellowish crust is wedged in the corners of both her eyes and her short lashes are dusty.

Still you saunter over and hear them talking about one of their usual subjects—sex. Rosa is whining, "But my *amá* says the only reason to do it is to get babies."

"I'd say that's a sad commentary on your old man," you say, plunging right in.

Aracely starts cracking up so hard she can't get her breath. She pants rabidly before collecting herself to say, "Like you're an expert. You never even got a hickey before." Aracely's one claim to sexual expertise is the fact that Lance Rivera planted a love bite on her during a showing of *Our Man Flint* at Studio One. The story goes that it was so dark in the theater that when he came back from the bathroom, he sat in the wrong row and began kissing Aracely instead of his date, Veronica. When the lights came on at intermission, Lance was horrified to discover his mistake. Many claim he gagged.

"Well," you say, pulling the record out of your book bag where you stuffed it to smuggle out of the house, "I'm not saying I'm the expert, but look what I have here, *The Straight Dope* from Father Cochran."

"What's that?" demands Aracely.

"A sex record," you tell her.

"My *amá* won't let me listen to any sex records," Rosa brays.

This is too stupid to respond to, so you just shake your head. *Virgin, about those friends, could you snap it up?*

"Ooh-ooh," says Aracely, taking the record from you and turning it over as you did to read the back. "When can we listen to it?"

"After school?" you suggest.

"I'll get in trouble," moans Rosa. " I know I will."

"But where?" asks Aracely, panting in excitement. "Where? Where?"

"My *amá* will find out, and she'll tell *apá* and I'll get put on punishment. You and Aracely don't care, but I never get to do anything fun. I'm always on punishment because of you guys."

"Let's go to my house after school. I can use Cary's record player."

"Will Cary be there?" Aracely has a perverted interest in your brother. "Will he?"

"If he is, he'll probably be in the bathroom." Your friend's interest in your brother is exactly equal to his dread of her.

"They'll all be pissed and make me go to confession and then watch my sister's kids the whole weekend. You guys don't ever care if I get in trouble."

At the same time and together, you and Aracely shout: "Shut up, Rosa!"

"Okay, okay, but where are we gonna meet after sixth period?" asks Rosa. "They don't let me walk to Sophia's house alone."

You plan to meet in front of the school by the Chalice Hilyard Memorial Bench—named for the studious lesbian, a junior who was beheaded when a semi jackknifed into her family's Volkswagen Beetle on the way to visit family in Seattle. The bench, shunned by others because of its morbid associations and because some girls are actually stupid enough to believe you can contract lesbianism from a wrought-iron memorial bench, is strategically located under an enormous willow which not only shades you, but allows you to watch the steady parade of bombs, low-riders, and regular family cars cruising the school. From there, you can watch who gets picked up by whom and keep an eye on the after-school action without being seen in the company of your hideous friends.

After first bell, you and your friends head for your separate classes. You head upstairs for College Preparatory English, while Aracely, in Business Careers, trots off for her first-period typing class. *La Pobrecita* Rosa, meanwhile, sinks down to the basement for Manual Arts and Home-making, where she will weave pot holders or keychains out of plastic strips until lunchtime. On your way to the stairs, you make a brief and reluctant stop at your locker. At Sacred Heart, girls have to share because there simply aren't enough lockers by half. You have to share one with Leticia Longoria, a pretty and popular sophomore, who keeps things like leg makeup, lip-gloss enhancer and sun-streak alongside the thin picture books in her half of the locker. It's not that you hate Leticia, but you dread her, the way a person like you would naturally dread someone who thought to put makeup on her legs. *On her legs, Virgin!* You know a person who is con-cerned about leg makeup is on a different plane altogether from you and your prayers to the Blessed Mother for miracles. You can't imagine what she makes of your eyepatch, weird glasses and thick, neckless body.

And today, as you brush past her and her small group of equally attractive friends, she exclaims, "Sophia, girl, how are you?" to their tittered amusement.

"Hi, Lucretia," you force yourself to smile broadly, showing a lot of teeth.

"It's Leticia," she reminds you.

"Oh, really?" you say twisting the combination on your lock. "I'll have to write that down somewhere."

"How's it going?" says Elizabeth Montoya, arguably the prettiest girl in the whole school with her honey-colored hair and green cat eyes. She's in some of your advanced classes, and she's the only one in the group who exhibits some evidence of brain activity. You bet if she didn't hang with this bunch, she might be a somewhat decent person.

"Yeah," adds Leticia. "We were wondering who you're taking to the Spring Fling? You know it's coming right up." Leticia gives a friendly grin, but her eyes roam to her sniggering group. "I bet you're taking some real cute guy."

"Spring Fling?" you ask, as though oblivious of the posters and banners that have been hanging on the walls all over school for a week or more. "Is it that time already?" You grab your heavy literature anthology and make to slam the locker, but stop yourself. "Oh, you don't need your *Stuart Little* or anything, Leticia, before I lock it?" You figure Leticia has accumulated close to a thousand dollars in fines on that children's reader which she checked out from the school library as a freshman and which she has been too embarrassed and too cheap to return despite the regular fine notices deposited in the locker. The book leans against a bottle of *Heaven Scent* in her half of the locker. "Need anything for first period? Remedial Reading, isn't it?" you ask.

She shakes her head, and you slam the locker shut, saying, "*Stuart Little*—you let me know how that baby turns out, okay, Lucretia, I mean Leticia. I always have to read these big books without any pictures." You hold up the anthology, a college text that's thick as a telephone book. "I have to read Hawthorne, Poe, and Melville. It's been a good nine or ten years since I got to enjoy anything like Stuart Little."

"Bitch," Leticia hisses, the smirk wiped from her face.

"Cool it, Letty," whispers Elizabeth.

"I ain't gonna cool it. She's trying to make like I'm a dummy or something. Girl, why don't you say things straight out? Why you got to act all smart all the time? Don't you know everyone's laughing at you? Don't you know what a joke you are?"

"Shh, Letty, shh. It's Rita."

You turn to see your big sister crossing the hall. Leticia and her friends shut right up. Your sister Rita, aside from being a silent, scary and very tall senior, is on the basketball team and notorious for fouling herself out through rough play against her opponents. If she's not afraid to throw someone across a basketball court in front of a hundred or more spectators, who knows what she'd do if you pissed her off before a mere gaggle of skinny girls? Elizabeth and the others start slipping away, but Leticia remains, staring angrily at you, her head swaying slightly from side to side like a cobra's. You realize she probably does need one of her teensy basic books from the locker for her first period, or she'd get the heck away too.

"You need some money, Sophia?" asks Rita, keeping her eyes on Leticia.

"I gotta dollar," you tell her.

Rita peels another dollar out of her wallet and stuffs it in your blouse pocket. "Here's one more," she says.

Leticia doesn't dare say anything in front of Rita, but if she could she'd probably promise to get even with you or at least tell you to go to hell.

"What's that smell?" asks Rita, sniffing the air.

"Smells like..." you also wiggle your nose gamily, and there it is—suddenly and unmistakably. "Phew!"

"Dog shit!" says Rita triumphantly. She leans toward Leticia. "Why you must have stepped in dog shit. You stink!"

Leticia glances down at her two-toned saddle oxfords and at the thick lip of brown grass-bearded dog stool adhering to one heel. "Shit!" she cries.

"You smell bad," Rita says sympathetically.

"Really bad," you agree, not knowing why you didn't smell it earlier.

Leticia pinches up her face, gives a frustrated shrug and limps off, favoring the shit encrusted shoe as though she had twisted an ankle.

"What's with that *payasita*?" asks Rita, using her favorite name for a girl who wears too many cosmetics—a little clown. "Why was she picking on you?"

"Who knows? Maybe her leg makeup itches."

"Leg makeup?" Rita, grins. "Do they really have leg makeup?" The only beauty product Rita uses is Chapstick.

"Leg makeup," you say, "scar eliminator, nose putty, butt vanishing cream..."

Rita laughs, glancing at her watch. "C'mon, stupid, I've just got time to walk with you upstairs."

* * *

At school, you've noticed you are spending more and more of your time trying to avoid Sister Barnabas, a huge lunk of a nun who has made up her mind to "counsel" you for "body image" issues. In fact, she's trying to get you to join her "group," fatties all, who sit around bemoaning that nobody likes them. She's singled you out because you are not only fat, but you have the added psychological bonus of being half an orphan as well. You know Barnabas probably cares— she's that type—but you also know she's working on a counseling certificate to get her lazy behind out of the classroom and into a nice, quiet little office. You can't see how— *explicame, Virgen*—how on earth, this nun, who is fatter than you by two and, let's face it, a nun, is going to be able to help you?

Nevertheless, Sister Barnabas is forever skulking around, lurking in corners, and tiptoeing up behind you. You're pretty huge, but you're slippery as hell. You have to be. You sneak into broom closets, crawl under bleachers, and dive into crowds without a ripple, ever dodging her massive shadow. Until today—*Madre mia, things have got to go better than this*—when she claps a meaty claw on your shoulder as you're headed for American Lit. Then in a moment of nunnish playfulness, she wraps the other moist hand over your glasses, bumping your nose and smudging your lenses most annoyingly.

"Guess who?" she lilts.

"Hmm...Sister Barnabas?" you murmur.

Barnabas squeals, "Of course, it's me!" Then, more seriously: "Who else did you think it *might* be?"

To her, everything is evidence you need serious help. "Sister Barnabas, I was just thinking about you."

"Really?" You never before noticed how round her bright blue eyes are and how deceptively normal they seem behind her stylish granny-frames.

"I was. I was just thinking how I'd like to come by and have our little talk just as soon as I'm done with midterms," you say, buying yourself at least another month.

"Oh, honey, you don't have to wait that long," she sighs. "And I bet you might even do better on the tests if you had a chance to get a few things off your chest."

"After midterms, Sister, after the test, I swear I'll come by to see you." And, whew, you've escaped again, but naturally, after all the horsing around with Leticia and her group, then messing with Barnabas, you are late again for American Lit, and Sister Cleophas, a musty old nun roughly the size of a garden gnome, has to make a big display of reeling her pocket watch out of the folds of her habit before cackling, "Third tardy this week, Miss Chacon."

"Oh, I don't think so, Sister. Maybe the second, but you really shouldn't count the time I slipped on the stairs. And today, I was talking with Sister—"

"Third tardy this week, Miss Chacon." She clasps a pen in her shriveled little fist and scribbles out a referral form.

"Go see Mr. Borelli, Miss Chacon, before you may return to my class."

You take the referral and begin your sad march to Borelli's office. Truth be told, Cleophas has been against you since you refused to kiss her last Christmas when one of the girls ingeniously strung mistletoe over her desk, and the entire class paraded up front—one by one—to kiss her dried apricot of a cheek. You were the only one to stay in your desk, pretending to be so entranced by "Benito Cereno." You thought it worked, too, but she's been so pissy ever since then that you know you were only fooling yourself.

You duck into the bathroom, hoping to hide out the entire period, and proceed to the next class as though nothing had happened, to "forget" about the referral, but opening the door to the girls' room, you notice Leticia Longoria furiously spritzing herself with Jean Naté. She looks up at you, and you hold your nose, backing away.

And now you have to deal with Borelli, an unsuccessful hairdresser who lucked into a regular salary as vice principal at Sacred Heart and now thinks he rules the known world. Perhaps he was once handsome, but now he's so bloated and so old no one, not even sister Cleophas, would give him a second look. Of course, he thinks everyone—especially fat homely girls like you—are mad with love for him.

Once inside his office, you make up your mind not to look at him, not to flatter him with your gaze. You stare instead at the books on his dusty shelves.

"Why are you always late?" he grumbles after a pause.

You don't know what's come over you, but you decide that not only will you refuse to look at the man, you will not speak to him either.

"Do you hear me?" he asks. "What's the matter with your eye?"

You don't nod or shake your head. You won't give him a thing.

"I asked you some questions, young lady, and I want answers."

You press your lips together, and your tongue curls, resting in your mouth like a slug under a rock.

"You're going to talk to me. You're going to speak when you're spoken to." His voice sparks with anger, and though you're not looking, you can tell he's leapt up from behind his desk. You hear his feet padding the carpet. You think he might even hit you and then you can go home early, catch the soaps, and maybe even sue the school. "Am I going to have to call a parent conference?" he asks feebly. "Because I will, young lady. You can bet on that."

You want to sigh because you can see this is going to take a while, but you don't. You don't make a sound.

* * *

It's really not your fault that your dad was working in the Harbor area and couldn't be reached, so Bette had to be called. And certainly not your doing that Bette came to the parent-teacher thing falling-over drunk. She whispers to you as you walk together to the special conference room that the night before she had dropped acid—half a tab of windowpane—and she had gulped about a jug of Sangria that morning just to take the edge off the acid. But when she got the call for the conference, she felt she had to come, and she even drove herself over though she said the streets kept pulling apart like strands of gray taffy. She couldn't find good shoes is all. Her dog Little Chilé (named for his constant and obvious state of canine arousal) keeps chewing up her pumps and boots, which are all Bette ever wears. The only pair he left alone were her wedding shoes—white heels charred like marshmallows from her wedding reception where she threw them into the fireplace after she and her husband had tossed in their champagne flutes, and she still wanted to keep throwing things into the flames. They smell like a pile of burning tires, which is why Little Chilé lets them be.

Wearing burnt and noxious-smelling shoes, and being stoned out of her mind, does not keep your oldest sister from defending you before the semi-circle of sisters congregated with Mr. Borelli in the airless conference room. Normally, Bette is quite pretty, with her long black hair and round cherubic face. She used to be a cheerleader at this very school. She used to be president of the senior class, but today, her hair is as snarled and strung-out as she is and her cheeks are gaunt and greenish. You have to admit she's not making much of a case for you. In fact, she looks like a lunatic, an escapee from Bedlam. You'll be lucky if they don't call the police to take *her* away. Out of the corner of your eye, you can see Sister Barnabas nearly smacking her lips at the sight of your depraved sibling—all the more evidence of your madness.

It isn't at all like Borelli says, that you were trying to instigate insubordination. How does a fat girl with an eyepatch instigate anything but mildly creepy feelings in others, *Virgen, digame?*

Some of the nuns, your teachers, pipe in with positive remarks about your grades.

But Bette blurts, "You people make me sick. Where are your balls? You don't have the balls! No balls!"

This seems more than slightly silly to you since: a) it is completely out of context, following comments on your decent grades, and b) she was addressing a group consisting primarily of nuns.

"An' I say you don't have balls," cries Bette, pounding on the table, "an' I mean it to the maximum!"

But you don't dare laugh. You just cough and take your glasses off to wipe them, somehow giving Sister Barnabas the idea you are about to weep, a clear indication you need a ton of counseling in a very bad way. Faster than a rattlesnake can strike, she pushes a box of Kleenex at you. Even though, truth be told, you are the most level-headed person at the table. When you decide to break down and talk, you are the only one with the presence of mind to call a taxi to take Bette home and arrange to have Loretta dropped off by your father to retrieve Bette's car later—Borelli plus all those wimple-wearers with nary an idea among them how to cope with the smashed older sister of a snotty, albeit creepy sophomore.

Yeah, you handle it, but you wish you had thought to have Loretta come to the conference instead of Bette. Loretta never drops acid or drinks Sangria before breakfast or ever wears shoes that are even slightly blistered, let alone the kind that look like they've been dancing with the devil in hell.

* * *

The dang conference lasts through lunch, so you go straight to your afternoon classes. By the time the final bell rings, you are hungry enough to rip your own arm off and eat that. You dutifully stop at your locker for the Father Cochran disk and then to the Chalice Hilyard memorial bench to wait for your two idiotic friends. Naturally, you are the first one there, since your friends are slow as mud and they're forgetful too. They may not show up at all. Ten minutes, fifteen minutes, twenty.

You are getting ready to tuck the record into your book bag and put on your blazer for the long walk home when you see her walking slowly toward you. Her stride is long and lazy like the tiger you have seen pacing in the zoo. And her hair is stippled by shade from the willow alternating with stripes of the sun's ghostly glow. She's smoking a cigarette, streaming blue smoke through her nostrils.

Most of the other girls and the entire parade of cars are gone. Only Maria Spinetti, the freshman who never bathes, sits on the front steps of the school, scratching her grubby knees and waiting for her equally filthy father to pick her up. So it's just you, Maria Spinetti and her. Deliberately, she moves closer, closer until she's standing over you, casting her cool shadow over your thick knees. She takes a pack of Marlboros from the breast pocket of her blouse and says, "You want one?"

"Sure," you say, but your voice sounds high and squeaky —an unintentional Minnie Mouse. "Thanks, Elizabeth."

She laughs, baring a row of even teeth that are so white they seem unreal. "You're funny, you know that?" she says, tamping out a cigarette for you. "Your voices and jokes. You are really funny."

"Funny-looking," you concede.

"No, you're funny, like gifted. You could be on Johnny Carson, I bet, telling jokes. The *Stuart Little* thing, that was hilarious, but I couldn't laugh or anything 'cause Letty was right there. I thought it was pretty funny though."

"Thanks," you say, still holding the unlit cigarette casually between two fingers.

"Here, let me light that." She extracts a matchbook and snaps a flame.

You puff to get the cigarette going.

"Hey, you hungry?" asks Elizabeth. "I got my boyfriend's car while he's at work. You wanna drive over to Tommy's for a hamburger?"

You swear your stomach has hearing because as soon as it hears the words "Tommy's for a hamburger"—before your brain can register the information—it starts groaning like a wounded dog. You cough to cover the sound. "I guess," you manage to say and drop the cigarette to grind it under your heel. "Okay."

"C'mon. He parks it around the block for me, so I can use it while he's at work. He works over at that body shop on Alvarado down the street. I've got my own key."

You're barely listening. You are like Wimpy in the Popeye cartoon when it comes to hamburgers. And Tommy burgers— slathered in chili, topped with warm pickle slices and precariously nested on a steamy disintegrating bun—are the best in the world. Never mind that you can see the cloud of green flies hovering over the chili vats through the greasy windows. And you force yourself not to remember in too much detail how Aracely got to laughing so much the last time you went to Tommy's that she snorted bits of her burger and chocolate soda through both nostrils. "Wait," you blurt, remembering something else. "I can't—I don't have enough money." The two bucks in your pocket won't even get you a full order of greasy fries.

"My treat," smiles Elizabeth, crinkling her cat eyes and showing all those lustrous teeth again. "C'mon, it'll be fun."

She approaches a primer-colored Chevy and unlocks the driver side door. "It's a bomb, I know, a real cholo-mobile," she says ruefully, "but it drives."

"Oh, it's fine," you assure her, remembering her boyfriend is one of the older guys who hangs around the school, comes to the school dances and volleyball games, like a jackal on the prowl always waiting for some pretty, simple young thing to stray from the herd. Pedro, Pito, Pepe—something like that—is his name. He has gray hairs already threaded in with the black and acne scars you can see from across the street. "It's nice of him to let you use his car." You climb into the passenger seat beside her.

"Yeah, it's convenient. But I'm definitely going to break up with his ass once my parents get me my own car." She twists the rearview to check her lipstick, rubbing it more evenly on her lower lip with a pinky finger.

"Sorry to hear that."

"Nothing to be sorry about. Have you ever seen him? He's a real oinker—ugly and gross. He keeps wanting me to touch his *chorizo*. And you know that ain't never gonna happen." She shivers and stabs the key into the ignition. "You mind if we stop at my house, so I can change first?"

"No. Go ahead."

"I live up near the park. Hey, can I show you something? I have this favorite place—a special place—I want you to see, do you mind? I mean, you don't have to be anywhere, do you?"

"No, no," you say, silently warning your stomach to shut the hell up. *Virgencita, the stomach, can you help me here?* You cover it with your book bag, hoping to muffle the sound. But the roar of engine does a pretty good job of deafening you and Elizabeth Montoya as you drive up winding roads into the park to see this favorite, this secret place.

* * *

You have to laugh. There's nothing else to do. Of course, Leticia Longoria, Suzy Gomez, Marina Hinojosa would be at this "special place." What did you expect? That Elizabeth Montoya, the beautiful, was going to start being friends with you, Sophia, the ghastly? You can't imagine why you had that unreal feeling, that heart-jolting shock on seeing these three appearing from behind the eucalyptus trees as you and Elizabeth lit fresh cigarettes in a copse above the big ravine in the park. You know exactly where you are, and you know which direction to take to get yourself to a payphone and call Loretta to come get you. You're not too worried, but you wonder why they look a little strange walking toward you. That's when you realize you can't see their hands. They're holding their arms behind their backs. Then you do get a little scared, but you have to laugh.

"What's so funny, huh?" demands Leticia, drawing a stick from behind her and hitting it against one palm. You're relieved it's not much of a stick, just the kind of thing painters use to mix up paints. Marina and Suzy wave tree-branch-looking things. "What's so funny now you don't got your big sister here to protect you?"

Elizabeth Montoya streams two blue strands of smoke through her nostrils. "I got her here, now I'm gonna go. I don't want no part of this." She won't look in your eye; she just turns and starts hiking back down the hill.

Letty lands the first blow, catching you behind one knee; it buckles, but you don't fall. The trio hoots. "Take off that patch," shouts Leticia. "Let's see you got an eye under there or what. C'mon, take it off."

You have to laugh.

But another blow cracks at the base of your spine, and you stumble to your knees.

"Think that's funny?" demands Leticia. "Take off the patch."

"Okay, okay," you say, fumbling to reach under your glasses and peel off the patch. "There."

"Ugh!" cries Marina. "That's *ug*-ly!"

"You're creeping me out," says Leticia. "Stick that thing back on."

"It won't stick now," you try to explain. "The adhesive..." Another cracking sound. Your nose gushes red. You feel your glasses dangling from one ear. "I can't see." A rain of dull thumps, and the glasses fall into the grass. You're gulping back blood. It's not as painful as you thought after the first, almost like it's happening to someone else or to some thing. Like these girls are pounding on a sack of flour, beating an old rug strung on a line far, far away in another city, at another time. You don't cry. There's no time. You try to say something, but your tongue is the one thing that really does hurt. "I can't thee. I can't thee without my glatheth."

You hear them grunting, cussing. They call you bitch and a fucking cunt and stupid and some other things you can't make out in the blur of blows and curses. They're asking if you think you're funny now, if you think you're smart. Through your blood, you smell their sweat, their sour body odors under the Jean Naté, the dog shit and hairspray. You can nearly taste menthol from the trees and the warm fresh-cut grass pressing under your nose as you roll to the ground. Rolling feels good, so you keep tumbling. You think maybe you can just roll away. The knoll is curved like a lap, and you start rolling down, down, down. The trees, the grass, the heavy clouds in the sky churn around and around as though you are a marble spinning in a kaleidoscope. Your skirt is hiked up to your waist, and you think you will never, ever get the grass stains out of your blouse, your panties. But still you let yourself roll. For a while, they are after you. Thumping and thudding on your back, legs, and stomach with their sticks.

Then someone says, "Shit!" And they stop, the voices disappear, but you keep spinning faster and faster, snagging your hair, your clothing on twigs, bushes, rocks, but they don't stop you, and you can't stop yourself. You don't even try.

You just have to laugh.

Frostbite

It's only about a mile to Our Lady of Truth or Consequences Catholic Church and not a bad walk, even if it is only a quarter to seven in the morning and already crackling hot outside, but Olivia, my wife, wants me to take the truck.

"You know better than to walk on those feet," she tells me. She's painting the eyebrows darker on one of the dolls that she makes for the craft fairs in Albuquerque and Santa Fe. This one's wearing a crocheted gown of magenta with many ruffled layers pulled over a spherical wire casing that covers the legs, making it look like some kind of woolly cake that's hatching a plastic torso and head out the top. Even so, the doll looked pretty good to me until Oly started in on the eyebrows. I see she's using one of my brushes—camel's hair, an expensive one—and probably my paint too, but I don't say anything. "You know what those doctors said." She takes a moment to wag the brush at me. "You want to end up an amputee? Is that what you want, *hombre*? And what if the disability people see you?"

She has the idea that if I'm not always sitting in the den with my feet propped on a pillow, disability will send detectives out to catch me and snatch away all my benefits. But I know my feet are still frostbit, and the toes will always be cold as marbles and bluish black in the webbing. They can haul me into court whenever they like, and I'll lift one foot, peel off a sock and show any judge in the nation. And that will be that. But there's no point arguing with Oly. So I just say that I like the way the doll's coming out.

"Do you?" she smiles, turning the doll to me so I can see

it more fully. "I thought the color of the yarn might be too strong."

"No, it's fine." The yarn is nothing compared to the heavy brows Oly has scored on the smooth peach forehead. *Hijolé!* It's Joan Crawford with bowed lips, which I know my wife will soon tint unevenly with ox-blood nail varnish, giving the thing a drippy vampire grimace. She does this with all the dolls, and I'm just grateful she doesn't use my brushes for that.

She replaces the doll on the table and stares me in the eyes, pursing her lips, so her apple cheeks are pleated in fine gathers on either side of her chin. The older my woman gets, the more Indian she looks. You can't say that to her, though. *No que no.* But with those watermelon-seed eyes, that shoe-polish black hair and the full red cheeks, you could throw a blanket and some turquoise on her and she'd be all set to sell postcards and kachina dolls near the railroad tracks in Gallup. "I still wish you'd take the truck, Rudy. *Es que* it's a perfectly good truck. I don't see why you got to walk everywhere."

"I'm going by Carmen's," I tell her, as if this explained it. "She's gonna walk with me to mass, and then when we get back to her place, we're driving out to Albuquerque to see Hortensia. You want us to stop for you?" Hortensia is our daughter, and I'm holding my breath, hoping so hard that Oly will want to go see her in the hospital. She hasn't been even once since the surgery.

"No, no," she finally says in a real fast voice and fusses with the doll.

"C'mon, Oly, you gotta see her. She's been asking for you."

"I can't, Rudy. You know I can't."

"I don't know why not. I been every day and Carmen too."

"I'm not ready. I'm just not ready."

"What's to get ready? You go and you be with her. You talk to her."

"You don't understand anything," says Olivia with a crack in her voice. "How will it be? Can't you see I won't know?"

"What? What won't you know?"

She's facing me now, and her eyes are shiny and bright, but I know my wife and she won't let them fill. "I won't know where to look. Where am I supposed to look?"

I let my breath out slowly, like I'm cooling coffee. "Well, I'll be back this afternoon," I say after a moment. I'm thinking if she don't want to go see Hortensia, then Carmen and me might go by the courthouse and visit my son Rufus before heading to Albuquerque. Was arrested last night on a DUI near Fourth and Main. They wouldn't let me bail him last night, and Oly was so mad I tried to get him out, she wouldn't talk to me until we went to bed, and then all she says was, "You ought to leave him rot in there or in those roach motels. We didn't bring him up that way, you know. This is his own doing."

"See you later, honey," I says, and I lean to kiss her forehead that smells like meat, gamy and raw, like fear. I want to touch her hair, curl a stray lock behind her ear. Instead I turn from her, head for the door, throwing one last look at the grinning doll on the table.

* * *

Outside the heat falls gently on my face like the white scarf Oly used to wind around her hair when I'd take her riding in the Jeep, before the kids were born. It would come loose sometimes and tickle my jaws like this morning sun. Already I can smell the piñons sharpening their needles for winter and the charred bottoms of ashcans smoking in the neighbors' yards.

Yesterday my grandson came to me while I was burning the trash in our back yard. I like burning the trash in the summer. The keen bite of sulfur, the snap of the blaze, and whirls of soot reminds me that autumn is near and with it the cooler weather I enjoy before winter comes and I have to stay in the house all the time on account of my feet. I had been standing there, dreaming a little and stirring the rubbish with a charred tree branch when my grandson approached. Hortensia and her boys live next door, and since they got no father, I been something like that for the both of them. I watched him a little sideways without looking up. He loped across the bare yard, vaulted the short cinder wall, reminding me of a young wolf or a coyote, some rangy feral animal zig-zagging toward me.

"Hey, good morning, son," I said, poking the flames.

"Grandpa, I gotta talk to you," he said, kind of shyly. "Can I talk to you?"

"About your mother?" Both boys been worried since Hortensia first got her results, but each behaved differently. This one, the younger one, grew quieter, thinner, and he got these dark half-circles under his eyes. The other one swelled like one of those Japanese blowfish, eating, eating all the time and sobbing like an overstuffed baby when he went to see her in the hospital.

"No, not really, but seeing you here, you know, kind of reminds me of that time Mom set fire to that jersey Sheila gave my brother." He glanced at me, smiling. "Remember that time?"

"I remember." Hortensia hated her oldest's girlfriend, a wild one from Las Cruces. Part Pima and part she-devil, the girl had already given my grandson two black eyes and a broken wrist before they had dated a month. "It was a Lakers shirt, *que no?*"

"Yeah, that's right. Remember how Mama said when she burned it, the ashes curled into the shape of a skull?"

"That's what she said." I nodded. "I didn't see it, though." I prodded the blaze while my grandson watched for a few moments before I said, "Why don't you tell me what's on your mind, son."

"Ah, it's probably nothing." He laughed a little weakly. "But I'm having these questions, you know."

"Questions?" I thought maybe the boy was having his doubts about God with Hortensia being so sick.

"Yeah, it's like I'm struggling, Grandpa. I'm really struggling with these things." He started pulling junk out of the pockets of his jeans—tissues, gum wrappers and ticket stubs—and feeding them into the blaze.

"What kind of things, son?"

"It's my sexual identity, Grandpa," he blurted. "I'm... having...problems."

"Oh," I says, beating a frozen-peas box into the heart of the fire.

"I'm just really struggling with this, Grandpa, and I had to tell someone because I can't stand it anymore. What do I do? Am I sick? Am I crazy?" He stood there staring at me with those wide dark-circled eyes, like he had just met the devil in person or had been haunted by ghosts.

Over Hortensia's house, I could see a thunderhead deepening, darkening, and a few fat droplets sizzled on the lip of the trash can. In these parts we get these short hard rains about every afternoon in the summer, just enough to dirty the windshields and puddle the ruts in the road. I was glad I thought to burn the garbage before the rain.

"It's God's will," I says after a while, hardly knowing, hardly thinking about what I would say.

"God's *will*? God *wants* me to have these problems? I can't sleep. I can't eat." His voice rose scornfully. "He wants that? What if it turns out I'm bisexual or even gay, Grandpa? What happens then?"

"That's God's will too," I said. "And he loves you. He always loves you, *m'hijo*."

"How come you always got to talk for God, Grandpa? How do you got the inside line on what he's thinking? And what's the big deal with God, anyway?"

"It's all we have, boy. All we have," I mumbled. It stung me how angry he sounded. "I didn't mean to make you mad." He shook his head. "It's okay, Grandpa. Just forget it."

* * *

I'm thinking about this as I walk the block and a half through the alley to Carmen's house, and I know I didn't do too good. I didn't say what I should have said. I still don't know what it is I should have said, but I felt kind of stiff and fake, and the boy knew it. He helped me burn the rest of the trash before the downpour, but we both knew I let him down pretty hard.

These boys, I don't know about them anymore. The one with that gal who beats him up and the other with the sexual identity business—both things I never even thought about in all my years.

Both things my own son never opened his mouth about. Of course, he never opened his mouth much to me, but when he did, he always started and ended with "sir." Taught him to salute when he was just three. He was cuter than that John-John, the President's son. But I don't let my mind go to my son right now. It's easier to think about Hortensia's boys. Easier, even, to think about Hortensia in the hospital, watching that little television on the wall and hoping they scraped out all the cancer this time.

The walk to my sister's is too short, I think. I pull up the latch to her chain link fence and drag my shoes noisily on the concrete slabs leading to the back porch. The red ants are bad over here. They flow across the walk like a moving trail of paprika. They're big, mean and live only to bite. Of course, they can't hurt my feet, but I stomp on as many as I can to keep them from getting inside and to make as much racket as I can, so I won't startle Carmen when I come in the back door with my key.

"Rudy," calls Carmen, heading for the door before I fish

out my key. "C'mon, I'm ready, let's go, so we don't be late. Here, put on your moccasins."

One thing I like about my sister is that she's always on time. Another thing I like is her white hair, which is thick and soft and more fully white than you would think possible for human hair. But the best thing about my sister is that she keeps my moccasins for me. Whenever I see her, I can change into the only comfortable footwear there is for me. Of course, Olivia won't stand me wearing moccasins, so Carmen keeps a pair for me at her house. She even goes to the Isleta reservation to buy me new ones when the old ones grow shaggy and scuffed.

Gratefully, I slip off my loafers and ease into the slippers. "Ah," I say, rocking a little on the balls of my feet. I don't know how the Indians do it, but these are the only things that warm my feet and give the toes a tingle of feeling. "*Gracias*, Carmen."

"*De nada*," she says, and she tosses the loafers into the back porch. "Now, let's go, little brother, or we'll miss the first prayers."

"Okay, I'm ready." And we set off down the driveway for the church.

"We picking up Oly before we go to Albuquerque?"

"No, not today," I say.

"What are we going to tell sister?" Carmen calls my girl "sister" and Rufus "brother," as though they're our siblings instead of my children.

"I'll just say Oly's sick, you know. That she's not feeling too good."

"You know, little brother, that girl's gonna start worrying about her mama, if you keep telling her Oly's too sick to visit."

"What am I supposed to say? That her mother can't stand to look at her since...since the surgery?"

"You know they have those things now that women can buy..." she pauses, concentrating, "prosthetics. Supposed to look natural, real. La Lurline got one on one side, and I can't tell the difference, honest to God, I can't."

"Am I supposed to bring some over to Hortensia?" I pretend I'm talking to my daughter, "Here's a box of chocolates, some flowers, and, honey, guess what I got in this bag for you. Put 'em on, so your mama can come see you in the hospital."

"I guess that wouldn't be too good," admits Carmen, shaking her head so the hair looks like dandelion fur ruffling in the breeze.

"Nah, won't work. It looks like I'm gonna have to fight this one with Oly."

"Poor little brother." Carmen lets out a long sigh. "The longer we talk, the gladder I am that I never married."

I think about this, and it's true. Years ago, when the kids were young, back when Oly was still smoking and happier most of the time, I used to feel sorry for Carmen, especially around Christmas, when Hortensia and Rufus would stare at their gifts with their mouths open like baby birds, trembling and glowing even from the lights on the tree. I used to wish Carmen had a husband, children of her own. But these days, I never feel sorry for my sister.

"It's sure peaceful for you all by yourself, *que no*?"

"Well, I admit that sometimes I feel disappointed in myself. But it never gets ugly, you know."

We get to the corner of Main and Becker, just about to cross when the police cruiser sails up, giving a little blurt of the siren and flashing the blue light. I check the signal again to make sure we're crossing with the green.

"It's Hernando," says Carmen, grabbing my elbow in case I try to step in the squad car's path. "Wonder what that *mocoso* wants." Carmen used to babysit the deputy until he started school. He was a fussy little tot who cried a lot for his mama. In her mind, he's still that whining snotnose kid under the uniform, the sidearm, and the badge.

Hernando Bergeson lowers the passenger-side window

32

and leans across the seat to holler, "Rudy, Rudy, you got a minute?"

"We're going to church. What is it?"

"Caught a circuit judge speeding near Tomé this morning, and he agreed to set bond on Rufus, if I tear up the ticket. You ready to come to the station, get that boy out?"

"Heck, yeah," I say, not looking at Carmen.

"Well, hop in, and I'll take you over to the station. You coming too, ma'am?" he asks Carmen, who's just standing at the curb, holding her handbag over her chest like a shield.

"I guess," she says, shrugging.

"You can ride in the back, ma'am, if you don't mind."

Carmen climbs in, scrooching way down and patting her hair as flat as it will go, so no one will recognize her riding in the back of the police car, when she ought to have been on her way to mass.

It's not a long drive to the station, but Hernando seems to think he has to fill every moment with chatter.

"Yeh, that circuit judge thought he'd beat the sun to Blue Water for some fishing. But I tagged him, just past Ortega's shop before the Y. He shoulda thanked me 'cause if he hit the Y at that speed, he'da blown a tire or two, you know. But, no, he's pissed—'scuse me, ma'am—pissed as a lizard. I was gonna write him a seventy-dollar ticket, rocket his insurance to the moon, just for being a sumbitch—'scuse me—but I remembered your Rufus and worked a trade instead."

"'Preciate that, Hernando."

Hernando waves it off. "Don't mention it. Hey, they got some ruins out there by the Y. That's what made me think of you and your boy, them ruins. Nice ones—crumbling pink adobe, tumbleweeds all around. You been out there? You seen those?"

I had, and I painted them a few months back, but I shook my head. "Out by the Y, you say?"

"Just *before* it. I seen them ruins and right away thought you might like to paint 'em. Then I got to thinking about your boy, and I hauled that old bastard—watch my French, ma'am—into the station to bond out Rufus, who's much the worse for wear, sicker than a prairie dog with a gut fulla rat bait and not talking that big talk like last night, not one bit, no sir."

I can feel Carmen's foot pressing against the back of the car seat, but I can't help myself. "Has he asked for me?"

"Shoot he's not asking for anyone, but maybe God or the devil to kick him out of his misery. You can see for yourself, we're here. I only hope that old judge don't get cranky and set too much bail on your boy. I left to find you before the hearing."

"Don't know how to thank you, Hernando," I say.

"Just paint them ruins I toldja about, Rudy. We all got our work." He pulled into a parking space back of the station and yanked up the hand brake. "I'm just doin' mine."

I don't believe I hate anyone. I believe in the New Testament and what Jesus said, and I try to love everybody. But I can't keep myself from blaming the National Guard. The National Guard is like a wife I stood by and loved, for richer for poorer, in sickness (always mine) and in health. It's like a wife I knew and I loved, but who turned into a savage, blood-drunk wolverine when I said I'd had enough and had to walk away.

I remember shipping off to Denver to handle these protesters. This was thirty, maybe forty years ago. Of course, I had my crewcut then, my green fatigues and the boots. Lord, I hate those boots even more than the Guard these days. We were given face protectors and told to make a wall, not to let the protesters pass. There was this one lady, pretty lady. Jane Fonda. I'd seen her in the movies. *Cat Ballou* and something else. I liked her fine, but that day in Denver, she spat on me. She did. Spat right on my face shield. A thick wobbly gob that wavered on my shield before rolling onto my shirt. And I remember being shocked, wondering how she could do such a thing. She didn't even know me.

Now I think she did know me, what I was.

But that day, I hated her, and I loved that Guard. I would have given my life for the Guard. No questions asked. I taught my baby boy to salute, to call me "sir" every time he spoke to me. I would have given my life...but not my feet.

I found that out years later in Montana one winter. Stranded, separated from my men on maneuvers, I tried to hitch, tried to stay the night in an abandoned shed. That's when I almost lost my feet. Your feet don't feel it when it happens though. Your ears hurt more, your shoulders cramp from bowing against the wind and the hands—they ache and ache. You don't notice so much that your feet are getting cold, but they take the worst of it.

And now I'm thinking how I hate the Guard. Hate, despise, and curse it. I would spit on it myself, if I could. That's what I'm thinking while I'm writing out the check for Rufus' bail. I feel the saliva welling in my mouth, the bile churning up from my liver, and that's what I'm thinking while I'm signing my name with the chewed-up ballpoint Hernando handed me from his breast pocket.

* * *

"Well, we missed mass," Carmen shows me her watch on the steps to the courthouse. "We may as well go back to my house, get the car and go to Albuquerque to see Hortensia."

"Let's wait while Rufus gets his things. He's gonna need a ride. Maybe he wants to go with us, see his sister."

Carmen clicks her tongue. I'm turned away, so I can't see her, but I can tell she's folded her hands over her chest and she's rolling her eyes, though they're squinted because the sun's even hotter now.

Just like me and Oly live next door to Hortensia, Carmen is a driveway away from Rufus. His wife Allesandra is forever running to Carmen's, telling on Rufus—how he's drinking, how he didn't come home, how he got fired as P.E. coach at the middle school, how her sons are crying for their daddy, and on and on. Allesandra works at the Home Depot, and I can just see her, flapping in her quilted blue apron across the drive to Carmen's like the largest jay of the season darting for seeds.

I'm folding my arms too and standing like the statue of Hilario Romero, the first G.I. from Truth or Consequences killed in action, World War I, when Rufus pulls open the glass door and walks, slowly and painfully, down the steps. The first whoosh of a passing car makes him wince.

"Son," I say. "Son." Rufus always favored his mother, but today he looks like a piece of uncooked chicken that's been left too long out of the refrigerator. His apple-cheeks are pimpled and yellowish, peppered with stubble.

"Yessir," he says, quiet-like.

"Call me 'dad,' okay?"

"Yessir."

"Son, you want to go with your auntie, here, and me, and go see your sister, go see Hortensia. You know she's out of the surgery?"

"Um...no."

"Yeah, she is. She got out a coupla days ago, and she's doing great, just great."

"I meant no, I don't want to see her, Dad...sir."

"*Sin verguenza!*" yells Carmen, swinging her purse like she can't take no more, and she hits Rufus with it—smack— across the jaw. "You are going to that hospital. You are going to see your sister, and you are going to be nice, you hear me?" She winds up like to whack him again, but I grab the strap to stop her. Rufus crouches, guarding his forehead, ready for the next blow. "*Pues*, I'm sick of it," says Carmen. "Just sick of it."

But my sister doesn't look sick. The color in her cheeks and the black of her eyes. She looks like she's ready to hike through the mountains to settle a score with a polecat.

"Get that *mocoso* Hernando to drive us to my house for the car," she orders. "I'll keep an eye on this one."

* * *

Carmen's not a bad driver, but I don't like to look at the road when she's spinning the wheel. I keep remembering the time I taught her to ride my bicycle, and she almost ran over the sister of Hilario Romero, war hero, on Fourth Street, just behind where they built the Dairy Queen.

"If you look at a thing," I had explained to her, "you're gonna hit it. So don't look at things. Just look at the road, where you want to go."

And she had bumped off on the bike, too tiny to do more than toe the pedals, but pushing anyway and wavering this way then that, until the Romero girl appeared, carrying a piglet under one arm and a newspaper tucked under the other arm. "Don't look!" I cried. "Don't look!"

But Carmen, her hair mouse-brown at the time, but always thick as a bush, wobbled on the bicycle straight into the woman's buttocks. Poor Carmen wept, and the piglet squirmed away, but Hilario Romero's sister was very kind. She took us into the house, cleaned and wrapped Carmen's scrapes, and gave us *bizcochitos* with *yerba buena*.

Still, I don't like to look when Carmen drives, so I turn back to my son, and I say, "How you doing?"

"I've been better, sir." He manages a smile, though.

"Well," I say with a full smile, "okay." Then I turn to look out the side window. Tumbleweeds, hard-packed earth, one yellow and black billboard. Heat shimmies, making mirages of deep emerald pools between the weeds, yet my feet are so cold they burn, even in the moccasins.

"You know, Dad. You gotta know I'm sorry for all this. I feel so bad. I wanna stop hurting Allesandra, the boys, you. You really gotta know how sorry I am."

"Look," I blurt, "there's a Stuckey's coming up. You wanna pecan log?"

"A pecan log?" snorts Carmen.

"Yeah, c'mon. It's just up a ways. We can take one for Hortensia. Rufus, how about it. You love those things."

"No," says Rufus, "I don't want one right now, sir."

Carmen grumbles, but she throws on the blinker, pulls off the highway and glides into a parking space by the glass door to the gas station/curio shop. I don't trust leaving the two in the car together, so I turn to Rufus, saying, "How 'bout it, son? Want to come in with me? Maybe you can help me pick out something for your sister? Something to go with the candy?"

He hesitates, looking pretty reluctant, even bad-tempered. For the first time, I'm struck by how ugly my son is. Big and meaty, he slouches in Carmen's back seat like a captive bear with his shaggy head of uncombed hair and the greenish shadow shading his loose jowls. When he frowns, he looks like he's fifty, instead of thirty-five. Fifty and sick with some soul-eating disease. I avert my eyes to his thick arm, resting on his lap. It is only a foot or so from my hand. If I reach over the seat, I can take his arm, squeeze it.

"C'mon, boy," I urge him.

He grumbles, but unlatches the door and swings it wide.

In the Stuckey's, Rufus wanders to the refrigerated beverage section, while I sort through the shelves of souvenirs. I don't think Hortensia especially wants a scorpion in resin, or a chamois-covered tom-tom. She certainly doesn't need an ashtray that says Land of Enchantment on it in the hospital. I remember Carmen is waiting out in the car, so I figure on just getting the pecan roll and maybe a soda for Rufus.

"Want a drink, son?" I call to him.

"Yeah," he says, a little too eagerly.

"Get yourself a soft drink, then."

"Oh."

I walk over just in time to see him, shoving a can of

Schlitz back into the cooler. How could he think I would buy him a beer? He has got this sickness bad. I'm thinking to call my brother-in-law's niece Selena, who used to lead AA in town until she got kicked out, I think. Last I heard, she was getting big in the Albuquerque chapters, though my brother-in-law told me the family was considering having an intervention to get her drinking again because she had gotten so irritating about AA, always shoving it down everyone's throat. I'm thinking maybe she might be able to help my boy.

Rufus brings a can of root beer to the counter, where I've set two pecan logs. "You sure you won't have a candy, son?"

"None for me."

While we're waiting for the clerk to show up, I say, "Maybe we can take your boys and Hortensia's boys out to Blue Water before fishing season ends."

My son pops open his soda and gives a disgusted look.

"What's wrong?" I ask.

"I don't like fish."

"What do you mean? You always loved to fish, and cooking the fish on a little fire outdoors. What do you mean you don't like fish?"

He opens his mouth just a slit. "Lay off, will you? Jesus, just lay off."

"Okay," I say in a low voice because the clerk is coming, "okay. We don't have to go fishing."

* * *

The rest of the way to the hospital, no one talks. Carmen puts on her tape of the sea sounds, and it makes my stomach queasy. I hear Rufus slurping his root beer in the back seat, belching, and then crumpling the aluminium can.

I'm wishing Carmen could put the car in reverse, and we could all travel backwards. Not just back through the miles, but through the years. Back, back to when Rufus and Hortensia slept in their old bedrooms with the paintings of the Guardian Angel who watches two children cross a rope bridge. What happened to those paintings? It would be so good of Carmen to take us back to their old rooms, how they were, and to those two paintings hanging above little brother and sister as they slept in their twin beds.

By the time we reach the visitors' parking lot at the hospital I'm ready to vomit from seasickness. I focus on my moccasins to quell the nausea as we make our way through the lobby and up the elevator to Hortensia's room. The rules posted on the double doors to the floor say that a patient can only have one visitor at a time.

"You go in first, little brother," Carmen tells me. "Me and Rufus will wait in the little lounge."

"I won't stay long, so you can have some time with her," I tell Rufus.

Hortensia leans, almost sitting, against a huge white pillow. Her face is white, but her eyes are large, shiny black like her mother's. "Dad!" she cries. "Dad, did you bring my boys?"

"Uh, no, but I do got a surprise for you, *m'hija*."

She's disappointed, I can tell, but she looks good, twice as strong as she looked yesterday. My Hortensia, she's a good girl when she's sick. She's no complainer. "Did they say when they're coming? The boys, I mean?"

"I'll bring them this evening," I tell her. Maybe Oly will change her mind by then.

"That's okay, Dad. I was just wondering."

"Carmen's here." I don't mention Rufus, thinking he will be the surprise.

"Oh, good! I've missed her. I've missed you all." She smiles, and I'm thinking I could bend and kiss her cheek, but I pat her hand instead, brushing my fingers against her IV tubing.

"What have you been doing?"

"Oh, watching stupid shows on television. That's all."

"What were you watching?" I ask, looking at the silent monitor suspended from the wall.

"This silly show about a woman who gives her baby up for adoption because she wants to be a professional dog breeder, and then years later, this girl comes to work for her and guess who she is..." Hortensia goes on and on, telling me the details of the television program she just watched. I listen, smiling a little, enjoying her talking, but not listening much until she says these words: "sexual identity."

"What's that?" I say.

"Sexual identity. It's when people are trying to decide if they're homosexuals or straight or what."

"I know what it is, *hija.* Why did you say that?"

"Don't get upset, Dad. I'm just saying I'm worried about my youngest, I'm worried about little brother. I think he's having some problems with sexual identity, and he's angry right now, Dad. He's really angry with me. He's not talking to me."

"What's he angry about?"

"The circumcision."

"The what?"

"The circumcision. He's mad because I had him circumcised when he was born. I tell him and tell him I didn't know it would upset him at the time."

"He's mad because he's circumcised."

"He says I mutilated him, I butchered him. And now, this sexual identity thing. Dad, you gotta do something. I can't while I'm stuck here. I can't do anything, but wait for him to come see me. And then when he comes, he's wearing eye shadow, Dad, and my Cover Girl blushing powder. I only hope I have some makeup left when I get home."

"Ah, it's a phase," I say, willing it to be one.

"And the other one, so in lust with that *changa*—I swear she's a beast, a violent ape—he doesn't notice a thing that's going on with his little brother. And I can't do nothing, Dad, not while I'm here hooked up to these things. You gotta do something with the boys, Dad. And Mr. Mewers, Dad, don't forget Mr. Mewers. I bet the boys haven't fed that cat once, let alone changed the litter box. Can you look after him? I don't want to get home to a dead cat."

"Sure, sure, Hortensia, calm down. I'll feed the cat. The boys are okay. I had a good talk with little brother yesterday, and I'll talk to him again. I'll bring them both by tonight. Don't worry about nothing, *hija*. Just think about getting better, okay."

"Is Mom still sick?" she asked. "One of the nurses told me that Rufus got arrested last night. You gotta get him in a program, Dad, a residential thing, where he has to stay put and not drink."

"Well, we're looking into it," I lie.

"He's gonna want outpatient weekends, I know, and a short stay close to his buddies, but you can't pick a program like a prom dress, Dad. This is a serious thing. I'm worried about my little brother."

I nod.

"You gotta take care of Mom, too, Dad. Are you going to be able to do all that? I don't know. I don't know. What about your feet?"

"I can do it. My feet aren't so bad with this weather. Carmen can help out, too. I told you she's here. She's waiting to see you. I better let her have a chance to spend some time with you since I'm coming back tonight," I tell my girl, edging out of the room. I blow her a kiss from the door.

"Thanks, Dad," she says, blowing me one back. "Thanks for everything. I'm sorry to get so worked up."

"It's nothing." I step out and softly close the door, as if she were sleeping in the room and I didn't want to disturb her. I feel so exhausted I want to crawl onto the empty gurney in the hallway and get myself a rest. My feet are burning with the cold from the air conditioning.

I can barely force them to shuffle toward the little lounge without whimpering a little like a shot dog. It's funny how

42

the animal noises help, even if the hospital people look at me a little oddly. In the lounge, I see Carmen flipping through the pages of a magazine.

"Where's Rufus?"

"Gone," she says without looking up.

"To the restroom?"

"*Que restroom, ni restroom.* To the bar, little brother, to the bar. He took off like a shot as soon as you went in to see Hortensia. Said he was going to the restroom, but that was half an hour ago."

"Which bar, do you think? Maybe we can find him."

"Don't even," says Carmen. "Let him go. It's no use, little brother."

"Maybe you're right," I sigh, dropping into the seat next to hers. "I don't think my feet can make it."

"Are they real bad now?"

I nod, fishing in my pocket for the pecan roll. "I told Hortensia I brought her a surprise when I thought Rufus would see her, so give her the candy. Tell her it's my surprise."

Carmen takes the pecan roll solemnly and opens her purse. "I got something, too," she says, fishing in the bag. "Something for you."

"Carmen?" I ask, scratching my head. "You ever think about things like sexual identity?"

She screws up her brow like she's thinking it over while she pulls a bright red and green blanket, a little rug really from the purse. She flaps it open and wraps it around my knees so it drapes over my feet, making an instant tent of warmth. She's still thinking, I can tell. Another thing I like about my sister is how seriously she thinks about things when you ask her a question. She waits and considers before saying what she thinks.

"*Como molestas*," she says at last. "Don't bother me with silly questions like this, little brother. Sexual identity, *ni nada*. I don't even know what you're talking about."

"You remember I used to like a drink, when I got back

from the army, before the Guard. Remember the fights I had?"

"You were a shorty. People picked on you."

"I was a drunk, a mean one like Rufus. Maybe this is something he gets from me. And then I was a hard father, remember that?"

"I don't know what saying and thinking all that helps right now, *hermanito*. I really don't. You try to do the things that help, coming to see Hortensia, getting Rufus out of trouble, watching out for the boys, *que no*? That's what's important."

I nod my head. When Carmen is talking, things make sense. She's a practical woman. I like how she reasons, what she says, but the best thing about my sister is how she tries to keep my feet warm.

A Tatting Man

Joaquin Benavidez, provided with a hand-sized mirror and a pair of manicure scissors, trimmed the snowy nose hairs persistently sprouting from the passages of his aquiline proboscis like tangles of a winter tumbleweed.

"For your novia," his wife had heckled him when she was alive—just one week ago, in fact. She had enjoyed teasing him about his attraction for the new English teacher at the Senior Center he managed. "*Eres un Don Juan*," she would say with a wink. "*Don Juan anciano.*"

"*Callate, vieja*, I'm too old for *novias*," he always murmured, as he did now over his shoulder to the vacant shower stall.

She would have volleyed more playful insults and jokes about his outlandish crush.

"I am Joaquin Benavidez," he liked to say when he finished brushing his teeth and spitting the mouthwash that never seemed to cover the calcium reek of his long amber teeth. "At joor service."

"Yeah," she would say, "and what am I? Yesterday's beans? And you ain't been at my service since World War Two."

But, that was a lie they both enjoyed. They had still been at one another's service after some fifty years of marriage. Albeit a gentler and rarer service over the last twenty years, it could still be a pleasant way to serve, up until the time of Tonia's death.

The previous Monday, Antonia discovered a rosary of ants cracking through a square of linoleum in the kitchen and, in her efforts to sweep the crimson insects back, she stumbled, landing hard and cracking her skull on the stove. Her last dance, Joaquin remonstrated himself, had been with a broom.

"*Tonia, te quiero*," he whispered as part of his grooming ritual these days. He put the compact mirror away.

* * *

The funny thing was that—with her lover Melchor unceremoniously booted back to Mexico by the Department of Immigration and Naturalization around the same time that Antonia was ceremoniously laid to rest by her ancient and wailing relatives, descended from the north like a covey of bedraggled crows—Mr. Benavidez and Regina, the new English teacher, had become a lot closer as human beings who experience loss and grief at the same time, will. They discovered they had much more in common than would be expected of an octogenarian former-restaurateur turned Senior Center Manager and an English-as-a-Second-Language instructor in her late twenties.

They could be found during class breaks with their heads huddled together. Mr. Benavidez smoked his pipe while Regina spoke to him quietly on the lawn behind the Senior Center. The fireflies flickered between them like miniature spaceships traversing a pair of odd planets.

"It's not that he was a bad person," she explained once, speaking of her most recent ex-husband, whom she dubbed for convenience, the Antichrist. "He had a hard life, Mr. Benavidez. Did you know he was abandoned with his brothers when he was four when their parents went on a drinking binge? Yes, it's true. They left those three children— he was the oldest, you know—all alone in an apartment for almost a week before social workers found them, filthy, starving, full of tapeworm and headlice."

Mr. Benavidez sighed, shaking his head.

"Then, he just got bounced from foster home to foster

home until he got put into that mental hospital when he was about thirteen..."

Arturo, who strained to be Regina's most precocious student, stared longingly at them from the picture window of the Senior Center. He knew enough to keep himself away or they would break off the conversation and wait patiently until the eager young farmworker embarrassed himself with his own prattle. So he merely stood behind the glass and watched them, trying to imagine their words, wondering whether they were in Spanish or English.

"It's like this," Regina said, another time on the subject of her different marriages. "In the beginning, it's like I'm on opium or something or even going blind. Everything's swimming in this rippling underwater world. It's not that I don't see things as they are; it's that they seem softer, blurrier like if I were scuba diving or something."

Mr. Benavidez, who had never been scuba diving, nodded compassionately.

"I mean, if I see a shark or a jellyfish, I don't panic. I just assume a current will come along and pull me away." Regina turned up her palms, helplessly. "Oh, I don't really know what I mean, Mr. Benavidez."

"*Te entiendo,*" Mr. Benavidez assured her, knocking the ash from his pipe and refilling it with pinches from his pants pocket. "I understand."

* * *

In the evenings, Mr. Benavidez had begun smoking the cigarettes Tonia left in a beaded handbag on the coffee table. Virginia Slims, they were called. Mr. Benavidez used to be irritated by the advertising for these cigarettes. Before— whenever he heard the insipid slogan—he would mutter, "Yah, you come along way, bebe. You can get cancer just as good as the mens."

Now, smoking these cigarettes marketed for women

brought Mr. Benavidez a coziness, especially after dark when he tended to feel more solitary in the house. Though he felt absurd taking up cigarette smoking in his eighties, the curling plumes of smoke smelled too much of Tonia for him to resist lighting at least one and often two. Filling his lungs with the acrid smoke, he could almost hear Tonia's slippers scritch-scratching over the yellowed linoleum in the kitchen. He could nearly make out the peculiar way she had of hum-whistling to tunes he never could recognize.

"Make up joor mine, mujer, are you humming or wheestling or what?" he would implore her. "Is that 'You Are My Sunshine' or 'Chingle Bells'?" he begged her to tell.

"Both," she always said with a smile that flashed the gold incisor of which she was so proud. "I'm humming an' I'm whistling 'You Are My Sunshine,' 'Chingle Bells,' an'...an' ...'I Wanna Hole Your Hand.'"

"You can't do that! Ain't nobody can't do all that!"

Again, the tooth would sparkle. "Who says?"

When Mr. Benavidez was wiping out the shelves behind the bathroom mirror, he toppled the small bottle of a scent called Rendez-vous that Tonia had relished and immediately the small tiled room filled with his wife's warmth and wit. He could almost feel her strong brown hands on his shoulders kneading the knotted muscles under his shirt. He spun around to face ... the aqua shower curtain gaily printed with burbling angelfish. Sheepishly, he set the vial upright and sopped the spill with his rag.

In the morning after shaving, Mr. Benavidez cast a cautious glance about the bathroom, kicked the door shut and gingerly dabbed a drop of Rendez-vous behind each ear lobe.

* * *

"These mosquitos are making a feast out of me," Regina complained that night. She swatted a plump insect into a rust smear on her elbow. "I notice they don't bother you, Mr. Benavidez. I thought I smelled repellant on you earlier in class. What kind do you use? Mine doesn't seem to be so effective."

"Tell me about the new fella," asked Benavidez. "I hope I don't hafta take the troca over to Truth or Consequences and duel him over you, nor nothin' like that."

"Who? Pablo? Nah, he's so nice, he'd probably grab the pistol out of your hand and shoot himself straight in the heart to save you the trouble. It's a little creepy."

"Last week you was in love. It was 'Pablo this an' Pablo that.' Now, what's this? Trouble in *paraiso*?"

"I don't know what's wrong with me tonight, Mr. Benavidez. Pablo is very good and kind and funny, but it feels weird, you know. Take tonight, Mr. Benavidez, when I get home Pablo will have a little dinner on the table for me and the newspaper folded to the parts I like to read. There'll be flowers in a little bowl and a fat yellow candle burning near the flowers."

Mr. Benavidez hosted the unexpected vision of his wife smiling, the gold tooth incandescing her brown cheeks. "*Pues*, what's wrong with that?"

"What's wrong with it, Mr. Benavidez, is that it's too nice. What if I don't feel like eating? What if I don't want to read the paper when I get home? What if I want to jump in the car and buy a bottle of wine to take to Mountainaire and drink it up there in the mountains, all by myself, crying and singing until the sun comes up?"

"Cryin' an' singin'?" Once again, Mr. Benavidez flashed on his wife hum-whistling in the kitchen, while she stirred the deep starry pot filled with beans.

"Oh, I don't know what I want! Look it's Arturo rapping on the window. Must be time to go back." Regina turned to walk toward the senior center.

"Cryin' an' singin,'" Mr. Benavidez murmured to himself. He knocked the cold ashes out of his pipe and followed her back to the class.

* * *

A few days later, Mr. Benavidez inexplicably returned early from the classes at the Senior Center. On that night, he had glumly pushed open the glass door to admit Regina and the students, forced a few unconvincing coughs and announced in a stage whisper that he felt ill. He turned without another word to walk back home, his head hanging, while his workboots shuffled over the parking lot.

Regina felt alarmed, but she had too much respect for the caretaker's dignity to permit Arturo to tag after him, as Arturo himself had suggested, to see what was truly wrong with the old man.

"He's probably just tired," she insisted to Arturo, knowing that, if she were feeling low, the last thing she would want would be an earnest face bobbing at her elbow, following her home. "He'll be back tomorrow when he's feeling better."

Back home, Mr. Benavidez carefully lowered the shades and lit one of the Virginia Slims he had bought earlier at the Quick Stop, where he informed the incurious clerk they were for his sister. He sank into the sofa and propped his feet on the coffee table to watch a *telenovela* he had overheard his wife discussing with a neighbor.

The dramatic series, called *Mari Mar*, featured a dim-witted but sexy juvenile, who appeared to have emerged from the sea one day, causing a goodlooking shirtless man to fall in love with her. This relationship, Mr. Benavidez gathered from his initial viewing, resulted in great consternation for the shirtless man's dignified family and friends, who abhorred the sultry sea teen's lack of sophistication.

Mr. Benavidez watched, amazed, as the young girl—who must not have gotten enough to eat in the ocean—devoured everything in sight in the shirtless man's high-class home and then made herself up like a clown to attend another high-class party that evening. Mr. Benavidez supposed the idea was to contrast her unspoiled innocence with the wily deviousness of her host's family and friends. But, really, the girl ate too much. He watched her stuff down a banana and hide the peel in an expensive looking vase, while he lit yet another cigarette.

A half an hour later, Mr. Benavidez witnessed the simpleminded protagonist rolling around on an oriental rug wrestling with another woman she had caught dancing cheek-to-cheek with her *novio* (who—by this time—had donned a shirt with white ruffles). All this came after the attractive teenager had gorged herself at the unattended buffet table, practically plunging her nubile arms up to the elbows into what looked like onion party dip!

Mr. Benavidez gasped as the credits scrolled over the two struggling women and the first strains of theme music overtook their cries.

He stubbed out his cigarette in the choked ashtray—how many had he smoked?—and reached for the TV Guide. He riffled the pages for the next night's listing, but was disappointed to find only the program's title and channel in the time slot. There was no hint how the fist fight would evolve. He dropped the small magazine to the floor and raked trembling fingers through his hair.

* * *

Regina's supervisors, Olga and Juan Carlos, agreed to extend Regina's summer contract through the year. Regina found she could take classes at the university during the day and—with a break to stop home for a late lunch and a nap—she was able to make it to the Senior Center in Farmington in plenty of time to teach evening classes which ran from Monday through Thursday.

Working in Farmington meant long hours away from

home driving to and from the Senior Center. The class lasted three hours week-nights. This left her very little time to spend with Pablo, who turned out to be very agreeable in any case.

Pablo could be so considerate and so thoughtful that Regina felt very provoked by his solicitous behavior at times. The constant can-I-get-you-something's interspersed with the what-do-you-need's were extraordinarily vexing to Regina, who tried to be a very nice person herself.

Through the keyhole in the bathroom door, Pablo would ask Regina—while she had her bath—if she would like a tall glass of ice water with maybe some mint or, no, how about a slice of lime in it?

"No, thanks," was Regina's measured reply as she turned the page of her book.

"How about the lime, then, with the mint?"

"No, really."

"Are you angry with me?"

"What?"

"Do I annoy you?"

"No," Regina lied. "You don't annoy me." She felt extremely irritated that Pablo—with the locked bathroom door and the billows of steam between them—could sense Regina's agitation and, even still, proceed to pester.

"Am I too sensitive to you? Does it bother you?"

"What? I can't hear you. I'm washing my hair now, Pablo. We can talk later."

* * *

The night after he first watched *Mari Mar*, Mr. Benavidez decided he could not go to class. He had to sneak over to the Senior Center before anyone had arrived for class and stealthily unbolt the glass doors so he could return home, unquestioned, to learn what happened that night to the alluring but imbecilic teenager.

He set himself up in front of the television this time with

a little dish of *bizcochitos*, a jelly jar of the sweet wine a neighbor had sent when Tonia died, and the inevitable ladies' cigarettes in the conch ashtray, all tastefully arrayed on the coffee table, just as Tonia would have done if they had decided to have a snack while watching television together.

Mr. Benavidez remembered Tonia pleasurably settling herself before the television set while he set out to open the Senior Center or to attend some task in the yard. He wondered for a troubling moment why Tonia never had asked him to join her in enjoying these serial programs that she not only relished but sometimes taped for reviewing late at night, while he slept. He shrugged without understanding.

Mr. Benavidez snapped on the set and settled back on the couch with a little smile teasing the corners of his mouth. First the theme music, then the rolling sea announced the emergence of the lithesome youngster from the frothy waves. The *novio*—as he had in the opening scene the previous night—was just starting across the screen on horseback when Mr. Benavidez heard knocking at the kitchen door.

"God-durn!" Mr. Benavidez hoisted himself with effort from the thick lap of the sofa. "Yah! Yah! I'm coming! *Ojalá que* joor not selling nothing and I don't have to get out the shotgun!"

"Tonia? Tonia?" a persistent and familiar voice queried through the darkened screen. "You ain't forgot the Sewing Bee? Tonia?"

Pulling the door wide, Mr. Benavidez greeted Mrs. Padilla, a neighbor, wearing her usual dark skirt and shawl with gym shoes and white socks folded at the ankle.

"Hi, Joaquin, so how come you're home, huh?" Mrs. Padilla demanded. "Where's Tonia? She ready yet?"

Mrs. Padilla, though a decade younger than Mr. Benavidez, was as senile as he had ever seen a person get without being relegated to live out her remaining days in a *cuartito* at the back of a son or daughter's already crowded house.

It was the store, Mr. Benavidez reflected, sadly, that done it. Mrs. Padilla had come from a terribly poor family. The kind that had only one pair of shoes to share among the thirteen or fourteen kids. The kind that felt a little ashamed at their relief when a baby died from the shits because it meant less competition down the road for clothes and food. Mrs. Padilla had been the beauty of the bunch—*la rubia* with eyes that changed like the sea mirroring shades of the inconstant sky—and as soon as she turned Mari Mar's age, Mr. Benavidez speculated, she married the local storekeeper and was catapulted to the pinnacle of Farmington society some sixty years ago.

The storekeeper was a gringo and at least three times his bride's age when they married. Naturally, he didn't last far into the second decade of marriage though they managed to produce many spoiled and selfish children. After her husband's death, Mrs. Padilla found herself rich, but alone until she met Jimmy Padilla, a gambling railroader ten years her junior. Against the warnings of her friends and family who insisted he wanted her only for the house and the store, Mrs. Padilla (whose other names Mr. Benavidez was at a loss to recall—he shook his head, wondering if he weren't getting a touch of the Alzheimer's, too) impetuously wed the young Mr. Padilla and they had several more spoiled and selfish children raised on striped hard candy from the big-mouth jars in the store.

True to the predictions of friends and family, Mr. Padilla gambled away the store. Mrs. Padilla entered her fifties store-less, living on social security plus a small allowance from one son who was miraculously untainted by the selfishness that spoiled his many siblings.

Mr. Benavidez, recollecting Mrs. Padilla's legendary days of snapping after losing the store, hesitated to remind the old woman in his kitchen that Tonia had passed away some weeks ago. "She ain't here," he finally murmured.

"Hang that dog!" complained Mrs. Padilla, who had

found speaking two languages too much trouble and gave up Spanish as a consequence. "How are we gonna get them tablecloths done?" she challenged Mr. Benavidez. "Huh? Tell me that?"

"What tablecloths?"

"Me an' Tonia is making the tablecloths for the raffle."

Tonia making tablecloths? Why had she been so secretive? "Are you sure?" he peered at Mrs. Padilla, who—since snapping—was not always the most reliable narrator in Farmington.

"She's got them right in here." Mrs. Padilla stepped into the pantry and emerged bearing beige folds of linen and lace, which to Mr. Benavidez' eye, were like gauze or spider-webbing. "And we got the fiestas coming next month. I can't do everything myself."

"But, they are bee-yoo-tee-fool," he whispered, fingering an end.

"It is Tonia got the touch," Mrs. Padilla admitted. "She got the talent. I don't know how she forgot about the Bee."

"You know how it is." Mr. Benavidez shrugged.

"There's only one thing then," said Mrs. Padilla, refolding the unfinished tablecloths. "You gotta come help out in her place."

"Are you—" Delicacy interrupted his speculation over Mrs. Padilla's sanity.

"Am I what?" Mrs. Padilla challenged with a lilt of her chin. "No, I am not crazy."

"I din't mean—"

"C'mon let's go, then. They're waiting over at the church. You watching *Mari Mar*? Put her on the VCR and you can watch her later. Here." She thrust the bundle of cloth into his arms. "I'll do it while you get ready."

"Jus' lemme find my shoes, Mrs. Padilla."

"There's not a lot of time, Joaquin. We got to hurry."

* * *

Regina was not sure why she agreed to marry Pablo. She knew there were considerable small cracks, or "fissures"—as she referred to them privately—in the structure of their relationship. The overlong smiles that ached her face at his silly jokes, the little temptations to nose the car in the opposite direction from the house after work and drive until she ran out of gas, the inexplicable impulses to do things like throw a full can of beer at the back of his head for no reason whatever—all of these things indicated to Regina that there might be, as Mr. Benavidez speculated, some "trouble in *paraiso*."

She considered it might have been the accident on the "Y" that convinced her to accept his proposal of marriage in spite of the problem-citas—as she also began to call them to herself.

The "Y" formed by two highways converging just outside of Truth or Consequences was an especially dangerous piece of roadway because of the many slopes and turns that prevented visibility. This danger was compounded by the extreme high speed or low speed of vehicles—from monster cars to tractors—traversing it. Also, no one had gotten around to paving certain stretches which resulted in the "Y's" nickname of "Blowout Junction."

Regina couldn't remember what bit of business or errand took her and Pablo through the "Y" that day, but as always she insisted on driving wherever they went. It had been Regina at the helm of her little car that rainy afternoon when she noticed a car merging slowly but certainly into the path of a station wagon moving at high speed. She recalled thinking that car would brake at a critical moment. But, it didn't. The two cars collided with the sound of crumpling metal and popping glass. Regina, always a circumspect driver, had only to apply the brakes from her safe distance behind the station wagon to glide to a stop before the wreckage.

The silence that followed the shrieking, grinding, shattering sounds was absolute. Regina and Pablo felt afraid to speak.

Then a rather plump woman in a powder blue jogging suit emerged from the passenger seat of the station wagon and ran in the direction the car had been traveling, away from the accident, away from Pablo and Regina.

"I wonder where she's going," Pablo said.

"Well, she doesn't seem to be hurt that badly. I suppose we'd better get out and see if we can help those other people." Regina did not feel up to chasing the woman in the jogging suit to offer assistance. And she really did not want to peer into darkened windows of crashed cars, for that matter.

"If we had a car phone, we could just call someone for help." Pablo was not eager to get out of the car either. "We could just dial for the police or an ambulance."

"I noticed a mobile home about half a mile back. They might have a phone."

"You want me to go call from there?"

"I could drive back there."

"And leave me?"

"Someone should stay," reasoned Regina.

"Let's go see how those other people are first, so you can give more information,"

"Are you sure we have to?" Regina asked.

"Well, the emergency people oughta know how many, at least."

"I guess you're right."

Reluctantly, Regina and Pablo climbed out of the car. Regina elected to examine the passengers in the station wagon. Since the woman sprinted away, Regina assumed no terrible harm had come to any other people still inside.

A middle-aged man, bald and puffy in the face, slumped

behind the steering wheel of the station wagon, rolling his head and saying softly, "Jesus, Jesus, Jesus."

"You're going to be okay," Regina told him. "You're going to be fine."

"Jesus, Jesus, Jesus."

"We're getting help. You are going to have some help very soon." She spoke in a loud, clear voice so that he would hear her between his cries.

"Jesus, Jesus, Jesus."

She saw a styrofoam coffee cup in a plastic cup holder under the radio and noticed a dark stain welling on the man's jeans. "You must have spilled your coffee." She touched his leg to see if it were burning from the coffee, but his leg was cool and clammy. A sticky rust smeared her fingertips. "We can get you more coffee."

"Jesus, Jesus, Jesus, I don't want to die."

"Hush, now, and rest. You aren't going to die," Regina assured him. "We're getting help for you."

"Jesus, Jesus, Jesus."

"We can get you more coffee, too."

"There's a baby in here!" Pablo called from the other car. The sight of the infant strapped in a babyseat, silent and bleeding from one round cheek, galvanized Pablo. He yanked open the door and released the seat from its belts; he pulled the baby seat a safe distance from the highway. "Go on back to that trailer and call for help! I'll take care of things here!"

Gratefully, Regina backed the car to nose it away from the wreck toward the trailer she had seen about half a mile back.

* * *

By the time Regina returned to the accident scene that afternoon, Pablo had managed to block off the area with flares he had found somewhere—she knew she didn't have as much as a jack in her car trunk—and to cover the victims with blankets. He'd also managed to locate a diaper bag and change the baby's diaper. He was feeding the baby formula from a bottle when he saw Regina and smiled, wearily. They could both hear the sirens in the distance.

"Did that man die?" Regina asked of the driver of the station wagon.

"No, he's in shock. I covered him up."

"But, he was bleeding so badly."

"Cut by the glass from the rearview mirror."

"The other people?"

"Person," Pablo corrected. "It's an old man, so drunk he passed out. I don't know where he was taking this little fellow. But I'm glad he brought the diaper bag."

When the ambulances arrived, Regina had to marvel at Pablo's calm utility in helping out the paramedics. He didn't blanch at the gore—the old man was badly slashed about the face and the Jesus-caller had a good deal more than jagged glass to worry about—nor did he turn away to stare at the empty, cricket-singing alfalfa fields when the elderly victim revived, retching and vomiting a foamy pinkish spew, as he was removed from the car. In fact, Regina completely forgot all about the problem-citas that had been worrying her for so long when Pablo handed the infant over to an ambulance attendant after sneaking a quick kiss on the baby's smooth head.

After the last ambulance pulled away with its siren blaring, Regina and Pablo headed back for the car and started the long drive home.

"Pablo, I..." began Regina, feeling somewhat chastened, "I didn't know you could be so...useful."

"It was the baby. I just wanted to help that baby," he admitted. After a few minutes of silence, he added: "Regina, do you think someday we might have a baby?"

"A baby?"

"Yes, do you think we might have a baby one day?"

"Look, Pablo," Regina leaned forward, pointing at a

pudgy blur of powder-blue loping steadily alongside the road. "Is that the woman from the station wagon?"

"Regina, I love you."

"Look, Pablo, look! She's still running."

"Will you marry me?"

Regina, with her eyes on the rearview watching the woman in the powder-blue jogging suit—her plump knees churning, her red cheeks puffing—nodded, accepting Pablo's proposal.

* * *

Mari Mar had just discovered she was pregnant and was on the verge of divulging this to the duplicitous stepsister of the high-class shirtless man.

"I wouldn't do it, Mari," warned Mr. Benavidez, from his perch at the edge of the couch. He reached in the pocket of Tonia's housecoat for a Virginia Slim. "If I was you."

Behind the washing machine one afternoon as he investigated to see what was making a strange sound like a rattlesnake caught in a snare drum, Mr. Benavidez found one of Tonia's housecoats. It had been her favorite—a soft peach printed cotton that had deep pockets on either side. He lifted it to his face to inhale the warm smell of cinnamon, perfume, hand lotion and the unmistakable coriander and crushed fern smell of Tonia herself.

Now, in the evenings, he found he was more comfortable shedding his khakis, workshirts and boots and slipping the worn housecoat, light as butterfly wings, about him. He liked the voluminous looseness of the garment as it billowed around him when he walked through the house. Each little gust brought a trace of Tonia to his nostrils. And, really, he considered he didn't look too bad for an eighty-year-old man in a woman's cotton housecoat.

"You are a fool." He wagged his finger at Mari Mar, who had grabbed the stepsister's hands to dance in gladness. Mr.

Benavidez could see one of the stepsister's jet eyebrows already arching in treachery. He lit the cigarette and set it in the ashtray with its crimson kiss mark about the filter. This night, he had experimented with a little face powder, some lipstick.

* * *

"Really, it's a simple thing," Mr. Benavidez explained in the classroom, holding the fragile stitching to the fluorescent lighting overhead. "If you ever been a fisherman like my old pops an' worked the nets like I done growin' up, then it ain't that hard."

"But it's so detailed and elaborate." Regina admired the lace work Mr. Benavidez stitched during class.

Since he had become adept at taping *Mari Mar* for viewing late at night when the loneliness crept onto his chest like some kind of odious animal—a muskrat or a possum—to press its weight against his lungs and his heart, Mr. Benavidez found that he not only kept the loathesome beast of loneliness at bay, but he was unfettered to return nightly for the English classes. His first night back, he was anxious to show Regina the stitching he had done to finish Tonia's tablecloth.

"It's called 'tatting' and I betchoo, if an ol' *pendejo* like me can lorn how to do this, then these young *chamacos* can pick it up in no time."

"It looks pretty complicated." Regina shook her head dubiously.

"I can titch you an' you can titch these folks. What do you think? They are almos' done with the piñatas." The piñatas, started as a class project months ago, for all practical purposes were finished. The students grew bored trying to stretch out the application of those final pieces of tissue paper over the last few classes. A few ambitious students, like Arturo, had even completed their second piñata.

"I will make some—how to say, those leetle *cosas en la sofa?*" Arturo was already fascinated by the new craft.

"Los doilies," Benavidez told him.

"I want make los doilies for my wife en Mexico." He pictured a central diamond design with smaller diamonds in each corner.

"Alls we need," pointed out Mr. Benavidez, "is the niddles, the string, an' the cloth."

"It's okay with me, Mr. Benavidez," Regina agreed, "with one condition."

"What condeeshun?"

"You teach the class."

"*Pues*, I ain't no titcher."

"You was a *jefe*, right, when you had the restaurant?" argued Arturo.

"Yah, but..."

"*Jefes* titch pipple," Arturo declared. "Dey titch pipple in the restaurant how to cook, how to peek up the tables, how to serve *la comida*. Eberytheeng!"

Mr. Benavidez scratched the top of his head, making a sound like sandpaper rubbing together. "You're right, ole' man."

"When will you start?"

"First, we need the *materiales*, hokay?"

"I'll work on it," promised Regina, formulating the argument she would use on Olga, her supervisor, ("Juan Carlos doesn't like the idea, but..."), then on Juan Carlos, Olga's boss, ("Olga thinks it's stupid, but...") to get consensus on a requisition for more supplies.

"What's this?" asked Mr. Benavidez suddenly, noticing the infinitesimal diamond chip on Regina's left hand. "You're gettin' married?"

"Sort of," muttered Regina.

* * *

Since the engagement, Pablo had become—to Regina's way of thinking—almost oppressively kind and thoughtful. It was nearly malicious the way he insisted on polishing her shoes, straightening her chest of drawers, throwing the trash out of her car.

"What's wrong," demanded Regina, "with the trash in my car?"

"What do you mean?" puzzled Pablo, who was in the midst of planning some treat—avocado stuffed with crabmeat or, maybe, ceviche—for dinner.

"What's wrong with a person having trash in their car?"

Pablo could see from the way she stood with her hands on her hips and the way her brow knitted that Regina was very angry. "Tell me, what's wrong with that?"

"Well, it might catch on fire," offered Pablo.

"Oh, c'mon, now. Don't give me that!" Regina rolled her eyes. "Trash in a car doesn't just burst into flame."

"It's messy, then."

"A-ha! Messy! That's your opinion, not mine! Who the hell are you to tell me what's messy?"

"What are you talking about, honey?"

"The trash! You took the trash out of my car!"

"I was only trying to help."

"Bullshit! That's bullshit! You were trying to tell me that I'm messy, pretending to be nice about it at the same time, and I think that's the most reprehensible, most heinous, most hypocritical...um, um, thing I can think of!"

"But the car had a lot of trash in it," protested Pablo.

"That was my trash," Regina thrust a finger at her chest. "That trash belonged to me. You had no right to touch my trash!"

"I thought you'd want the car cleaned out. I thought you'd be happy."

"You had no right! That was my trash, and I want it back! I want every piece of it back!" Regina wheeled around and stomped out of the house, heading for her newly-cleaned car.

Pablo rushed to the window and called through the screen, "Regina, I'm sorry!" The car windows were rolled up, and he couldn't be sure that she heard him. "I'll get the trash back, honey! Every bit, I promise!"

Funny, thought Regina, how sometimes you can think about a person and that person will suddenly appear even if you hadn't thought of him or seen him in ages. Her mind skimmed over a few other pesky details about Pablo when it turned, unexpectedly, to the Antichrist. She realized unhappily she was acting a little bit like him. She had even used the same bullying tone on Pablo that the Antichrist had used on her. Hadn't she been kind, though not as relentless, as Pablo to her former husband? She remembered a morning her ex-husband boxed her ears until they bled; she had just set the breakfast table with blueberry pancakes, fresh orange juice, and coffee...

She had not thought about or seen the Antichrist for several months. Her shock, therefore, was intense on seeing him step into the deserted crosswalk that evening right in front of her car, incongruously cradling a red and white striped bag of popcorn to his chest. Regina had been driving fast and, though she slammed her foot on the brake, the car slid. She had to swerve to miss bouncing her ex-husband with her front fender. Meanwhile, with his eyes wide and his mouth agape, he threw the bag of popcorn into the air and scrambled back to the curb.

He looked so comical, tossing up the sack of popcorn and scurrying across the street, that Regina had to bite her lip to suppress the laughter rolling up her throat. The popcorn seemed to fly in an arc and sail a little with a gentle current before scattering in the street.

The Antichrist charged back across the street toward Regina's car, shaking his fist as though he still had some jurisdiction over her actions. He seemed to have forgotten, thought Regina, putting the car into reverse, that they were divorced.

"What the hell is the matter with you, you stupid bitch!" he roared.

Unable to think of anything better to do, Regina gave a friendly wave of her hand and backed the car away from the intersection. As soon as she could, she turned the car around and found herself on the familiar highway to Farmington, though it was not a night for teaching class at the Senior Center.

* * *

Mr. Benavidez poured himself a little glass of orange juice and replayed the taped episode. It was usual for him to view a single installment two or three times depending upon when he became sleepy.

About half an hour later, his head dipped onto his chest and he fell asleep on the sofa with all the lights and the television on. He woke soon after with the sharp rapping on his kitchen door. He rubbed his eyes and lit a cigarette, before he realized he had a late-night guest who would not go away.

"I'm coming. Hold your horses," he muttered, lumbering to the door. He remembered his dress and the cosmetics as he pulled the door open, surprised to admit an equally startled Regina.

"Mr. Benavidez?" she asked, stepping back to discern her old friend under the face powder, the lipstick and the cotton frock. "Mr. Benavidez," she said, again, after a long pause, "I didn't know...you...smoked cigarettes!"

"Yes," admitted Benavidez, recovering only slightly from the horror of being caught in his wife's clothing and makeup, "I guess I got some real bad habits."

Soy la Avon Lady

It's already dark by the time David drives me home. I was going to take the Greyhound, but my brother was coming from Barstow to L.A. anyway to get some supplies for the horse motel. Normally, I can't stand being in the same city with David, let alone the cab of the same pickup. He's one of these guys thinks there's only one way to look at a thing, and he's the only one can see it that way, so you may as well forget it because if you're not him, you won't never understand. My brother wasn't always like this. Was the horse motel made him an ass. Everyone knows he was just a sawed-off volunteer fireman and fry-cook at the Denny's on the business route before he married that widow, la Betty Crocker, and got her to convert her dead husband's ranch into a horse motel. Now he's Mr. David Martinez, business-man extraordinaire, though, no matter how often he showers and changes his clothes, he always smells a little like his horse motel. I talk to him about it. I even try to get him to take a little Avon for this problem.

As soon as I get in the truck I rolls down my window to let in some desert air and I says, "You know, David, we carry some very effective men's colognes."

"That's the problem with this country," he starts in, pointing out a primered Chevy loaded to the gills with Mexicans.

"Now, I know you like the Skin-So-Soft for fishing."

"Keeps the mosquitos off." He nods. "Look at that. Can't even goddamn signal. Learn to drive, *mojados!*" he shouts out the window.

"Yeah, well, we have some real good aftershave and soap, too."

"Listen," he says to me, sighing. "You're what? Forty-eight? I know I got a couple years on you, and I'm hitting fifty. But a good fifty, a solid fifty. I got my business, and I got my health. But you, look at you. All that makeup. I know you're my sister an' you're a chick. I seen your twat when mama used to give us a bath together. But I have to be honest here, you're big enough to play for the Forty-Niners. And you're running around like some overgrown campfire girl in drag for Godsake, selling cookies. Ain't no one uses Avon no more, except to keep mosquitos off. It's gutdamn irritating to hear you turn every conversation into a sales pitch. Whyn't you just settle down and stop bugging folks."

So that kind of puts me in a sour mood, even if it is coming from David, whose entire fortune and well-being comes from his settling down, marrying la Betty Crocker. Come to think of it, he's probably given me the best advice he knows. I only wish he could follow the second half of his own great advice because as soon as he made his little speech, he started in on the time Johnny Carson called him up at the horse motel.

"Now, I ain't sayin' I planned it thataway," says David, a grin cracking under his red beak of a nose. "Now, I'm not saying I arranged the call, but you gotta admit it was a pretty gutdamn strategic bit of public relations."

I just rolled my eyes, rubbing my fingers over the upsidedown "M" scarred on my forehead. David calls it my "W." His way of seeing things. Anyone else'd tell you, despite all the Avon fill and foundation, the powder and whisper blush, what I got is an inverted "M" up there, for my name, for Molly. Like some kind of cockeyed monogram. I trace the path of weals through one eyebrow and up toward my hairline, rising in the middle like a reverse widow's peak. Then I stare out the window at the neon-haloed car dealerships, K-marts, pizzerias, and dry cleaners blurring past along the highway. I have been back and forth between Barstow and L.A. at least a thousand times. There is no really scenic route, but you'd think that over time there would at least be a slightly less ugly way to go or that a person could get used to the boringness of it all.

The time Johnny Carson called David I happened to be watching the show. I was half-crocked from that wine you buy in a carton, I admit, but even I, stumbling in my negligee before the blue-gray haze of my black-and-white set, even I could see that old Johnny had just called my brother up to laugh at him. I have to jam a soup spoon between the wall and a critical place bulging out of the back of the set to get a good picture, and that night the spoon had popped out. So Johnny's smirking eyes boiled through a blizzard of static. Even so, those pebbly eyes clearly smirked, and I could even see Johnny bite back his lipless, lizard grin as he chatted on the phone with my brother.

"Johnny was pur-ty surprised to find out we have a horse motel in Barstow. Told him it was the only one in the state. Still is," David turned to nod at me in agreement with himself. "But, man, was he shocked about the elevator. 'State of the art' I says to him. 'State of the art.'"

Around that point in the famous conversation, I remember Johnny passing the phone to that big guy, the one who looks like a refrigerator wearing a suit and who laughs at everything Johnny says, that what's-his-name, on account of he, Johnny, that is, had to double over with spasms he made like he couldn't control.

"People need a horse motel, I 'splained to him," David goes on. "They's rodeos and horse shows and all kinds of reasons to take a horse somewhere overnight."

The thing is, though an idea like a horse motel sounds pure ridiculous to someone like Johnny Carson, who has like a castle in Malibu and makes jokes about how much alimony he has to shell out, and even to a person like me, who sells Avon between temporary secretarial jobs, plenty of people seem to truly feel the need for lodging their horses at my brother's motel.

"You know how much business shot up after that show aired?" David demands after he wound up the full retelling of his telephone conversation on the Tonight Show so many years ago.

I nod, closing my eyes and scrunching myself into a ball against the car door, so David might think I'm drifting off to sleep.

"How much, then?" he persists.

"A lot," I'm yawning by now.

"Gutdamn straight."

We pass a batch of black-and-white cows alongside the highway, grazing and staring without much curiosity at the passing cars.

"Hey, you remember when we first moved to Barstow? You were just a little thing, black as a bullfrog. Yammered your ugly little head off in Spanish. Scared those old folks in that diner. Remember? Musta thought they was being invaded."

"You're nuts. I never spoke Spanish."

"Don't tell me you don't remember. You were at least four or five. Coupla years later, I remember, we went back home for a visit on the train. Was on the train. You were staring out the window and pointing a dark little finger at a cow. You ast, 'Is thet a kay-ow?'" David does his best Southern drawl, which is purely pathetic. "I'll never forget. You were still as black as a bullfrog. An' I remember you had those floppy yellow shorts. A bullfrog in a pair of yellow shorts."

I let David laugh, enjoy his little make-believe story. Pulling my jacket over my shoulder, I let myself drift off. I must have slept the rest of the ride into the city because the next thing I remember is David shaking my shoulder and saying "end of the road." I thank him for the ride, and as usual he doesn't wait for me to fish my key out of my handbag ust came here for the

, then." She hands me

ctor now. This is an

while I'm filling in

astern—maybe even

nto the waiting room

s in that choppy way

ng to die if he doesn't

to fill forms.

eaching over to take

while I examine your

w and hoping there's

i."

k momentarily."

said "momentarily,"

l sure he's Lebanese.

twins, both butchers,

row me the leftover.

bloodstained aprons.

dump them both and

nymous Nordic type,

sk if he had a brother.

hing. She was in the

he didn't go through

d Grandma. And her

the glaring wait area,

ling station near the

or find my way to my apartment door before peeling off like some teenager playing chicken at a stoplight. And I live in a pretty rotten building, to be honest. If David was any kind of decent brother, he would have at least walked me to my door.

I have to step over all the usual wadded-up disposable diapers, fast-food wrappers and beer bottles, finally feeling my way along a mildewed mattress propped against the wall near my door. There's a cluster of Mexicans in undershirts, jabbering at each other and drinking cans of beer under the street lamp just across the way. Anyone might jump out with a switchblade and rob me of my Avon case, which was all I had of any value, as David, naturally, had forgotten to pay me for the bottles of Skin-So-Soft he ordered.

I make it to the door okay, but once inside I slam my hip on the telephone table, knocking the phone on the floor and scaring poor Fabian out of his little cat wits. "It's okay, Fabian, it's just me," I says in a calm voice because Fabian has pretty bad asthma, and stress can cause him to have an attack. I set my case on the floor and went to pet Fabian's thick gray fur. His breathing is already growing shallow and ragged. "Damn," I says, but quietly, and I drew him in my arms. He struggles and squeezes out of my grip, running around the house and hacking like he was trying to bring up a hair ball.

I pick the phone off the floor and dial real quick. The line rings twice, and then I hear a loud and gruff "Yah!"

"Uncle Enrique?"

"Yah!"

"It's me, Molly." Fabian, though heaving and retching, bounced from the couch to the coffee table like he's place-kicked by some unseen demon.

"He-e-e-ey, Mulligan! *¿Como estas?*" Like a lot of old guys, my uncle never quite trusts telephone wires to carry his voice over any kind of distance, so he has to holler his head off into the mouthpiece.

"Uncle Rique, it's an emergency! Can you come over and

take me to the hospital right now?" I have to hold the [
at least a foot from my head and shout back.

"Of course, *hita*, are you okay? Wanna ambulance

"NO! I just need a ride!"

"I'm coming right now!"

I don't mention it's Fabian that needs the hospital,
know my uncle Enrique isn't the kind of uncle who p
too much for information, particularly personal inform
He probably thinks I'm bleeding to death from a b
abortion, and if that's the case, he'd just as soon not kn
particulars.

I catch up with Fabian in the bathroom where he'
ging over the plunger behind the toilet. I pull him out
him in a bath towel and bring him to the kitchen, w
pour myself some handy carton chablis into a coffee
stand there drinking the wine and cuddling Fabian v
wait the few minutes it takes my uncle to drive over. Fa
plump body shudders as he gasps, struggling to breath
is the worst attack he has ever had, and I'm scared he's
die before Uncle Enrique gets here.

But still I could feel him fighting for air as I carri
to the door when I heard Uncle Enrique knocking. I'd
on the outside light, and Uncle blinks on the threshold
tell when he makes out the towel-wrapped bundle in m
because he quickly shifts his eyes away. "It's Fabian,
Rique, he's having an asthma attack!" I push out the
door.

"Fabian?"

"My cat! He's gonna die if we don't hurry." Say
words makes my voice crack, and the tears leap out
eyes.

"A cat? Is that what you got there? A durn cat?"

"It's Fabian. You remember Fabian?"

"I remember the movie star." My uncle scratches h
making a raspy sound with his fingernails. "Singe
wasn't he?"

"Have you been here before?"

"No, my usual vet is closed now. [
emergency hours."

"You'll have to fill out these form
a clipboard.

"But Fabian needs to see the d
emergency," I says. "My cat might d
these papers!"

Just then a nice-looking Middle
Lebanese—man in a white coat steps
from a door behind the counter.

"What is the matter here?" he as
foreigners have.

And I says that I think Fabian is gc
get help now and that I don't have tim

"I will look at the cat," he says,
Fabian. "You can fill out the paperwor
cat, Miss—"

"Martini," I says, smiling a little n
no lipstick on my teeth, "Molly Marti

"Okay, Miss Martini, I will be ba

My heart flutters a little when h
and he puts his dark eyes on mine. I fe
My sister Gloria once dated Lebanese
and I'd hoped she'd marry one and t
They were so darling in their matching
But Gloria decided she would rather
have a child out-of-wedlock with an an
who I never even met, let alone got to
But Gloria's like that; she can get an
back seat when we had the accident.
the windshield like me and Barbara a
skin is as white as the heart of a radis

Uncle Enrique blinks his way into
saying, "I had to park clear at that f

freeway." He sits beside me and picked up a copy of *Cat Fancy* to thumb through. "Where's Fabian?" he asks.

"The doctor's looking at him. You got a pen, Uncle?"

He leans over to reach into his side pocket and pulls out his key chain with at least three million keys attached to it, a Swiss Army knife, a bottle opener, a teensy sewing kit and a little bitty pen and pencil set. He hands me a pen the size of a toothpick, saying, "Here you are, *hija*."

I take that itsy-tiny pen and start filling out the forms, while my uncle chews on his tongue and reads an article in *Cat Fancy*.

After a while, Uncle scratches his head. "Gotta story here," he says, "about a Siamese cat s'pose to beat up a grizzly bear to save the life of a *dog*. You believe that?"

I shrug and write something unreadable under "Current Employer." I didn't like to put Avon or "it varies" in case the doctor should look over my form.

"Says the cat jumped on the bear's head from a tree and scratched its eyes. Blinded him," Uncle continues. "I guess it could happen. But to save *a dog?*"

As I was signing the last sheet, the doctor appeared again. "Miss Martini," he says, "I am so terribly sorry."

"Martini?" asks my uncle, looking around though we're the only ones in the waiting room.

"This is my uncle," I says, not wanting to hear the doctor say anything else.

"Yes, it's good to meet you. I have some bad news I am afraid. Your cat has died. Of course, there will be no charge. I could do nothing to help him."

I remember how my mother threw herself on Grandma's casket when they were ready to lower it in the ground, and afterwards the aunts really criticized her for that because my mother is kind of an underachiever emotionally, so when she makes a display it's usually for show. Back then at the funeral, even I, in my turban of bandages which was coming unraveled and the gauze was falling in my face, even I could see my mother was making a show, and I felt so embarrassed I wished I could shrink up like a pine nut and roll into the earth right besides Grandma. But in the animal emergency hospital that night, I thought of my mother when I fell into that doctor's strong Lebanese arms, and I realized the truth about my mother's scene at the graveside: it was only part show.

"Miss Martini, please, please," says the doctor, patting my shoulder with one hand, but pushing me upright with the other.

"Name's not Martini," scoffs my uncle. He's often impatient with foreigners. "It's Mar*tinez*."

I have Uncle Enrique drop me at the VFW club. I'm way too depressed to go home and put up Fabian's little rolling toys, his catnip mouse and wash out his double-sided dish.

"Are you sure, *m'hija*? It's pretty late."

"Yeah, I'm sure," I says, remembering I had no money. "How 'bout you come and have a drink with me?"

"No, no, no way," he says. "I gotta go to court tomorrow. Remember my friend Kiko? He gotta ticket. I said I would drive him."

"Isn't Kiko the one who rides a bicycle?" I says, recalling a fat guy in a Dodger cap, teetering on a Schwinn. "He doesn't even have a car. How'd he get a ticket?"

"Riding under the influence."

"Oh... You could still have one drink with me," I says.

"Oh, no. I better not." Uncle Enrique pulls along the curb in front of the VFW and leans again to reach in his back pocket. "You need some money, *hij*a. I got a little extra." He hands me a twenty-dollar bill. "I'm real sorry about the cat, that Fabian," he says as I got out. "You take care of yourself, okay, Mulligan?"

* * *

"Hey, it's Molly! Molly Martini! We thought you was still in Barstow!" My best friend Charlene waddles over and climbs a barstool near the door to wrap her fat, freckled little arms around my neck.

"Hi, Shorty," I says, smiling a little, but sadly, so Charlene will know right off that I'm feeling down. I call her "Shorty" because she's a dwarf, a "little people," that's what she likes to be called, anyway, and not a dwarf or a midget. She's not just one of these shorter folks that everyone exaggerates about when they call her a dwarf. She really is under three feet tall. Her mother was a dwarf, an actress who had a part in the *Wizard of Oz*, and her father was a dwarf too, but I'm not sure what he does for a living. We met one time at a funeral for another dwarf we both happened to know and got to be friends at the bar afterwards.

"What's wrong, Miss Martini?" Charlene squeaks, seeing my sad smile.

"I lost my Fabian tonight," I says, starting to sob even before Willie, the bartender, can slide me my drink.

Well, you know, I cry a lot that night, and I have to say I drink a bit, too. I go through that twenty pretty fast, even though some people buy me drinks. Turns out it's our friend Fisher Boy's birthday, and his wife Millie, an ex-school photographer from Visalia, has a cake for him and a half a case of champagne. So you know I drink my share of that, and I eat a wedge of cake the size of Charlene's ox-blood prayerbook. I know they're the same size on accounta Charlene sets her prayerbook on the pool table alongside of my paper plate.

Fisher Boy has his own bottle of champagne, and he sits at the bar nursing on it like a baby. Has a bunch of friends with him, some guys I don't recognize. But old Fisher Boy won't talk to anyone 'til he's finished his drink. This heavy guy—bald on top, but with long hair, wearing a leather vest and no shirt underneath—lumbers up on the stage over past the shuffleboard table, his bootheels blasting like gunshots. He grabs the microphone, which wails in my ear painfully. Then he taps it some, causing a couple of thunder rolls. "I jes' wanna say," he mutters into the netted bulb of the mike, "we all of us here—all us veterans and friends of veterans in this club—come together to honor one of our own on his birthday. Now, don't matter if you fought in double-ewe, double-ewe one, two or three—"

I shoot a look at Charlene. I'm never good with numbers, but I'm pretty sure we'd only gotten to two with the wars. Charlene had her stubby index and middle fingers out, counting under her breath.

"Korea or Nam. Was in Nam myself, and I ain't proud of what I done. I raped. I pillaged. I even helped burn down some villages. And, in general, I ain't proud of those things, but I am proud to be a veteran of a foreign war and proud to be a member of this club and mostly proud to be a friend to this man we honor tonight on his birthday. Getcher ass up here, Fisher Boy! Willie, somebody, help him up the steps."

Fisher Boy steps up two of the stairs without help, then falls to his knees and crawls up the remaining two and over to the microphone. The rapist and pillager lifts Fisher Boy to his feet and pushes him toward the microphone stand, which Fisher Boy clings to as if it's a masthead on a ship tossed around in a storm.

"Hallo, everybody! I'm Fisher Boy, an' I'm a drunk!"

Everyone laughs, and some folks hoot back, "Hello, Fisher Boy!" It's like a reverse Alcoholics Anonymous meeting. Pretty funny, really, if you consider the circumstances.

"What I want to say is, first of all, I wanna thank my good friend, Lyle, for the innerduction—"

"Lowell," hisses the rapist and pillager.

"Huh?"

"Lowell. My name's Lowell."

"Oh, yeah, right. Well, anyway, thanks a lot. An' I wanna thank everyone for coming tonight, though you were probably coming here anyway and just found out it was my birthday a few minutes ago. What I got to say is, I'm seventy-eight years old, an' I'm a veteran a' World War Two. I don't think we got to Three yet, Lyle, but I ain't been payin' too much 'tention. I was a clerk typist in the army, an' I din't get any opportunities to rape an' pillage too much, but I wisht they had invented white-out then because I ruint a whole lot of forms. Man, you shoulda heard the guys cuss when I screwed up their passes. Holy Moly! Anyway, point is, we're all here, and it's my birthday. So have some cake and have a drink!"

Fisher Boy hoists his champagne bottle and pours the dregs down his chin, darkening the front of the new t-shirt his wife has given him. The front of it says, HERE COMES FISHER BOY! and the back reads, THERE GOES FISHER BOY! I think it's pretty clever, almost as funny as the baseball cap someone else has given him with a fake ponytail attached to the back.

We all clap and sing 'Happy Birthday', then 'For He's a Jolly Good Fellow' and clap some more. While I'm beating my hands together for old Fisher Boy, Charlene dug a sharp little elbow in my rib cage. "Guess who just come in?" she hisses.

"Who?" I says, looking around.

"Suzy Q."

"Oh, no." Now, if I feel sad about losing Fabian, I feel almost worse when Charlene tells me my baby sister had just come into the VFW. Suzy Q is good or bad, hot or cold, dark or ... only dark, actually. But, you get the picture. She's never in-between on anything, not ever.

When Suzy Q is good, she's at home, taking care of those three little half-Japanese children of hers, making a super-tasty supper for her husband Dean, and keeping that house so clean you could conduct major surgery on her bathroom floor, behind the toilet, even. But when, Suzy Q is bad, Lord, you sometimes have to scrape her off a gutter and throw her in the drunk tank at county for at least a week, if you can find her. Last time she was bad was around Christmas. She went missing for a week, and poor Dean had to hire a private investigator to find her in some by-the-hour hotel room with a skinhead junkie from Altoona, who was, Dean says, not sorry at all to cut her loose.

"Where is she?" I ask Charlene.

"Over to the back. That tall booth she likes."

"I guess I oughta go and talk to her," I says, real slowly, so's Charlene can interrupt and argue me out of it.

But she says, "I guess you oughta."

I make my way to the back of the bar, pulling off the party hat someone stuck on my head. You can't have a serious talk with someone like Suzy Q wearing a polka-dot cone spouting pink and green streamers over your hair.

Suzy Q favors a booth near the ladies room, one of the older ones that hasn't been reupholstered with scotch-guard like most of the others. The VFW used to be a decent kind of bar at one time, with wood floors, stained glass windows and real near-leather booths. But they covered the wood with parquet and sold the stained glass and only a few near leather-booths remain. People generally don't like to sit in them, though, because they tend to make your buttocks and backs of your legs sweat, and then you stick, so you make bathroom sounds as you peel yourself out of your seat.

But I doubt if my sister sweats all that much. She reminds me of a long cool glass of ice tea. Her clear copper skin chills your finger tips when you brush against it. And you can almost hear the ice cubes rattle when she walks. She even smells like a sprig of mint, a wedge of lemon. With her long brown legs, her wide eyes and Cleopatra-flat black hair, my baby sister could be a desirable woman if she wasn't so criminally insane when she was bad.

"Hullo, Suzy," I says, thinking how lovely she looked in a peppermint-striped shift—ice tea in a slender barber's cup.

"Amalia," she says, putting out her frosty fingers to delicately shake mine. "How good to see you." Suzy has the habit of whispering in a breathy way when she talks. You can barely hear her, and you can't help but hear every word at the same time. She has the kind of voice that I imagine would be just perfect for reading stories in the tabloids out loud. *Woman Gives Birth to Baby with Dog's Head*, would sound just right coming out of her mouth.

"Where's Dean?" I ask, noting the near-finished gin and tonic near her elbow. Poor Dean doesn't like Suzy Q to drink for all the obvious reasons.

"Dean?" Suzy Q repeats like it was a foreign word. "Dean? Dean?"

"Your husband, Dean Fujimori. Where is he? And the kids? How are the kids?"

"Bartender!" she roared right in my ear.

"Golly, Suzy, you about took my hearing out."

"Another, please," she says with a smile when Willie appeared at her elbow.

Willie nods, giving me a nervous look. "Um, are you sure?"

"Perfectly sure," whispers Suzy, pulling a roll of twenties out of her handbag. "Just keep them coming, will you?"

Willie hesitates. "How long are you staying?"

"Not long," says Suzy. "Not very long at all."

"You aren't going to do the ladies room like last time, are you?"

"Don't be silly," Suzy laughs.

"'Cause they said they was gonna cancel my policy, that kind of thing happens again."

"I'm not staying long, Willie. I promise. Just bring me another, please."

Willie retreats in an undecided way, like he didn't get to

say all he had to say, but he brought the drink in a few minutes anyway.

"So," says Suzy Q, staring at me from head to toe. "So, Amalia, how are you these days? My, you've grown a bit."

"Thyroid," I says. "And my metabolism's changing."

"I see."

"Heard you had some trouble around Christmas," I says, taking a chance.

"That!" she giggles. "That was not trouble. Nothing near trouble. I'll tell you what trouble is. Trouble is that people don't even know what trouble is and what trouble can do when it wants to, and that, my sister, is real trouble."

"Well, Dean was pretty upset."

"Dean?"

"Maybe you want to go home, Suzy, after your drink. Maybe I'll go with you. I haven't seen the kids for a long time."

"Listen, Amalia, do you remember when we were kids? Do you remember that skinny little tree Dad tried to get to grow in the front of the house? I keep thinking about that tree."

"What about it?" I remembered my father brought home what looked like a twig one day from the nursery and said we were going to have shade for the house in a couple of years. He propped that twig with a two-by-four, watered it, fertilized it and even built a short white wire fence around the base to keep dogs off. I can still see him, coming home from work in his rumpled overalls with his lunch-box and heading straight for the hose to feed his tree.

"That tree never had a chance, Amalia, the way we treated it."

"What do you mean?"

"You don't remember how we bent it and pulled the leaves, dancing around it like it was the Maypole. You don't remember that?"

"Maybe a little. But we didn't kill the tree. A tree like that can't survive in the desert."

"You were the worst one, Amalia, hanging on that tree and singing at the top of your lungs at anyone driving by. You remember that song you always sang."

"You're making this up, now." I was starting to get mad. Many of my conversations with my kid sister tend to go this way: she claims to remember something stupid or shameful I did when I was drunk or when I was a senseless kid, and I get all upset about it.

"I think it was from *West Side Story*," she persists, tapping her long red fingernails on the tabletop. "What was it? Oh, I know. It went like this, 'I wanna be Americana! I wanna be Americana!' You sang that all damn day long, every day one summer. Don't you remember? It was perfectly hideous! You would wear one of Mama's floppy skirts and pearls—I remember the pearls—and pin yellow yarn to your head to give yourself long blond hair. Then you'd scream 'I wanna be Americana!' at the top of your silly lungs at any car went by. God, I was six years younger than you, but I wanted to die from embarrassment. The whole neighborhood must have thought the natives were *very* restless that summer." Suzy laughs, lighting a cigarette.

"You know what. I do remember that summer. But it was you, Suzy Q, it was you sang that stupid song over and over and over and over and—"

"Don't be ridiculous." Suzy takes a huge swallow of her drink and a drag on her cigarette. "You were the one."

"Drop it, Suzy. Drop it, please." My eyes fill, blurring my long cool ice tea sister with her cigarette and her drink.

She snaps her fingers. "What does Uncle Enrique call you? What is that little nickname he gave you?"

"Mulligan."

"Just what does that mean? Mulligan?"

"I really don't know."

"Oh, I know, doesn't it mean 'do over'? Like in golf,

when you make some horrid error. It's so bad, they call it a 'mulligan,' and you get the chance to try again."

"I'm not sure. I don't know golf."

"Good name," says Suzy, mashing out her cigarette.

"Suzy," I hear someone say. I glance up at Dean, standing by the booth and holding out his hand toward my sister. "Suzy, let's go home. I had to leave the kids alone to come here. Let's go home. It's late."

"How did you find me?" Suzy asks, half-rising from the booth, then sinking back down.

"Willie called me."

"You shit!" Suzy yells across the room. From where I sit, I can see Willie give a little shrug.

"Let's go home, Suzy. I'll make you a bath and light some candles. It will be so nice." Poor Dean keeps his hand out, so Suzy can grab it and steady herself to walk out. My brother-in-law is almost as large as a sumo wrestler, and I have no doubt he could have whipped Suzy out of the booth by her hair and tucked her—hissing and spitting like a cat—under one arm to carry out to the car. But Poor Dean favors a gentle approach with my sister—soft words, tender touches, candles and warm baths.

Suzy whispered some curse words, then she takes Poor Dean's hand and lifts herself noiselessly out of the booth. "I was ready to come home anyway," she says, looking at me. "It's so goddamn boring here."

* * *

Of course, I have to dance with the rapist and pillager after a few more drinks.

"I never danced with a raper and pillagist before," I admit as we hoof to some tune about Lubbock, Texas.

"Jes' call me Lowell," he says, smiling, and I notice he is either handsome in an ugly way or ugly in a handsome way. He had two full moons that stuck out on his chin, looked just like a stubbly baby's bottom and squinty green eyes hummocked in gooseflesh pouches. It sounds bad here, but if you blurred your eyes you might look at Lowell and think of Robert Mitchum. A bald Robert Mitchum with shoulder-length locks of dirty blond hair. You have to use your imagination some.

After a few more dances and a lot more drinks, I guess Lowell isn't so bad for a rapist and pillager. In between the dances, I tell him about Fabian, and he says he feels bad for me. He says he's done some time, and he can really appreciate a gal like me, then he winks. He offers to give me a lift home. So I tell him where I live, and I say good-bye to everyone. Charlene grabbed my elbow hard with her sharp little fingers as I'm on my way out. "Miss Martini," she says, "Miss Martini, you be careful. 'Sa full moon," she says. "Take care of yourself." Then she looked at Lowell and raised her eyebrows, rubbing her turned-up nose.

Turns out Lowell had a motorcycle. And, boy, am I glad I'm drunk because you can't get me on one of those things sober, I tell you. Lowell starts out a gentleman and lets me mash my big old hair under his greasy helmet, which is real good of him. Then I climb on behind Lowell, and the thing farts off down the street. Now, I don't drive. I never have, and I never want to, so I don't pay much attention to directions. I don't think it's too strange when Lowell gets on one freeway, then another. But along about the third freeway it seems like a lot of time has passed, and I know I don't live that far from the VFW.

With the rushing wind and the sounds of traffic—yes, there's traffic even in the middle of the night—it would be pretty useless to holler: "I think you're going the wrong way!" or "Where the hell are you taking me?" And anyone who's ever ridden the back of a motorcycle on a freeway knows there isn't any way of getting off or making the driver stop. So I just clutch at Lowell's lardy sides and thank God Above I'm loaded, or I would have been plenty scared.

It's one of those oily nights, when even the leaves of the oleander bushes along the freeway seem slick and slimy. A fish-smelling fog from San Pedro crawls over, clouds car windows and fuzzes the street lamps. Of course, I'm about dead blind anyway without my glasses. My mother is totally blind, and I expect I'll be there, too, one day. It runs in the family. But the fog muffling the moon and my eyes tearing up from the wind in my face makes it near impossible to see where I am. Just the sensation of moving downward, descending, makes me think we're headed toward the Valley.

I recognize the In-and-Out Burger at the off-ramp that leads to my cousin Elaine's house in Sylmar, where I always went for Thanksgiving and Christmas dinner. Awhile back, In-and-Out printed up a mess of bumper-stickers for advertising. Then some brilliant jokers had the idea to scratch out the "B" and "R" from "burger," and to this day you can spot all these cars with "IN-AND-OUT-URGE" pasted all over their back bumpers. Real hilarious.

I'm glad Lowell's getting off the freeway. Maybe he can drop me at Elaine's. I try to give people the benefit, you know. Maybe he's confused by my directions or too drunk to figure them out. He takes us to a little park not too far from Elaine's house. One of those small grassy jobs with the sandlot swingset near a baseball diamond and bleachers.

"My cousin Elaine lives near here," I says, climbing off the bike, my legs still atremble from the vibration of the engine. "You wanna take me to her house?"

"Let's take a walk," says Lowell. Then he grabs hold of my hand, leading me under the bleachers.

"What is that horrible stench?" I says because suddenly I smell the nastiest maggotty smell, like hundred-year-old banana skins layered with fertilizer, then soaked in soured milk.

Lowell just jerks a thumb at a nearby dumpster, and before I can say another word, he jumps all over me, and we both tumble in the dirt. Then he starts grunting and dry-humping my hip like a badly behaved hound. "Jesus," I says, "get off me, will you?"

His hands are all over me, squeezing my bra padding through my blouse, stroking my hips and reaching under my skirt. "Cuss me in Spanish," he moaned. "Cuss me in Spanish."

"What?" I says, pushing his hands away from my skirt.

"C'mon, baby. Cuss me in Spanish, bad boy," he says again.

"Will you get off me!" I holler. "I don't even speak Spanish! Get off before I yell 'rape'!"

One renegade hand shoots up my slip, and he froze.

"I mean it," I says, "I'll scream 'rape'!"

"My, God. What is this?" he asks, sitting up. "You *are* a chick! I thought—"

"What did you think?"

"At the bar, I thought they said... You look..."

"What? Tell me?"

"No offense, but chicks ain't my thing."

"Just take me to my cousin's house, and we'll forget all about this," I says, smoothing my skirt, "or you can be looking at some pretty serious trouble."

Old Lowell doesn't say anything to that. He just stands up and brushes the dirt from his Levis and starts walking back to the bike. I get up, too, and follow after him, but it's hard to keep up because I'm wearing these lamé heels that kept sinking into the soft dirt, stalling me. "She just lives a few blocks from here. I can show you how to get there," I says. But I can tell by the hunch of his back and the blank look of the hairless cap of his head that Lowell isn't listening at all. And sure enough, he pulls that smelly helmet over his own head, climbs on the bike and sputters off without me.

"Shit," I says, "shit, shit, shit." Then I take off my heels, but not my pantyhose as there was a clammy feeling from the fog which leaked into the valley, and I start to walk, block by block, to Elaine's house. And I get lost and keep getting lost. The soles of my hose are shredded, only a few tough threads keep them from rolling up my ankles. I wander around looking for Elaine's place until the foothills glow like coals in the barbecue from the sun coming up. I tell you Sylmar is one hilly place, where I do not recommend tramping around in nearly bare feet. There's all these same-looking stucco houses made to look like Spanish-style adobe, some huge yards, horse property even, and at least twenty-five million loud barking dogs, snorting and throwing themselves into the chainlink as I pass by.

Somewhere I take a very wrong turn, then another and another. The ranch-style houses disappear, replaced by liquor stores, dry cleaners, Mexican markets and apartments like concrete blocks scrawled with graffiti. The signs, the billboards, the street names change from English to Spanish, and the few folks I see rushing out to work are short, dark and completely uninterested in me. I might be invisible as far as they're concerned. It's almost as if they hood their eyes against me. And I feel like I'm intruding in some foreign country, like I'm in the heart of Mexico or San Salvador or some place even more dangerous.

Then I get the idea that I've died, that Lowell has snuffed me by the dumpster, and it's my soul wandering unseen in these foreign streets. I always was slow to understand things in school. Maybe I have died and am just too shocked or too stupid to realize it. That's when I see a burnt-down gas station, which has a phone booth still standing at the edge of the charred lot, so I bolt across the street to see if it would work, and I hear the shriek of brakes and feel a whalloping thud against my thigh, which sends me sprawling to my knees. A lowered Chevy breathes hotly in my face. The driver blasts the horn like an afterthought, and I stand up, waving to show I'm fine.

"Maricon!" the driver, a young man in a white uniform, screams at me before speeding away. That's when I know I'm not dead; I'm only in San Fernando or maybe in Pacoima.

My hip hurts. There's probably a king-size bruise forming
on it, but nothing's broken, and I check both ways before
continuing across the street. The phone looks to be more or
less unburnt, so I lift the receiver to hear the most wonderful
sound you can hear when you're lost and you've finally found
a phone booth—a dial tone. I reached into my handbag,
fishing for my emergency quarter, which I found
straightaway for once. I push it into the coin slot, but the dial
tone persisted. Thirty-five cents, a little sticker under the coin
slot reads, announcing the rate change. I only had the one
quarter.

I have to call someone collect. Charlene and the others
will be snoring it off—deaf, unconscious even until early
afternoon. Elaine will have left for work by this time. There's
only one person I can think to call collect this early, so I dial
the number. The operator has me give my name after the
recorded message asks whether charges will be accepted.
Then I hear my uncle Enrique, his voice husky with sleep,
but very clear, when he says, "No, no, no, thank you," and he
hung up.

There are some things that are beyond crying about. Now
I could cry and cry and cry when I lost Fabian. That's sad,
but not too unbelievable. After all, he was an old cat, and he
had the asthma pretty bad. Of course, I'll miss him, but I will
get used to it. There are some things I will never get used to
like being in a foreign country not twenty minutes from
where I live, like almost being raped by a biker who mistakes
me for a transvestite, like being hit by a car and then called
maricon, like having the one person who never lets you down
say finally and at last, "No, no, no, thank you," and mean, *no
more, please, I don't want no more of you, Mulligan.*

I walk some more, but I don't know or care where I'm
going. Then I notice this tiny old woman, wearing a dotted
jersey dress and black high-top shoes like my grandmother
used to wear, with the skinny black laces threading all the
way up to her shins. She even has a rope of silver hair snake-

coiled at the nape of her neck like Grandma's famous bun. Only thing is, her posture isn't too straight like Grandma's. Grandma used to walk around like she swallowed a broomstick, and it made her so straight she could barely bend. In fact, she used to unlace those high black shoes in the house, peel off her stockings and pick up fallen objects with her toes, rather than stoop for them. Remembering that feels like letting a warm breeze roll over me, a desert breeze fragrant with the smell of mesquite and piñon. So I follow that old woman, thinking she might lead me to a place that I would know where I was.

The aunts said I was her favorite grandchild. I used to pull a stool to the sink to try to help her with the dishes, but she would set me down, saying washing dishes wasn't work for me. She spoke only Spanish, and I don't know how I understood her, never speaking the language myself. Now I think we must have communicated through the bones. I remember brushing her long silver hair until it snapped and sparked with electricity, and I remember toying with the bottles and tubes on her dresser, rouging my cheeks with her compact and spritzing my neck with her atomizer of scent.

And in the car, we rode together in the front seat with Barbara, who liked to drive. We always rode together in the front, holding hands, Grandma and me. It made Gloria so mad, but Suzy Q was too young to care. Grandma liked to see who was out and about and make comments on everyone she saw. And that last day, a Sunday, we were coming from mass, she was the one to point to the station wagon bearing down on us like a cannonball, and she said, *"¡Aí borracho!"* That's what she said, and I did know that word. I got gooseflesh remembering it while I followed that strange old woman in San Fernando or maybe in Pacoima.

I remember smiling, waiting for my grandma to make a joke about the drunken man, but instead there was screaming, then an explosion of glass and metal and a red veil poured over my face. The newspaper said my grandmother had died on impact, but there weren't any reporters there; they didn't know. I was there, and I crawled all the way out the windshield, pushing the veil out of my eyes. Everyone was quiet, as though under a sleeping spell like the kingdom in that fairytale. Then I heard my grandmother's voice praying. Her vein-corded fingers groped, and I took her hand between my palms. I looked at her face, but I couldn't see her, or I don't remember. I did hear her, though. I heard what she said when I took her hand. *"¿Quién es?"* she whispered. *"¿Quién es?"*

Thinking about this, remembering all this, I've followed the old woman into a small fenced yard. She notices me when the springs of the gate squeak, slapping it shut behind me. She pinches at the sides of her skirt as though ready to shoo me away in case I came too close. I smile at her and turn my palms upward to show I mean no harm. I can't know what she thought staring at the wreckage of my make up, my dusty skirt and shoeless feet. *"¿Quién es?"* she calls out. "Who are joo?"

A hurricane of words seems to funnel into that tiny fenced yard, whirling and teasing about my head. They were in all languages, and I felt as if I knew them, each one. I can reach out and grab an armful and the Chinese, the Hindustani, the Dutch, the Swahili and the French will be mine and mine forever. If I wait and if I'm quiet, the Spanish will come, too. Then I can speak the language everyone says I know. I know if I wait and I'm quiet, the Spanish will come back to me.

The old woman has asked a very good question, and we both deserve an answer.

The Crown on Prince

"Mom?" Teddy called hopefully as he slammed through the kitchen door. His mother's car was missing from the carport, but so strongly had he willed her to be home all day that he believed she would be there somehow, even if her car were not aligned with his stepfather's primer-painted old Mustang. "Mom?"

"Not here," mumbled his stepfather, Hammond, from the depths of the refrigerator.

"Where is she?"

"How should I know?" Hammond pulled a purple onion from the vegetable bin and began to cleave it to bits with a large, spangly-bladed knife. "Working, I suppose."

Teddy wrinkled his nose. "I don't like onion."

"Who asked you?" Hammond's voice rasped on Teddy's nerves like one of those rusted files hanging on a strap in the toolshed.

Teddy couldn't figure how his stepfather always managed to sound sissy and nasty at the same time, and why he never talked to him as harshly when his mom was home. This was something Teddy just couldn't seem to communicate to her.

"What do you mean he talks differently?" she would ask.

"I don't know, he just sounds like it's such a big deal to have to use his voice on me when you're not here, and you're never here, Mom."

"Where is my mom?" Teddy asked again, absently, yet hoping for a different answer.

"I told you, working." Hammond narrowed his pouchy little eyes as if wondering whether Teddy was an idiot or merely being obnoxious.

"Are you making dinner?"

"What if I am?" Hammond turned to hack the onion.

"Nothing, I guess...." Teddy hated when Hammond made dinner, usually a pulpy mess of vegetables peppered with strong spices, covered with onion and doused with garlicky oil. Hammond seemed to know a thousand recipes for foods that Teddy and his sister Tina made no pretense of eating. "When is she coming home?"

"I don't know. Whenever she feels like it, I guess." He rolled some mushrooms out of a plastic bag and began to behead them mercilessly.

"Oh," said Teddy. "Guess I'll go to my room."

"Don't you have any work to do?" Hammond seemed to believe kids Teddy's age should always be working, serving adults in some way. And Teddy, who worked harder than most kids with his landscaping jobs and his personalized training to become the shortest basketball star ever, felt too angry to respond. "Off the top of my head, I can think of a few garbage cans that need emptying," Hammond persisted, "and a whole mess of leaves that need raking."

Teddy dragged his bulging backpack to his bedroom. "Homework," he mumbled over his shoulder. He would throw himself on his bed, stare at the dusty peaks and dips of plaster in the stucco ceiling that reminded him of meringue pie, and think of how he could use the hedge-clippers on Hammond's big crooked toes.

Maybe Teddy fell asleep, but after what seemed a few seconds he stirred to Hammond pounding on his bedroom door and darkness parting the curtains by his desk. "Ted," barked Hammond, "I'm going to the library, Ted. You hear me, the library. Tell your mom, if she bothers to ask."

Teddy mumbled, closed his eyes again and turned to the wall. Minutes later, the persistent bleating of the telephone roused him. He stumbled from his bed and cracked his knee on the door frame trying to get to the phone. He ran from the kitchen to the back bedroom to finally find the cordless phone wailing in the bathroom, of all places, on the toilet tank, where Hammond probably had left it.

"Mom?" he breathed eagerly into the mouthpiece.

"Mom?" an unfamiliar voice repeated. "Is this Safe Room?"

Teddy, blinking sleep from his eyes, glanced at the innocuous-looking tub, the soft beige wallpaper and the cream-colored tile. "Yeah, it's pretty safe."

"Look, I never called here before. I don't know how you do these things, but—" the voice whispered. "Look, it's my husband. Well, he's not really my husband, but he's acting crazy."

"Acting crazy?" echoed Teddy and the clean tile reverberated.

"Yeah, really crazy. That's why I called," the breathless voice rushed on. "He says he's gonna kill me and he's gonna kill the baby. He already smashed my head with the remote on accounta I got a little Kool-Ade on it."

"You have a baby?"

"Yeah, but it's not his, see, so he wants to kill it. It makes him so mad when it cries. Look, he's downstairs at the bar, see, and he swears he's gonna kill it if it's still here, you know, when he gets back."

"It? What do you mean?" wondered Teddy.

"I already told you, a baby, just four months old."

"No, I mean, is it a boy or a girl? Does it have a name?" For some reason, Teddy flashed on the image of a baby boy nearly two years old, standing barefoot on the sticky seat of his highchair, cold, cod-stinky diapers slapping at his small buttocks as he reached out his arms and cried, "No, no, no!"

"Pookie, about four months old."

"A boy?"

"Listen, I don't care if he does kill me. I'm going to prison next week for possession anyway. But, I gotta save Pookie. Look, can you come over here? Do you people do that? Can you come over here and get Pookie? Can you do that for me, please? Oh, God, tell me you'll come get my baby. Hear that? That's him coming!"

"I'll get the baby!" Teddy shouted into the phone. His hands trembled like he had palsy, and sweat tickled his hairless armpits. "You have to tell me where—"

"I'll take Pookie to the gas station at Prince and Vernon, you got that?"

"Prince and Vernon." It was about a mile and a half from his house. Teddy could be there in about seven minutes on his bike, but how would he bring a baby, four months old, back on the ten-speed? He pushed the question from his mind. "I'll be there."

"Okay, I'm trusting you, girlfriend, you hear. Oh, God, he's here!"

Teddy heard a cry that twisted through his stomach like a sharp blade. And it reminded him of something. He remembered another baby in the deep tunnel of a memory, buried long ago. Then the line went dead.

He twisted the tap and splashed water on his face. He had to hurry.

Hammond had returned already, or maybe he hadn't left for the library. Teddy found him in the kitchen again, mixing a drink in his special silver shaker. "No, she's not here yet," he said in a bored, sing-song voice.

"I have to go. Tell my mom...that, that, that I'll be right back."

"Did you throw out the trash? I know you didn't rake, but tomorrow is trash day."

"I don't have time for trash," he said, directing a meaningful glance at his stepfather. Gladly, Teddy left Hammond standing over the sink with his mixing vessel and a glass with some green olives and ice in it on the counter. "I forgot something," he lied. But when he said it, it felt true.

It wasn't until he wasted a few minutes searching the garage that Teddy remembered his bike had been stolen a few weeks ago and he had been riding his sister's old discarded girl's bike with the stuffing busting out of the worn vinyl seat and the bent frame that made him look like he was limping as he rode. He sincerely hoped that woman on the phone would not be standing around the gas station waiting for him. He couldn't bear to hear her laughing at the front tire squeaking in one direction, the back in another.

He hadn't even ridden it out of the driveway before he heard great hacking howls of amusement from Old Andy, who had chosen this humiliating moment to parade his Yorkshire in front of Teddy's house.

"That's sure a stoopit-looking bike, son," he gasped, pointing at Teddy.

"Yessir," agreed Teddy. Teddy figured Old Andy must be close to a hundred years old and feared the old man could drop down dead any moment. So he forced himself to be agreeable. Besides, he was sorry for the elderly man being led through the neighborhood on a skinny rhinestone lead by the not-much-less-feeble Yorkie.

"You look like one of those clowns at the circus on that thing. You oughta have a long horn that goes, 'Arrugah! Arrugah!' with a bike like that."

"Yessir," Teddy squeezed another strained little smile. "Well, gotta go, sir." Teddy saluted Old Andy, who had served in World War One and had written a very dull book about his experiences. He even paid some company to publish it and kept it tucked under a bony elbow on his walks, trying to find someone he could talk into reading it. Teddy wobbled off on the mangled bike, before Old Andy could think up some new reasons for Teddy to read his war book.

Teddy almost made it without being noticed to the big intersection which would shield him in anonymity, when he heard a soft, but distinctive, "Teodoro, Teodoro," from the bushes at the edge of the church parking lot. Spumes of blue-gray cigarette smoke curled up from the thick brambles. Teddy pushed at the pedals of the bike, but a stout brown arm struck out like a club and grasped the handlebars.

"Where you goin', Teodoro, eh? Where you goin' in such a hurry, man?" A bull-sized boy followed the brown arm out of the bush. Not Esteban, moaned Teddy inwardly.

Esteban was a boy Teddy knew from school who was so large and heavy he had to sit at the teachers' desks in every class. Teddy's mother liked to say, "Here comes the boy with *chi-chis,*" whenever she saw Esteban lumbering across their lawn. Esteban had flaps of flesh as plump as a woman's breasts that bounced against his mountainous stomach when he walked. He was always doing things like stealing cigarettes from the gas station or blowing up frogs with cherry bombs or knocking mailboxes off their posts with his baseball bat.

Esteban thought that he and Teddy should be great friends because they were the only Mexican boys in school. "*Compadre,*" he'd say when he saw Teddy, or "*Que tal, amigo.*" He never seemed to notice that Teddy was always busy doing homework whenever Esteban came over to play, nor did he notice that Teddy took long routes to avoid running into the hefty boy when going to and coming from the nearby church playground.

The only good thing about Esteban was that he was the only person other than Teddy's mother to call him by his full name—Teodoro.

His mother had picked that name for him before he was born. His father wanted to call him Victor, as the family legend had it, so that whenever he fought he would be prepared to win. Somehow knowing before he was born that Teddy would be the kind of person who would never want to fight, Teddy's mother decided to christen him Teodoro. "It sounded so lovely," she said, "like the Spanish *te adoro* which means: I adore you."

When a nurse brought his mother a sheaf of papers to fill in before she took Teodoro home, she didn't hesitate to fill in the birth certificate application with the name of her choice. Some months after Teodoro's birth, his father was entreating him to crawl. "Victor," he kept saying, "you can do it, champ. C'mon, Victor. That's a boy, Victor."

"Victor?" his mother had asked, wryly. "Why do you keep calling him Victor? His name is Teodoro."

"Oh, no it isn't."

"Oh, yes it is!" And she had hurried to find the birth certificate, to fling it in her husband's lap.

"I'll bet Dad was pretty mad," Teddy always said at this point of the legend. This was a story his mother loved retelling.

"You could say that," his mother would reply, tracing, always tracing the herringbone etching of scar tissue under her jaw as she spoke. "But it was sure worth it."

"Eh, Teodoro," Esteban wheezed in his ear while he still gripped the bike. "Eh, Teodoro, guess what I got here." The stout boy pulled a few Polaroid photographs from the breast pocket of his straining t-shirt. "Ever seen anything like this?" Esteban breathed heavily, waving the snapshots so close to Teddy's face that he could not focus on them for a few moments. Then he saw.

They were pictures of a wide-eyed woman with brown hair. In the first one, she stared in terror at the camera. In the next shot a hairy ham fist held a bloody knife to her throat; her eyes were closed. In the third photo she was lying on a bed in a shiny green dress, her head a sickening distance from her torso, separated by sheets splotched with great puddles of black-clotted gore.

Teddy made a sound that frightened him and hit the pictures from Esteban's hand. As they sailed to the dirt, he stumbled forward on the bicycle. "Hey!" cried Esteban. "What'dja do that for, man? My uncle brought these all the way from Mexico. You're gonna get them all dirty." Teddy could still hear Esteban's cranky complaints trailing after him, blending with the whine of the rusted bike chain as he rode bumpily across the church parking lot.

As Teddy pumped the pedals, he tried to regulate his

breathing to match the thrusting of his heels. He feared he would fall off the bike in a faint or vomit. That Esteban, he shook his head, what a huge creep. He was the kind of kid who was biding his time, just waiting to get old enough for prison. Teddy's mother liked to say that Esteban was a "walking heart attack" because of his weight and the smoking. "Here comes Cardiac Arrest," she'd say when she felt redundant from saying, "Here comes the boy with the *chichis*." But Teddy disagreed. Esteban's type gave heart attacks much more often than getting them.

Teddy had a vision of Esteban as a massive adult thundering like Godzilla through an imagined metropolis, innocent bystanders fainting away at the sight of his rude, bulky presence. He shook the image from his head, shuddering, nearly losing his balance on the lopsided bike.

Pay attention, he admonished himself. The tottering nearly drove the bike tires over a handful of carpenters' nails strewn near the newly-constructed church marquee which spelled out a curious message about making reservations for "Smoking or Non-smoking" sections of the hereafter. Still struggling to push Esteban out of his thoughts, Teddy thought the fat boy would no doubt opt for "Smoking."

Teddy rolled the front tire over a single upturned nail which had strayed from the scattering. The mournful hissing of punctured rubber brought Teddy off the bike. Damn, he kicked the bike in fury, catching his raggedy tennis shoe between the spokes. Shaking his leg to release his foot, Teddy hoped no one was watching his ludicrous dance with the falling bicycle. He glanced about cautiously and saw only Esteban marching slowly but certainly over the church lawn, the Polaroids still clutched in his dimpled brown fist.

Quickly, Teddy leaned the bike behind the marquee so that it was mostly concealed from the street. Then he turned on his heel and ran as fast as he could toward the intersection.

At first, he thought he might evade Esteban and head home to cajole Hammond into giving him a ride to the gas station. But his imagination wouldn't work to supply him with the words he would need to get through to Hammond. Walking the remaining nine concrete blocks in the late afternoon sun seemed a far simpler project than the task of extricating a small favor from his stepfather. No, Teddy would rather walk, and when he got to the intersection he just might hitch a ride to the gas station.

The idea of hitching a ride was a major decision for a boy like Teddy. As a small child, Teddy had feared strangers deeply. When he was in kindergarten, his mother bought him a picture book called *The Dangers of Strangers*, which had been a bedtime favorite. He never tired of the eerie ink drawings of treacherous adults—men and women with shadowy faces—luring youngsters into their cars "never to be seen again." He always remembered that part. It seemed worse than dying, the idea of never being seen again.

As recently as last summer, Teddy had hesitated getting out of the car to buy tickets to a popular movie while his mother parked. "What if someone tries to kidnap me?" he had asked seriously. For the world seemed a place brimming with dark darting strangers ready to swoop down on a solitary boy and whisk him into invisibility forever.

Lately, though, he sometimes felt he was in fact losing some of his visibility or that he had somehow failed to materialize fully, appreciably, whenever he tried to speak to Hammond and his mother or even to his sister, Tina, for that matter. Teddy remembered being the boy who brought everyone together when they were living with his father, before his mother married Hammond. Teddy recalled being the one to make everyone smile at his silliness, the one to hug the anger away. "He is the cuddlingest boy," his mother would say, responding to his outstretched baby arms. Before he left the family, his father even wrote him a letter saying that Teddy had "done a good job," but even he couldn't hold them together anymore. Teddy had the feeling that the more he grew, the more invisible he became and he just wasn't big enough, strong enough, or smart enough to stop it.

The decision to hitch a ride, though a major one, was a natural one for Teddy. He no longer really believed anyone would kidnap him. Who, after all, would want him? And who would come looking for him when he was gone?

Yet, his thumb wobbled indecisively as he jutted it from his fist. Car after car whooshed past. Teddy walked backwards as he hitched, believing he might cover the entire distance in this fashion.

After two blocks of hitching and walking, a small station wagon scooted to the curb and a woman with sand-colored hair reached across the passenger side to roll down the window and ask, "Are you running away?"

"Not exactly," said Teddy.

"Me, too," she replied, unlatching the passenger door. "Where you going?"

"Prince and Vernon Street. The gas station."

"Hop in."

Teddy climbed down into the car, noticing its weight from suitcases and boxes jammed into the flattened-out back seats. He had to scrooch into the seat with a vacant bird cage.

"Just put that cage there on the floor," the woman told him. "You can set it on my purse." Teddy obediently settled the cage on an over-spilling black handbag at his feet. "I only had it on there while Chamaco was waiting for me to load up the car."

The woman nosed the car back into traffic and Teddy turned his best smile to his new companion. Teddy was a great smiler renowned for the infectious nature of his *sonrisa milagrosa* as his mother called it. But his famous grin dipped a little when he saw that the woman had been crying. Her nose was puckered and pitted in the garish car-light like some hideously overlong strawberry and her eyelids were fat and purplish, the rims traced in blood pink.

"Why are you sad?" he asked.

"Listen, I bet you know what *chamaco* means," she said, wagging a finger. "I bet you know why I call him 'Billy.'"

That was when Teddy first noticed the parakeet huddling on the woman's shoulder. The plaid yoke and collar of her shirt were splotchy with runny traces of the bird's droppings. The blue-feathered face peeked out, the black eyes punctured Teddy's soul like target darts.

"Good boy!" the bird whistled. "Good boy!"

"Darn it, Chamaco, that's right in my ear!" the woman cried. The bird danced briskly on her shoulder pad and snuggled again under the collar. She turned briefly to Teddy as the car idled at a red light. "I saw you walking with your thumb out and I thought I could talk to you," she said. "That's why I stopped. I thought I could talk to you and you would know what *chamaco* means."

"Because I look Mexican or something?"

"Yes and no," she hesitated. "Because you looked scared and because you looked like you would understand."

"Doesn't *chamaco* mean "kid" or "half-man" or something like that?"

"Not quite a person, I think it means," she said. "There's your gas station across the street. Do you want me to pull in?"

"No, please, just leave me here. I'll walk."

"I lived in Mexico for a while," the woman said, pulling to the curb. "I know how it is to be in a place where no one speaks your language. But I learned. I learned to speak Spanish. Do you speak Spanish?"

"A little. I know a few words."

"I'm teaching him to talk." She jutted her chin towards the collar that hid the parakeet. "Aren't I, Billy? Billy, the kid."

"Thank you for the ride," said Teddy, extricating his legs from around the cage.

"No problem."

"Good boy! Good boy!" piped the parakeet.

"Don't be sad, okay?" Teddy called before slamming the car door.

The small station wagon sped off. Though Teddy couldn't be certain because he only saw the shadowy back of her head and the parakeet brazenly strutting across her neck, he had the idea the woman was crying again.

As he crossed the street to the gas station, a number of questions cropped up in his consciousness like thorny weeds after a deluge. Where exactly would he find the baby? How would he get the baby home? Should he have called the police? The police could be touchy in these situations, it occurred to Teddy. They might accuse him of kidnapping. And what would he—a thirteen-year-old boy—do with a baby, anyway?

The weather seemed to change as soon as Teddy stepped off the curb with the green walk signal. Cottony clouds the color of iron teased the last slatted strands of sunlight and blocked the sun obstinately. Steamy splotches of rain bounced off his round flat nose.

"Great," he murmured, wiping his nose with a pinch from his t-shirt sleeve.

He noticed a phone booth on the far corner of the parking lot and thought he might use it to call for help when he found the baby, but remembered he had, as usual, no money in his pockets. As a safeguard against spending the money he earned, he kept it tied in a sock between his mattress and box spring. It was a great deterrent; but as a consequence he never had any money when he needed it. Teddy hoped 911 calls didn't cost the caller from pay phones. He had never made one before.

He walked cautiously around the square white gas station convenience store. Diesel fumes wafting from rainbow puddles stung his nose. Teddy hoped the baby would not be too wet. The rain fell heavily now, soaking his thin shirt and fine black hair.

Around back of the station, Teddy saw the usual trash

bins and oily bits of scattered trash. A nest of weeds half concealed a crushed cardboard box. Teddy jogged toward the rain-darkened carton. "Pookie!" he called, wondering if four-month-olds recognized their names when they were spoken by strangers. "Pookie?"

But the box stood empty. A swath of cloth—burlap or a blood-rust tatter of blanket?—was caught in one corner. Teddy lifted the rain-swollen box and shook it as if to upend and dislodge hidden clues. In frustration, he raised the box over his head and hurled it with all his force toward the garbage bins. It struck the metal stem propping a bin flap open and collapsed it as neatly as a kick-stand before disappearing into the huge container with an extremely satisfying slamming sound.

A clap of thunder reverberated the metallic blast. Teddy raked the littered alley with his keen thirteen-year-old eyes for any traces of a baby. That was when he noticed the two shadowy humps rising from the bushes near a wall behind the station.

Rottweilers! Teddy jumped and dashed for the garbage containers. The slavering dark beasts snarled. Teddy could almost feel their hot breath through the seat of his worn Levis. But he was a good sprinter and a great jumper from practice in his personalized basketball training program. He leapt up on the bin like a deft lizard. The two hounds howled and snapped like demons dancing at the base.

"Shoo!" cried Teddy, feeling only slightly safer atop the metal bin. "Go home!"

The dogs continued to bounce at the bin, throwing their thick brutish bodies at the metal sides. Teddy thought he heard sounds and movement from within the hollowed container. He remembered reading a news story about a baby discovered among garbage and considered that the distressed woman on the phone might have hidden Pookie from the dogs inside the bin.

He pried open the flap he'd slammed tossing the box,

rasping his knuckles on the rusted metal as he pulled it wide. Teddy could see nothing in the shadow, but he could hear rustling and, now, squeaking sounds—the kind a baby rousing from sleep might make.

"Pookie?" his voice echoed in the damp hollowness. "Pookie?" He perceived a distinctive squeak. The dogs, exhausted by now, sat panting watchfully. Their ears perked at attention.

Teddy saw no choice but to climb into the bin and search about with his hands for the baby. He lifted the flap to prop it and swung a leg into the gap when the squad car flooded the dark wet alley with its cool blue-bright throbbing lights and eerily whining siren. Though the sun was only beginning to set, a couple of flashlights found Teddy's blinking face like glowing magnets pointing polar north.

"Step out of the trash, son!" a megaphone blared. "Keep your hands above your head and do not make any sudden movements."

"The baby!" cried Teddy. "There's a baby in there!" Confusion suffused his brown face with sudden heat from the lights. He blinked his wide black eyes. He felt like a sleepwalker awakening in very bizarre circumstances.

"Step out of the trash! Keep your hands above your head!"

As Teddy climbed out of the bin, the officer wielding the flashlight poured its light into its shadowy depths. In a corner near a greasy paper bag, a nest of newborn mice writhed blindly, mewling like kittens under the bright beam.

Teddy knotted his fingers over his head as he had observed arrested people doing on television in realistic crime shows. He hoisted his leg out of the bin and slid down the slanted siding. The rottweilers had vanished, yowling in pain, at the approach of the screeching squad car.

"What did I do?" asked Teddy.

"You have the right to remain silent," recited a young

police officer, his fat cheeks sprinkled with light brown freckles, as he grasped Teddy's elbow.

"But what did I do?" Teddy wanted desperately to know.

"You have the right to an attorney—"

"I didn't do anything. I was just looking for a baby."

"If you cannot afford—"

"Knock it off, Harold! Can't you see he's just a kid?" An older officer in glasses took hold of Teddy's other elbow and it seemed for an awful moment they might have a tug-of-war that would snap him in two like a wishbone.

"That's just it, Dennis. A kid is a perfect foil." The younger officer relinquished his hold on Teddy.

"Son, what exactly were you doing in the trash there?"

"This lady called my house. She told me to come get her baby. She said her husband, well, not her husband, but her boyfriend said he was going to hurt the baby. She was going to put the baby behind the gas station."

"Hold on a minute, son. Why did the lady call you in the first place? Do you know this lady?" The older officer called Dennis removed his cap to scratch at his liver splotched, hairless pate.

"No, I don't know her. She just called." Teddy felt he could talk until the sun came up the next day, until the cows came home (as his mother loved saying), which would be a very long time since they owned no cattle, and he would never be able to explain adequately why he had been rummaging around in a trash bin after dusk.

"I think he's lying," commented the younger one, Officer Harold Hekkleman his name-badge read.

"Son, were you looking for aluminum cans to recycle?" Dennis asked. "You know it's against the law to take trash for profit?"

"It is?" Teddy, his hands still clasped over his head, asked in amazement.

"Is it?" asked Officer Hekkleman, also intrigued.

"Of course, it is. That trash is the property of the station 'til trash pick-up day."

"But, it's trash pick-up day today!" exulted Teddy, remembering Hammond's directive. "The trash men work their way west, don't they? Our neighborhood is tomorrow. Look, look at all those recycling bins upside down across the street. Today is trash day!"

"Cut the crap, son," the gray cop sighed.

"Who do you work for?" Hekkleman demanded, suddenly. "Just tell us who it is you're working for."

"Lots of people," Teddy shrugged. His fingers, still laced behind his head, rubbed upward on his damp scalp. The rain, which had been abating, stopped as unpredictably as it had started.

"Name names."

"Well, the Harringtons next door, the Van Brocks down the street, the Platts, Old Andy—but I don't remember his last name, those two unmarried ladies with the really steep backyard—"

"Sweet Jesus, Dennis, it's bigger than we thought," the younger officer struck his forehead with his palm.

"Just what is it you do for those folks?" asked Dennis, who seemed like he already knew.

"Different things depending on the people, the weather, and their yards," recited Teddy. "In the spring and summer, it's almost all strictly mowing. Late fall and most of winter, I rake. Things like that. Can I show you my card? Can I put my hands down and show you my card?"

The policemen, fascinated, nodded in unison.

Teddy reached into a rear pocket of his Levis and produced a slim plastic case from which he extracted two business cards. He handed one to each of the officers. "I also feed and walk dogs and I water plants. In case you ever have to go out of town."

"Regular little entrepreneur," the one called Dennis pronounced the word in a way that made Teddy think it was some kind of dinner in a fancier restaurant than Teddy usually liked.

"Looking to expand?" Harold narrowed his eyes.

The older officer scratched his belly and burped. "My gut tells me this kid's legit."

"Oh, yeah?" Harold countered, "then what's he doing here this time of day?"

"Look at his shoes, Harold. He's wearing cheap sneakers from K-mart, for God sake!"

The younger officer did a double-take when he glanced at Teddy's shoes. For the first time in his life, Teddy became almost glad that his mother had shod him inexpensively. "Gosh, kid! How much did those shoes cost?"

"Sixteen ninety-nine with a coupon," said Teddy.

"Kid, you been set up," Harold smirked.

"And what about you, guys?" was Teddy's deadpan reply.

The old officer guffawed until he started wheezing, holding his sides in pain. "Harold, go into the store there and get me a milk. No, make it a Maalox. We better take this kid home and make some kind of report. Get the kid something, too." He turned to Teddy, saying, "It's a little service the county provides."

"Want anything, kid?" called Harold over his shoulder as he headed for the convenience store part of the gas station.

Teddy thought a moment. He thought about all the things he wanted, ranging from his yearning to have his mother at home, waiting, looking at the watch on her slim brown wrist and worrying, to his desire for less embarrassing sports shoes. But, his stomach rumbled like the reconvening clouds overhead and he said, "Candy, I suppose. Chocolate, anything without coconut!"

"This is a drop-off spot, son, " Dennis explained, stroking his stomach through his uniform with broadly splayed fingers, long and patchy with wiry gray hairs. "This is the crack postal service in town, you see."

Teddy's literal mind fixed on the idea of an excellent post office. "But there's not even a mailbox—"

"Kid, kid, either you are smoother than my wife's sweet behind or you are one mighty stoop-it son-of-a-gun." The older officer took off his hat for good and began fanning his face with it as he leaned against the squad car.

Thinking of Old Andy and the crooked bike, Teddy hung his head and admitted, "I guess I fall into the stupid son-of-a-gun-category."

"You heard of crack cocaine? You heard of drug dealers?"

Teddy nodded both times.

"This is the time and the place they drop the cash and they drop the crack. We had a tip."

"You don't think there ever was a baby?"

"What baby?"

"A woman called my house. She told me...well, never mind. I just wanted to help the baby, that's all."

"There never was a baby, kid."

But here the experienced policeman named Dennis made a mistake. There had been a baby, a boy, standing in his highchair, arms outstretched, crying: "No! No! No!" as he helplessly watched his father fill his mother's ears with blood and push her out of the apartment, cursing: "Whore! Slut! Bitch!" while she clawed at the door. "My children, my children! Please don't hurt my children!"

"Got you an Alka-Seltzer." Harold pitched a box at Dennis.

"You ninny! I can't take a seltzer with ulcers! And what am I suppose to dissolve it in?"

Nonplussed, Harold tossed a wrapped bar into Teddy's hands, saying, "Here's a Coconut Crispy, kid."

"Let's run this kid home and see if we can't catch a burger before shift-change."

The officers drove Teddy home, alternately complaining about being underpaid for overtime and discussing their chances of seeing the tail end of a baseball game after work.

Teddy sat silently in the back seat, his mind skimming over the afternoon like a pebble skipping over water. He thought of the desperate woman on the phone, old Andy with the Yorkshire, Esteban and his photographs, the crying woman with the parakeet, even the rottweilers, and, of course, the two policemen who were driving him home. He wondered what the neighbors would think, seeing their lawn-maintenance provider escorted home in a squad car. He hoped it wouldn't hurt business too much.

Mostly though, he thought about his mother. He longed for her to be home so strongly that when the cruiser pulled behind the carport and he saw that her car was still absent from its oil-stained slot, he lied to himself, believing she would be inside, waiting for him somehow, even if her car was not.

After Dad Shot Jesus

Ofelia was the one to wake me up with the phone call. It was a Saturday night and, naturally, I didn't have a date. By eleven o'clock, I was already in bed with five small-sized sponge curlers wound into my bangs to give them some bounce in the front for ten o'clock mass in the morning. I remember a dream of looking into the cat's mouth and he had a real bad tooth—brown and bloody. When I touched it, he started to scream, "Bree-bree-bree-ee-ee!"

Then I realized it was the phone on the little white heart-shaped table by my bed. I snatched up the receiver and heard Tía Ofelia's calm, quiet voice.

"You better get over here quick," she said. "Your dad's shot Jesus."

"Wha-uh?" I croaked in a strange, rusty voice.

"*Pues*, is this Concha, or what?"

I cleared my throat. "It's me, it's Concha. What happened?"

"Your dad shot your Tío Jesus. You better come get him." She hung up.

I threw off the quilts and jumped out of the bed, feeling like a fireman when the alarm is pulled. I pulled my terry bathrobe over my nightgown. No time to dress. But I did shove my feet into my running shoes. I already had my socks on.

I was a little bit confused, still, from my tía's chopped-off call. I knew my father had no big love for Jesus—none of us did—but I didn't think he hated him enough to put a hole in him. And who was the 'him' I was supposed to come and get? Dad or Jesus? Surely, they'd call an ambulance to pick up Jesus and the sheriff to come for Dad. For a crazy minute, I even considered the phone call a prank or a ruse. I remembered how las tías had tricked Tío Manuel into coming over for the surprise party they threw for his seventy-fifth birthday by telling him Josefina had broken her foot and needed a ride to Truth or Consequences Regional. But it wasn't my birthday for another two months and I'd only be turning forty. The tías didn't tend to scheme celebrations until you were in your mid-seventies, and they considered you might not be around for the next one.

I decided to take the car. Usually, I just walk across the highway to the railroad tracks and turn on the dirt road named for my grandfather, Juvenal Reyes Drive, to stroll the quarter-mile alongside the chirping alfalfa fields to the farmhouse. I like to walk everywhere because I don't have any affection for my car; don't trust it that much, neither. This, to me, qualified as a special car-driving occasion so I flap-flap-flapped in my untied sneakers into the garage to see if she would start. Already, as soon as I slid onto the cool plastic seat, the door tried to slice off my leg before I could pull it in all the way.

The car actually started the first time, and as I backed her out of the garage I tried to remember if Dad had given any cues during the day that might have tipped me off that this kind of thing might happen. At the school where I teach fourth grade, once in a while we have a kid that goes *loco* and the principal sits down with us teachers and we try to figure out how we might have noticed behaviors that could have helped us prevent the problem. One time, for example, a kid in the eighth grade spit three times—ping, ping, ping— into the empty wastebasket every morning for about a week before he brought the claw hammer to school that he used on a classmate during the nutrition break. The county school psychologist paid us a visit after that one and told us to be on the lookout for that kind of thing. Ritualistic behavior, she called it.

I couldn't think of anything ritualistic Dad had been doing lately. Unless you count fishing. Dad fished almost every Saturday unless there were monsoon conditions. Even a regular steady rain wouldn't stop him. Come to think of it, he was pretty ritualistic about fishing every weekend and sometimes in the middle of the week, too. We almost always had bass or at least catfish for dinner. The good thing about Dad was that he cleaned his catch himself and never left a mess in the sink. And he always used the air-lock plastic bags to keep the fish from stinking up the ice cream.

I stopped myself from thinking of Dad in the past that way, eulogizing him for never leaving a mess. Just because he'd shot my tío didn't mean he wouldn't be standing in the kitchen again soon, whistling some made-up blues tune and shaving scales off a big one with his special knife.

But Dad hadn't seemed especially troubled or depressed lately. In fact, Dad is one of the happiest people I know. He always comes into the kitchen early in the morning, singing and tap-dancing a little on the checkerboard linoleum until I yell at him from the bedroom to knock it off. "Last ni-i-i-ight," he sings at the top of his lungs, drawing out the "night" dramatically, "the moon was so mel-low!" And he's famous for his verbal drumroll: "See-mi-da-watta-tee-ta-da-reeta-TAH!" often accompanied by the rapid beating of dinette chair upholstery. Then, there are his jokes:

"What did the monkey say when they cut off its tail?"

"I give up, Dad."

"It won't be long now."

Should I beat him to the punchline, he deadpans me like I'm the lunatic and says, seriously, "No, it didn't say nothing. Monkeys can't talk."

No, Dad never seems sad, exactly. Of course, he'll bawl at anything—movies, weddings, funerals, even First Holy Communions and graduations—but he never seems terribly sad or upset at those times. I get the idea he likes crying and the attention he gets sobbing and honking his red nose into his big-as-a-tablecloth hanky.

One time, though, right after Mom died and he was trying to figure out how to write a check, I saw steam on his glasses and these big tears welling where the bifocals bit into his cheeks. He pushed the glasses up onto the top of his head where they slid off from the baldness to clatter on the floor.

"I can't even write a check," he mumbled. "I never wrote no checks before. Where do you put the name?"

That was when I told him to come and live with me in the house that I had Tío Santiago build across the highway and the railroad tracks from the farmhouse.

Of course, because of Dad's smoking—the cigarettes and his cigars—I had to have Santiago build the *cuartito* about seventy feet from the main house in back. Dad even helped design it with the little front room, bedroom, and full bath. He didn't want me to put in a kitchen, though. "It's better to be on time for dinner," he always says, "than to be invited."

I was smiling a little, thinking about Dad as I bumped the car over my grandfather's drive. I could see the flesh-toned walls of the adobe farmhouse lit by the softly glowing windows like one of those Japanese lanterns. I saw my *prima* Barbara's pickup sitting on its tireless rims in the mud-rutted drive in front of the garden alongside Santiago's Buick with the long strand of chrome trim hanging off one side. The comfortable sight of these familiar car relics slowed my heart a little.

Tía Josefina jumped off the glider on the screened porch to open the door for me. I could tell she wanted to be the one to brief me.

"Your dad brought a gun into the house." She clenched both of my hands and raked my face with her bright eyes, holding her breath and searching my expression to see if I could comprehend the significance of his act.

"Dad brought a gun into Pueblitos?" I asked, using the formal name of the family home. It was then that I understood what the real problem was. The problem was not that my father had shot Tío Jesus, but that he had broken a rule.

Josefina sighed and released my hands. "Exactly," she said, nodding, sadly. "What would Reina have said? Think of it." Then I understood that Dad had not only broken a rule, but he had broken my abuela's rule.

My grandmother, Lorena, died thirty years ago this past June. She was killed in a head-on collision with a drunken driver while riding in a car driven by my cousin Barbara. Though Reina died over three decades ago, she still ruled Pueblitos in her absence as firmly as she had when she was alive. It was as though she had only stepped out for a hair appointment and would soon return to dole out some pretty serious consequences for the goings-on while she was away.

Reina fought long and hard for her power in Pueblitos and she was not about to give it up just because she had died.

"Where's Dad?" I peered into the house over her shoulder and I could see the living room full of people. "Did they already arrest him? Did they take him away?"

"He's in the kitchen eating."

"*Eating?*"

"He was hungry so I gave him some *papas con caldo.*"

"I better go talk to him."

"You better take him home, Concha. This is a very serious thing. We can't have him coming in here with a gun like that."

I clasped her bony elbow, and together we crossed the threshold, heading for the kitchen. I nodded to my Tía Ofelia, who lived at Pueblitos with Josefina and Santiago. She sat on the red rocking chair that had been Grandpa's, her arms folded. She was rocking slightly with a weary, but satisfied, look on her long camel-like face.

I waved at my Tío Santiago seated at the end of the dining room table. He lifted a slice of white bread to wave back. He slowly cudded a cheekful of his nightly loaf of Langendorff as I passed him, and, on the other side of the room, my Tía Aurelia, Jesus' wife and Dad's sister. She was on the piano bench with her back to me. She is entirely blind, yet she turned to roll the milky marbles of her unseeing eyes gently over my face.

"Is that you, Conchita?"

"Yeah, it's me."

She smiled, quaking a thousand tributaries in the complicated relief map of her walnut-colored face. "I could tell from the sneakers. They bounce with little vibration."

"Tía, I'm so sorry about Jesus."

She shrugged as if to let me know these things happen, then she reached for my arm to pull me close. "Don't worry about it," she whispered. "*Es nada*, I assure you." Tía Aurelia had been a school teacher for sixty of her eighty years. She had amazing control of her students, better than most sighted teachers. Aurelia, known for her terrible honesty, once told the Superintendent of Schools at assembly that he was "a sausage-shaped catastrophe ready to boil over into a thousand tiresome tantrums." But I couldn't help feeling she was glossing over the shooting that night to spare my feelings.

Barbara stepped into the front room from a side bedroom. "Hullo, Concha! What are you doing these days?"

"I'm teaching fourth grade."

"Teaching! Wow, that must be interesting work!"

"It can be."

Some of the family believed it was the accident that killed Grandma that started the slow but sure unraveling of my cousin's mind. Others believe it is the half-dozen prescriptions for psychotropic drugs her psychiatrist writes every month that did the trick. I hold with the second group. After a second or two, she spoke again:

"So what kind of work are you into, Concha?"

"I'm teaching fourth grade."

"Wow! That must be interesting work!"

"It can be."

I moved past her into the kitchen, where I found my father at the table, sadly spooning potato soup between his liver-colored lips.

"Dad!"

"Concha!" He dropped his spoon and rose to embrace me. "Did they tell you what I done?" For a wild moment, I wondered if he really thought it was a coincidence that I turned up late at night in the kitchen at Pueblitos in my nightclothes, curlers, and tennis shoes. "I shot your Tío Jesus!" he sobbed. "I dint mean to, really."

"There, there, Dad." He was hugging me pretty tight and wrenching my neck a little. I could smell the Jack Daniels rolling off his pores like a poison fog. "I know you didn't want to hurt him."

He jerked away from me angrily. "Hah! Natcherly, I dint wanna hurt that *sin vergüenza*! Hah! I wanted to kill him!"

"Dad!"

"I mean it, too."

"Dad, what happened? Why did you do this?"

"That shipskate! He won't pay for nothing! And I mean nothing. Not gas, not coffees, not cigarettes," he persisted, counting off on his brown-spotted fingers. "That man has never paid for nothing."

"Hmmm." I should have known. Uncle Jesus had an inflexible policy of never splitting, let alone picking up, a tab in any situation whatever. But, even the lowest fourth graders in my special Touch-and-Read group could have told you that riddling Jesus with bullet holes would sooner bring you a life sentence without parole at New Mexico State Prison than even tempt him to offer a round of drinks at the Railroad Club in town. It's bad luck to even look at my tío during the school's Easter candy drive. "Did you kill him? How is Jesus, Dad?" I hate it when my voice gets impatient. "You didn't kill him, did you?"

"*Pues*, ask him yourself. He's right behind you."

Jesus stood in the doorway with a narrow strip of Band-Aid over one eyebrow and a sheepish look on his round little face. He always reminded me of an owl with his dark-ringed yellow eyes and the small hook of his nose. Now he resembled a foolish owl, blinking in an uncertain way as though he hoped he hadn't been caught eavesdropping to find out the real reason he had been shot.

"Hello, Concha," he said slowly, taking my hand to shake it feebly.

"Shipskate!" hollered Dad. "No-good!"

"Dad!"

Josefina and Ofelia ran into the room. "You better take him home," Ofelia hissed, stepping between the brothers-in-law.

"What did I do?" Jesus shrugged, the wings of his shoulders hunching. Clearly, he enjoyed the immunity being shot had gained him.

"Liar! Shipskate!"

I muscled Dad out the screened back door, which wasn't too hard as he is usually pretty obedient with me. The tías whisked Jesus off into one of the darkened bedrooms. "This is very serious," Josefina whispered in my ear during the struggle.

"The bullet hit *Blue Boy*," Ofelia told me on the back doorstep, "right in the pants."

One of Reina's most cherished possessions was the framed print of Gainsborough's *Blue Boy* she had purchased in a museum gift shop several decades ago. Reina liked the painting of the beardless boy in satiny knickers so much she bought copies of the print whenever she could to give her children, other relatives, and friends as gifts on special occasions. It got so you couldn't walk into a house in Truth or Consequences without finding the predictable *Blue Boy* smirking down at you from a wall in the front room. And all the *Blue Boy*s were different shades to my eyes. Reina's was a rich peacock blue, while the neighbor's was navy and

Aurelia's was more sea-green. My *Blue Boy* was a curious electric blue. I kept him in the closet because he gave me sharp little headaches.

"Dad, you shot *Blue Boy*?" I guided my father to the car.

"Such a shipskate," he muttered.

"But you knew that, Dad," I told him, rolling the big car over the mud creases in my grandfather's road. "You've always known that."

"I can't stand it no more! Pull over, I got to irrigate."

Dad hopped out of the car with the wrench he kept in his pocket to turn on the valves of the pipes in the fields to water the alfalfa late at night when it hadn't rained the previous night. It was his responsibility to the farm, and he always kept it. My Tío Manuel, may God watch over his soul, used to say my dad was fanatical about duties.

"You tell your father it's his job to stand in the field like a scarecrow for a year, and in Chanuary chew got churself a popsicle out there."

While we waited for the fields to be wet, I cleaned out the glove box of my car which was already neat but for a box of Milk Duds Dad must have slipped in to melt all over the street map of Albuquerque. Eventually Dad climbed in beside me and unscrewed the dome light with his Swiss knife to figure out why it sometimes stutters.

"You know," I said after a bit, "you can't go back there for a while."

"It's the hinge switch, not a loose bulb, like I thought."

"Dad, you can't go back to Pueblitos like you used to. You can't go back there tomorrow or the next day."

"Don't be silly." He dusted the fixture with his tiny whisk broom.

"I'm not being silly, Dad, I know you listen to me. You can't go back."

"How long?"

"I don't know how long. They haven't said yet."

He got out of the car again to turn off the pipes and we drove home without talking.

I couldn't sleep good that night. I fought the quilts and thought about my grandmother, Lorena. Before I fell asleep, I kept remembering little things about her. I didn't know her too well. I was only ten when she died. But I know the stories.

I know how she was married before she was fourteen by prearrangement to join two strong farms side by side. I know that her mother was widowed and completely blind as a young woman, but running the farm competitively in New Mexico. Blindness in the women runs in our family. I am the only one without glasses. My great-grandmother was blind and a little younger than I am when she married off my grandmother to consolidate the farmland. Then she took a trip to Mexico and just disappeared. No one knows where she ended up or if she died. They say she was a very kind person.

They don't say that about my grandmother, Lorena. She married a man adopted by childless rich people, which probably meant she married the illegitimate son of the husband by an Indian servant. And Lorena was furious, they say, furious to be married and furious to be treated like another servant in her husband's home. She couldn't pass a well or a ditch, for that matter, without saying, "I want to drown him here and the mother, too."

Mad as she was, Lorena knew how to wait. She knew how to be patient and how to have babies—twelve of them— as a defense against her barren mother-in-law.

What I do remember of Reina is her blue breast welling out of her nightgown as she slept in the back parlor in the big bed with Ofelia. I was surprised she didn't sleep with abuelo, but later I heard him snoring, and I couldn't blame her. She must have been over seventy, and her breast was blue from the glow of the little black and white television set Santiago watched while his mother and sister slept. It was blue, but so beautiful, firm and moist like the bottom of a morning glory where it tucks into the stem cup.

I also remember the bull. One time they had a bad bull—a big, mean, snorting cloud of brown dust—at Pueblitos, and my grown tíos in their forties scrambled up the trees in the green apple orchard when they saw he was loose. I laughed when I saw abuelo dump his trowel and plaster to scuttle up the *cuartito* wall he was patching. He shimmied to the roof really fast like some goofy character in a slapstick comedy. Then Reina spun out of the kitchen to flap the bull back into the paddock with her apron just as if it were a cloud of mosquitos. Like abuelo and all of the tíos and tías, that bull obeyed her right away. I recall how it just backed itself into the corral like a big truck in the face of mean, little Reina and her flying blue gingham. No questions asked.

Her name "Lorena," I found out, means "famous in battle, renowned in war." Once I looked up names in this name booklet I bought at the grocery to find a name for the cat just after one of my students gave him to me. I wanted to call him something good. I know my dad's name, Espiridion, means "the spirit" and I wasn't going to find that in any book. I think Reina made it up.

"Concha," of course, is just a shell.

I ended up calling the cat "Herb" because he's so ritualistic about conducting his business in my herb garden, and to stop one of Dad's less tasteful jokes:

"Have you seen Herbie?"

"Herbie who?"

"Herbie Hind!"

Now I can say, "Yeah, I seen Herbie. He's sleeping on the hood of the car."

* * *

In the morning, I was the one to get Dad up for mass. During my fitful sleep, my sponge curlers had committed a rebellion on my scalp and had driven two large locks on both sides of my bangs into these half-moons springing out on both sides of my head. Frowning into the bathroom mirror with my sleep-swollen face, I looked very much like an irritated guernsey. I plastered both sides with intensive jets from my herb garden spritzer and clamped them severely with bobby pins.

"Get up, Dad! Goddamn it, we're late for mass!" I strode through his *cuartito* to the bedroom and threw the door wide open. I wanted to "See-mida-watta-teeta-dareetah!" *him* one good one for a change.

I thought for a minute something was finally going wrong with my eyes because it looked like Dad had two heads and some really lumpy pillows under his sheets.

"*Hija*, you remember Felipa?"

Felipa? The one my sisters called "Flipper" after the laughing porpoise on television because she was almost as bald as Dad and even more slippery? She always wore dark sunglasses, even in bars late at night; that's why I didn't recognize her. The unfamiliar eyes pinched like half raisins into her bland, doughy face as she blinked awake.

"*Hija*, Conchita. How are ya, honey?" she yawned.

"My name is Concha and I am not your honey."

Crunching gravel under my teetery heels the whole way, I marched to mass alone. I could feel from the prickliness of my scalp the side tendrils fighting the hairpins the whole way.

In church, there was that nice quiet cool that I love so much and I just knelt there and prayed kind of non-specifically. The church gradually filled and my tías nudged their way into my pew.

"Did you tell him?" whispered Ofelia.

"He knows," I whispered back.

"Was he upset?" Josefina asked.

I shrugged my shoulders. Who could tell?

Father Griego gave such a good sermon last Sunday about

community involvement and community activism that I went straight home and volunteered on the Homework Hotline. But this Sunday, he kind of floundered around, throwing guilt at people who hadn't donated enough to the roof fund—men who preferred their expensive cigars and vain women who wasted money on hair dye and fancy clothes instead of giving to a worthy cause. Las tías shifted uncomfortably in the pew.

Then he started in on those who speak ill of others. I really wasn't listening much until he said, "It is so easy to see the devil in other people, isn't it?" and he cast his eyes hungrily around the church until they stuck on me with those rebellious locks of hair climbing into mean little horns on either side of my head.

"The demon we see in others is our own demon rearing its ugly head."

Then he giggled, pretending to cough. I put my hand over my face and sank more deeply into the pew. I will say that Father Griego did try to keep his eyes off my hair from that point on, but he wasn't very successful. Eventually I tiptoed out the side door, so he could collect himself.

I felt so low, leaving church before Communion, that I decided to take myself over to the drugstore for a double scoop of chocolate chip ice cream. Sundays must be awfully slow at the drugstore because they let all the regular help go and it was just Chester Vigil, owner, druggist, and head of the school board to run the whole show. He was wearing his little red bow tie and building a pyramid with cans of geriatric formula when I walked in.

First thing he said was, "Heard your dad shot your Tío Jesus."

"Grazed him," I murmured, searching the frosted case for chocolate chip.

"Hope that's not going to make a problem for you with the superintendent around contract time."

"Where's the chocolate chip?"

"Finished off, noon Saturday. Got a new one you might

like—chocolate chip cookie dough. Got bits of brown sugar dough in it."

"Give me a triple," I said.

"No," Chester refused. "It's too rich. I'll start you off on a single." He patted a small brown dome of hard ice cream onto a cone that was too stale to crackle. "That'll be one dollar, Concha."

"One dollar!" I sputtered. Singles are only a quarter.

"Your Uncle Jesus was in here 'bout fifteen minutes ago, had a triple rocky road and said you'd pay." Chester pulled a receipt out of the register. "Wanted me to start him on a tab."

I shook my head and pulled a dollar in nickels and dimes from my coin purse. It had started already. "Chester," I said, "no tab for Jesus, okay? Just act like you don't hear him if he asks again, got it?" I hated to ask the head of the school board that kind of thing, but I could easily see Tío Jesus bankrupting me with triple scoops.

Chester nodded, sweeping the coins off the counter with his big soft hand. "Before I forget, Concha, your Tío Jesus needs a ride to Las Lunas this afternoon to see some relatives. Said to pick him up after lunch."

"*Hijolé!*"

"Look, Conch, I know you're a good teacher. My Lupe still says you were her favorite. But it don't matter, Concha, how good you teach come contract time if you got a dad arunnin' around shooting folks and stuff like that."

I hung my head. "I talked to him about it already."

"Where he get a gun, anyway?"

"From his work. You know how he started taking those prisoners to different prisons." My dad had been hired about a year ago by the Prison Board to transport these criminals by plane, usually from one end of the country to the other because they couldn't get along in their original prisons. He said he liked the travel and he'd met some real nice guys, good card players, too.

"I don't know, Concha. And that Felipa woman, that barfly. I don't like it none."

"Then you're lucky he's not your father, Chester, aren't you?" I said it right to his face. Then I walked out.

* * *

After lunch, I found Jesus sitting on the glider on the porch at Pueblitos, fanning his face with the pale straw hat he liked to wear. "Hello, Concha," he said in his high, mild voice that reminded me of the noise Herbie makes when he's waiting for his tuna. He put out his puffy little fingers for me to pump gently. My mother, God rest her soul, used to say Jesus had the handshake of a pudding. And yet he insisted on shaking hands with everyone all the time, like he was running for county commissioner or something.

"How are you doing, Uncle Jesus? How's the *scratch*?"

"You mean my gunshot?" he asked, gingerly touching the skin around the bandage. "I dunno, Concha, maybe I oughta go to a specialist in Albuquerque 'cause I got this mean headache ever since your dad shot me. Like maybe some brain cells got tumbled around and got bruised."

"Bruised?"

Next, my cousin Barbara came sailing out from the living room, smiling wide and squeezing her empty eyes against the sun. "Oh, hello, Conch. What are you up to these days?"

"Teaching fourth grade."

"Teaching!" She clapped her hands in delight. "That must be interesting work!"

"It can be." I turned back to Jesus. "What's this about Las Lunas?"

"Concha's taking us to Las Lunas," he told Barbara, then he rose feebly from the swing-seat, holding the piece of tape above his eye. It wasn't even full size, just the skinny flesh-tone strip I use in class on the kids with paper cuts and imaginary *ayas*.

"Well, I'm ready," she said, clutching her handbag to her chest and taking her father's arm. "It's so nice of you to take us, Concha. You're lucky to have the day off. What kind of work do you do, anyway? I'll bet it's something really interesting."

It was kind of shameful being in the car with Tío Jesus and Barbara, mainly because of the way he treated her.

Right off the bat, he started in on her driving.

"It's real nice of you to drive us to my sister's house like this. I can't go with Barbara in the truck on accounta she might kill me the way she drives."

Barbara didn't say anything. She just stared at the dashboard like there was a fascinating message for her written on it.

"And she can't remember nothing. Ain't that right, Barbara? You tell her something and poof! It's gone."

"Tío," I finally said, "I can't concentrate on the road with you talking."

"You want me to shut up," he shrugged, "just tell me to shut up."

"Shut up," I said.

I was thinking about my dad and how nice he treated me, asking my opinion and listening to me like I'm some big authority or some kind of genius because I teach fourth grade. I was remembering how he talks to other people about me, building me up so that when they finally meet me they're always a little disappointed.

I wondered how long he would be banned from Pueblitos and how much longer I would have to haul Jesus around before I worked my dad back into the good graces of the tías. It could take a very long time.

Once, one of my cousins married a man who carelessly brought a six-pack of beer into Pueblitos. We were having Thanksgiving or something like that over there. We were all hanging around waiting to eat, when this cousin-in-law marches in with a six-pack sweating the paper bag into pieces. It was like time stopped—nobody moved, nobody talked, nobody breathed. My cousin Clarence had been tossing cashews from the little crystal candy dish on the sideboard into his mouth, and it seemed like they just hung up there in the air for a bit, while we all stared with our mouths open at this cousin's husband and the beer under his arm.

Finally Ofelia had been the one to speak. "Reina don't allow liquor in the house."

"Oh yeah, who's Reina?" he had asked casually, like it really didn't matter one way or the other.

He was hopeless because even after we told him who Reina was, he couldn't understand how someone dead for over a quarter of a century could still call the shots. Eventually, though I'm not sure it's one hundred percent related to the beer-bringing, my cousin divorced him and nobody blamed her for it, not one bit.

We rode the twenty minutes or so to Las Lunas in silence. I was thinking that the drive wasn't too bad. You could see the hills jutting out of the fields like dinosaur backs and a few rainbow striped mesas shimmering in the heat. I always like to look at the cows standing around under the low-growing oaks and cottonwoods.

Something about a cow under a tree that makes me breathe just right. I think of Ferdinand in the red picture book my fourth-graders love. Ferdinand is a bull who just likes to sit quietly under the cork trees and smell flowers. I saw some cows like Ferdinand on folded legs under the leaves on the way to Los Lunas. Yes, I enjoy that drive. I even liked Jesus' relatives that lived in Las Lunas, especially Gino. But what would happen when Jesus started wanting me to take him to Santa Fe and to Taos where his two brothers lived?

I knew I wanted to get Dad back into Pueblitos and away from the influences of Felipa and women like her, but did I want to spend all my free time driving all over New Mexico to put him back in good graces? It seemed that since my mother died, Dad had sworn off clean and decent women in order to chase after trash like Felipa, who had great-grandchildren already and every one of them in Special Ed. Pueblitos was really the only place he ever got exposed to nice women like the friends of my tías.

"You forgot to turn," Jesus murmured, as I dreamily drove onto Main Street.

As a mean trick, I swerved wide in a dramatic, tire-screeching U-turn and made the old car lumber over the median.

"*Válgame Dios*," whimpered Jesus, bracing himself with his fat, speckled fingers against the dash.

Then I pretended the car was out of control. "Oh, my god!" I said and jiggled the steering wheel back and forth so that the car wobbled all over both lanes. Next, I started tapping the brakes making the car lurch forward a few feet and jerk to a stop. "Oh, no! It's the brakes!" I cried. It was Sunday afternoon with no one else around, so I kept this up a few blocks, Jesus cringing, cursing, and clutching to the upholstery and Barbara giggling like a little kid on a roller coaster, until I felt pretty silly and I had to quit. Besides we had nearly arrived at the house of Jesus' sister, and I didn't want his nephew Gino to see me.

Gino is about the most wonderful person I know in the world, and I'd hate to have him accidentally lift the blinds and see me making a fool of myself with the car on his street.

I parked the car like a reasonable driver would and pulled down my little visor mirror to pat my hair down once more while Uncle Jesus glared at me.

"I like your hair like that," Barbara said. "It looks so friendly, like a little puppy with its ears perked up."

Uncle Jesus turned his owl eyes on Barbara. "Whyn't chew ask Barbara what kind of work she does, Concha? She's always askin' you."

"Stop it," I said, flipping up the visor.

"Nah, go on. Ask her."

"Stop it."

"Okay, I'll ask her. What kind of work chew do, Barbara? Tell Concha."

"Stop."

"I...don't..." Barbara stared at her hands, as still and bluish as a corpse's in the car light. "I...can't...work." I jumped out of the car and rushed around to her side. I opened the door. "Come on, Barbara, let's go find Gino and make him get us some ice tea." I pulled her arm and she climbed out. "Whew, it's hotter than a forest fire out here."

Gino, when we found him, was lying in the hammock out back reading from a little paperback with elephants on it called *The Bhagavad Gita*. One of the things I love most about Gino is that he is always reading something, and that makes me feel good as a teacher. The book looked like something to do with India, and Gino, stretched out shirtless in the macramé sling, looked like some kind of maharaja, long and brown, lazily stroking his stomach.

I joke with him a lot, but I think I am in love with Gino. But he is, sadly, *joto* through and through. "Gino," I say to him, "when are you going to stop being that way and let me have a romance with you?"

"You don't want a romance," he says, "or else you wouldn't waste your time with me. You're an apprentice maiden aunt, studying under Ofelia and Josefina."

I don't like it when he says that because he is so often right about so many things that it scares me.

After we had a few ice teas and put Barbara in the front room with her glass and a tall stack of fashion magazines under the rather purplish Blue Boy, we went back outside to talk a bit. I told him about what happened last night at Pueblitos. He asked, "Do you know why your dad shot Jesus?"

"I guess Jesus wouldn't pay for drinks at the Railroad Club." I glanced over my shoulder to make sure my tío was still in the house talking with his sister. I didn't want him eavesdropping again. "Something like that," I added.

Gino shook his head impatiently. "Jesus had nothing to do with it. What Jesus did or didn't do is entirely irrelevant."

"He said that Jesus was a cheapskate," I explained.

"Come on," Gino urged. "You're smart enough to figure this out."

"It wasn't really the shooting," I said, remembering Josefina's face when she took my hands. "It was the gun."

"That's right, the gun."

"The bad thing was he brought a gun into Pueblitos."

"And what is a gun?" Gino leaned forward eagerly. "What is a gun after all?"

"A weapon, something to shoot with."

Gino looked at me like I was being stupid. Then he tried again. "Who uses guns?"

"Police?" I shrugged. "Criminals? Bad men?"

"Where is the gun, now?"

"I...I don't know. The aunts have it, I suppose."

"Do you suppose your dad brought the gun into Pueblitos to shoot a hole in the stagnated woman-world of that household and let a little chaos in? I think so. I think your dad tried to rip open a space so that the people—Josefina, Ofelia, Santiago, even you—could get some air, and maybe even escape a little. I think your dad tried to free you people, but he was the only one to get away." Gino was excited now. His black eyes glowed and a little spittle flew from his soft red lips.

I thought about what he said. I even had a picture of my dad lifting an invisible layer of atmosphere like the skirt of a circus tent and beckoning me to sneak out with him. I was quiet a long time, thinking while Gino waited. Finally I just shrugged and chewed on a piece of ice. "That's not the way it is," I started to explain.

But Gino interrupted me. "Then, you better go back. It's getting late."

He picked up his book and settled back in the hammock to read. I got Barbara off the porch and called to Jesus. We piled into the car and I drove toward the highway. We hadn't gotten more than five blocks before the car betrayed me as I always knew she would. I coasted her to a street right near a gas station.

"Out of gas," observed Jesus, looking at the gauge.

"Oh, no," sighed Barbara.

"I got a gas can," I said, climbing out of the car. "It takes about three dollars' worth to get home," I added. I had about twenty dollars in my purse, plus about half a dozen credit cards. "Jesus, got a few dollars?"

Jesus hunched his bird shoulders and swiveled his head, staring at the windshield.

"Golly, Concha," Barbara despaired, "I'm not allowed to have money."

"Jesus," I persisted, "how 'bout it? Are you going to give me a few dollars for gas or are we gonna have to walk?"

My uncle sealed his hooded eyes.

"Okay, Barbara," I said, "c'mon, let's go."

My cousin stepped out of the car, smoothing her lap. "Where are we going?"

"Walking."

"I like to walk." She smiled, taking my arm and falling in step beside me. "Do you walk a lot where you work?"

I started walking us back to Truth or Consequences, then I turned us around and we started back for Gino's house. He could take us home. Or we could stay there the night and maybe I'd call up a substitute and take the day off tomorrow to go on a picnic up to the caves with Barbara and Gino. I needed a break.

I was tired of paying for everything, for everyone, every time; so I left my uncle, an eighty-year-old man, who'd recently been shot by my father, sitting in a blazing-hot car without water, without even a newspaper to read. He could walk over to the gas station and call his sister or his other brother if he wasn't too mean to spend a quarter. I had no intention of ever coming back for him that hot afternoon. And I didn't feel so bad stepping over the weeds and ant hills cracking through the sidewalk, never once looking back.

Love Can Make You Sick

Estella glanced at her cousin Selena and looked away quickly. Selena wore a yellow dotted-swiss sundress with spaghetti straps, which not only exaggerated the stark lines and angles of her large bony frame but looked—with its floppy ruffles and buckling pleat—as if her cousin had yanked the chirpy dressing from her kitchen windows to stitch on some straps. Curtains into a dress, Estella shook her head. It was exactly the kind of impulse likely to overtake Selena.

"You remember Selena?" Estella asked her husband Rob. She jutted her chin in her cousin's direction. Selena had cornered Aunt Carmen near the barbecue at this garden get-together after their grandmother's funeral. Carmen's lips were forming a gentle "o" of surprise while Selena clasped her elbow and spoke excitedly into the older woman's ear.

"But she looks exactly the same," exclaimed Rob. "Why, I'd know her anywhere." Though he had not seen Selena for nearly twenty years, the fact that she looked exactly the same was far from a compliment, to Estella's thinking. The same fanatical glow stamped her cousin's gaunt cheeks and pupil-less black eyes that had marked her as the most obsessive and unpredictable drill-squad leader that Truth or Consequences High School had ever known. "Shouldn't we go say hello?"

"Let's not," murmured Estella, taking a cracker from the appetizer tray on the picnic table. "We don't want to interrupt. She's probably in the middle of telling Aunt Carmen how she became an alcoholic."

"Selena an alcoholic? But she didn't use to drink."

"Still doesn't." The cracker held a viscous creamed soup and tuna concoction. Estella stifled the reflex to gag. She looked for a place on the checked oilcloth to hide the uneaten portion.

"Then I don't understand." Rob shook his head as though to clear it.

"Selena doesn't drink, never has."

"Then why on earth would she be telling your aunt she's an alcoholic?"

"That's just the way she is." Estella shrugged. There was hardly any explanation for her cousin's rabid passions. Selena had little notion how to behave appropriately, and she seemed quite blind to the social cues friends and family heaped on her. Even then, Estella could see Carmen gently and ineffectually struggling to extricate her elbow from her niece's greedy grasp.

Selena still had no idea how hurt Carmen had been when she neglected to wear Grandmother's cameo to the Watergate hearings, that Selena had forced Carmen to tell her beloved mother—now departed—a lie.

"In a few minutes, she'll be over here to tell us all about the twelve steps and everything," Estella promised Rob. "For Godsake, don't contradict her. That will only encourage her to argue."

The afternoon sky, gray as gunmetal, grumbled overhead, and a few splotches of steamy rain sizzled on the flagstone slabs leading to the back porch of Carmen's house. The heavy air reminded Estella of thick linen, sprinkled damp and hissing under the iron. She held the hope of another summer storm like the one the previous week that churned rust-colored currents through the arroyos, flooding Main from First through Third Streets, and stranding motorists atop their pickup trucks and car-tops until the sun streaked through the block-like clouds, gradually parching the great pools into puddles. In the wake of that flashflood, Estella felt sure even a short heavy rain would send people jogging for their cars.

She wanted so badly to lie down in her quiet bedroom with the curtains drawn.

"But I don't understand why a person who doesn't drink—who never drank—would go around telling people she's an alcoholic," persisted Rob.

"You remember how she was at the wedding," Estella reminded him. Rob had met Selena for the first time when he met Estella. His brother Dan had married another cousin of theirs, and they were all thrown together the week of the wedding. Rob had been the best man for his brother, Selena one of the bridesmaids, and Estella the flower girl. Since she was only eleven at the time of the wedding, Estella naturally lost touch with Rob until they met again at the hospice nearly a year ago. After her recent move back to Truth or Consequences, this gathering after her grandmother's funeral was the first family function to which Estella brought her new husband, who—she felt certain—had been far from impressed with her relatives the first few encounters.

Surveying the gallery of faces crowding her aunt's backyard, Estella admitted to herself they were not an especially impressive group. Her uncle Santiago sitting stiff as a mummy with both his legs and arms in casts from falling off the roof of Becker-Dailies Department Store; Severito standing off by the back gate with his dusty pack of hounds; Carmen's niece Natalia wearing diaphanous scarves and dancing by herself without music; the old aunts nested in lawn chairs, fingering their bluish tresses and bickering noisily; cousin Rigoberta and her husband Tiny tossing a softball back and forth near the garbage cans (Estella had hoped vainly that Rigoberta would remove her baseball cap for the funeral service)—there was no denying the family was an odd lot. But Estella felt Rob had gotten an especially skewed view of them during the week of the wedding those many years ago, especially that night on the *llano*. Estella often thought that experience had pushed poor Rob into the ministry. She knew he had seen things on the *llano* that night he never wanted to see.

"Who's that over there?" asked Rob, indicating a burly man with a clump of thick curly hair that sat awkwardly on his head and then dangled like an animal pelt as he dove into the ice-chest.

"That's Jimmy. Remember Jimmy? He was Selena's boyfriend back during the wedding."

"Is he a relative too?"

"By marriage. He married Selena. Remember they were engaged?"

Jimmy popped open a beer can. Estella thought he must have felt their eyes on the blue dress-shirt straining over his bulging back because he pivoted, hoisting his can to toast Estella and her husband. They waved mildly in return. Jimmy's face was as mottled as a flap of ham.

"My God, what happened to him?" asked Rob, who after twenty years was even trimmer and more ascetic looking than he had been as a younger man.

"He's a lawyer now," explained Estella, "very rich, wants to run for something, commissioner of something. You've seen those Circle D's all over town, the hamburger places? Jimmy's family, the Durans, they own all those."

"So Selena's doing pretty well."

"Was doing pretty well. They're divorced."

"I'm sorry to hear that," said Rob, conventionally.

Jimmy drained his beer and tossed it like a basketball into the garbage can, startling Severito's dogs into a frenzy of barking. He reached for another can.

"I'm not," muttered Estella, but Rob didn't hear her over the howling hounds.

Selena, abandoned by Carmen who had gone to implore Severito to put the dogs in the garage, marched toward Estella and Rob. Selena's arm was outstretched—in the manner of a karate expert ready to break some bricks—to shake Rob's hand.

"So you're Stella's new husband," she blurted. Estella felt she hit the word "new" a little hard, perhaps making sly reference to her previous marriages. But, really, she assured herself, Selena is incapable of subtlety.

"Selena, do you remember Rob? He's Dan's brother, remember? He was best man at Dan and Barbara's wedding," Estella told her.

Selena flicked her hand in front of her face as though to brush away invisible gnats. "Yes, yes," she said, disinterestedly. "It's nice to meet you."

"Same here," returned Rob.

"But you've already met Rob," Estella reminded her. "You met him at the wedding."

"Yes, that." She shook Rob's hand, crushingly; then she forgot to let it go. Estella could see the tips of her husband's fingers whitening under her cousin's grip.

"How are you, Selena?" he asked. Estella cursed herself for not warning him to avoid that question.

"Well, I'm doing better. One day at a time, you know. One day at a time." She grinned, baring overlong teeth and a good deal of gum. "Did Stella tell you I'm an alcoholic now?"

"No, I—uh," Rob stammered.

Selena shot her cousin a look of reproof. "Well, I am. She doesn't think I'm an alcoholic because she says I don't drink. A person can have a terrible disease without other people knowing about it, can't they?" she challenged. "Well, can't they?"

"I suppose so."

"Selena," Estella argued, in spite of herself, "I've seen you try to take a sip of wine at Communion. You have to hold your nose. You don't even like rum cake!"

"I should know if I'm an alcoholic!" cried Selena, throwing her hands into the air like an opera singer in a dramatic moment.

Rob stepped back, alarmed. He scanned the crowd in the yard for any signs of disturbance from Selena's outburst, but no one took any notice. This type of thing was very much to be expected from Selena even before she decided to become an alcoholic.

Selena then grabbed for Rob's elbow and began the detailed story of her alcoholism. Estella, who had heard it all many times before, meandered over to the ancient aunts—Josefina and Ofelia—in their lawn chairs. They were quarreling over Rigoberta, arguing about how much weight she had gained.

"She's pure fat," said Ofelia with a satisfied frown. "Pure fat."

"She was pregnant, remember? That wasn't too long ago," reminded Josefina.

"Last year it was pregnancy," admitted Ofelia, "now it's pure fat."

"Here's Estella. Come here, honey, sit with your tía." Josefina beckoned her to a space on the long folding chair she occupied.

"This one's too thin," complained Ofelia. "You look sick. It ain't healthy, that kind of thin."

Estella lowered herself into the lawn chair with Josefina. She put her head against her aunt's shoulder and listened to the elderly woman's voice buzzing through her bones as Josefina disputed her sister's criticism. "It's the style now. It's been the style for going on like fifty years, Ofelia. All the girls are thin."

"Not Rigoberta," snorted Ofelia. "She ain't thin."

"Maybe not so much Rigoberta," conceded Josefina, "but it is the fashion."

"Not this *flaca*. This is sick-thin. And, look, her eyes all yellow like that."

Estella closed her eyes and let her mind float back to an afternoon in Seattle, her apartment there, a room, really. The man she loved—not Rob—married someone else, but she followed him anyway to that dark, wet city. That afternoon, he came to her as she knew he would. *You've been crying;*

your face is a mess. They were chigging, skin-popping because they weren't junkies after all. *She's hurt you again, I can tell.* He had a good job with a major hotel chain—a secretary, an office and a view of the sea, and Estella modeled for department store catalogs. *You can wipe your tears on my dress.* She could still see that dress hanging from a peg on her door—a cornflower-blue cotton shift worn whisper thin, tremulous as a butterfly wing in the breeze.

"Estella, Estella," Rob hovered anxiously over the lawn chair, holding her sweater. She had begun to shiver and sweat. "Do you want to go home."

"I think she's sick," said Ofelia. "Something's not—"

Josefina silenced her sister with a glance.

"Go home," Estella murmured, thickly. "I want to go home."

As Rob helped her into her sweater and guided her out of the yard, Estella could hear distinctly Selena telling Santiago that she, too, had fallen off a building one afternoon when she'd been drinking heavily.

* * *

Reading the newspaper at breakfast a few mornings later, Estella came across a brief bit about Jimmy.

"Hmm... Looks like Jimmy'll have to wait until he gets acquitted," she mentioned to Rob, "to run for the commissioner thing."

"Acquitted for what?"

"Caused an accident. Says here, he was driving on the wrong side of the road."

"Wrong side of the road? Why?"

"You figure it out."

"Maybe I should have a talk with him."

"You could," said Estella, doubtfully. "I wouldn't waste my time. Even Selena had to give up on him."

"What makes you say that?"

"I told you how she's like a dog with a bone." Estella smiled, envisioning her cousin talking through a great knucklebone lodged in her teeth. "She's so persistent; she's relentless, really. It's there in her face. You can see it. Didn't you ever see her on Watergate?"

"What?"

"Remember Watergate? Didn't you ever watch the Watergate hearings on television?"

"Of course, that was a turning point in the history of the presidency—" he began.

"Yeah, yeah," said Estella. "But do you remember seeing Selena on television during the hearings? She was the secretary to our distinguished senator—what was his name?— from New Mexico back then."

"Was she really?"

"Yeah, and it was terrible for everyone."

Selena had been on television every afternoon, affecting a deceptively ordinary look on her long angular face and sitting primly at the side of the distinguished senator from New Mexico. But she couldn't fool Estella. Day after day, Estella stared apprehensively into her father's little black and white portable set, and she could see the lunacy and passion in her cousin's eyes as plain as the very plain print on the dresses Selena almost always wore.

She just couldn't stay away, thought Estella, that long hot Watergate summer. Selena had to be the center of things. No one from Truth or Consequences had ever been on national television before. Selena's daily appearances during the Watergate hearings became one of the most nerve-wracking experiences the town had ever undergone.

"See Selena on Watergate today?" Estella would hear people ask in the supermarket, at the bar and at the coffee shop, voices dropped to invite dark confidences.

"Yeah, she was okay, but that lipstick was too much."

It got so you couldn't have a casual conversation with the checker at Piggly Wiggly without preparing for it by watching the hearings. Estella didn't think many people in town really knew what all the fuss was with Watergate. "Maybe something to do with the President," most would reply, if asked. No one cared that much. But to miss Selena on television was just plain negligent. Estella had the job of watching Watergate while her father was at work.

"She was wearing a pantsuit," she had reported once as he walked in the door, before he even had time to change out of the striped overalls issued by the railroad.

"*Hijolé, pants!*" He had struck his forehead with the heel of his hand and paced the living room. "*Pants*? On television?"

"Lots of girls wear pants," she told him. Estella herself wore only cutoffs and raggy shirts the whole summer, but she might as well have paraded around nude for all he noticed about her clothes. "They were a solid color, dark, probably navy blue."

"Earrings?"

"Yes, earrings."

"Not those dangly things?"

"No, they were studs."

"Ahh," her father had sighed, mollified. Then he tensed. "But what did she do?"

Rob asked Estella the same question, not fully comprehending the problem of having Selena on national television.

"She just sat there," said Estella, "writing things down in her tablet."

That answer had relieved her father. Like most people in town, he felt a good deal of anxiety knowing that Selena was on television every day. It would not be unlike Selena to grab a microphone at any moment to blurt some bizarre statement, mystifying Congress and the nation. After a while, people began to resent Selena and the burden she imposed by appearing daily on television. It was almost as though they believed they were responsible for preventing any acts of strange behavior through their vigilance.

"But what did she do?" Rob persisted. "What did she do?"

"It's not what she did," explained Estella, "it's what she didn't do. Don't you see? It would have been a hundred times better if she had muscled her way to a microphone and started ranting. Then people could stop waiting for her to act out; they could relax."

"I swear I never even noticed her," claimed Rob.

Estella reached across the table and gave his hand a warm squeeze.

"And she never wore my grandmother's cameo. Not even once!"

* * *

Selena called that afternoon while Estella was trying to compose a sermon for Rob. She had complained that a recent sermon seemed unfocused and a little meaningless. "It was like you were just saying whatever came into your head," she had told him, "and it didn't make that much sense." So Rob had challenged her to write a sermon for him. Something on love, he told her, something on the power of love. She was slumped before the typewriter staring at the keys when the phone rang, and Selena asked her cousin to go with her to an AA meeting in Albuquerque.

"Why don't you go to the meeting here in Truth or Consequences?" Estella asked, meanly. "Why do you have to drive clear out to Albuquerque?"

"There's supposed to be a wonderful meeting—a really good group—out in Albuquerque. They say the speakers are just fantastic!"

"They kicked you out of the Alcoholics Anonymous in town, didn't they?"

"They don't kick people out of AA," Selena informed her. "But there are an awful lot of cynical people in this town, that's for darn sure."

"Why do you want me to go with you?"

"It's a good meeting. I thought you might be interested. You can really get a lot from these meetings. Of course, you don't have to go," she added. "I know you don't really take me seriously."

"C'mon, Selena, I take you as seriously as the next person," Estella prevaricated. "I guess I can go with you." She hadn't been to Albuquerque in a long time, and she thought she might persuade Selena to take her shopping or to a movie after the meeting. Besides, Estella had never been to an AA meeting; she felt curious. She was getting to that point of considering all the things she might never have a chance to see.

And Estella mustered a soft feeling for her cousin, who had been the first one to run over in her tasseled drill-squad skirt the day Estella's mother died. Selena had arrived with a box full of board games—Monopoly, Scrabble, Parchesi, Aggravation (Selena had a particular genius for Aggravation.) Estella's cousin came day after day for more than a year it seemed, moving game pieces and rolling dice with the little girl until well after dark. What would it hurt to accompany Selena to her meeting? Besides the sermon wasn't going too well.

"Great! I'll be straight over to pick you up."

Rob was on the phone in his office when Estella barged in to tell him she would be going out. She could tell from the gentle tone he took and the encouraging questions he asked that he was talking to one of the churchgoers who had a "problem." This was his special area, dealing with these people in trouble. He was really a counselor at heart, thought Estella, remembering how they had found each other again when Rob was volunteering at the hospice. Rob was the only person to promise to help Estella and to keep his word.

"I'm going with Selena to an Alcoholics Anonymous meeting in Albuquerque," she mouthed for Rob to lip-read.

He cupped a hand over the mouthpiece and whispered, "Why?"

Estella shrugged. "She wants me to go with her. I thought I might do some shopping while we're out there."

"Don't let yourself get too tired, okay? Make her bring you home if you feel dizzy. Or call me; I'll get you." He removed his hand from the receiver. "Yes, Mrs. Escamilla, that is a hard situation. What could you have said differently to prevent the Ortegas from getting that idea?"

Mrs. Escamilla! Estella rolled her eyes. That garrulous old drunk. She would waste Rob's time for hours, going on about her neighbors and their dogs. What she really needed was an overnight in the drunk-tank at Farmington. Estella couldn't bear moaners like her. They made her skin prickle with impatience. If Estella were on the phone instead of Rob, she would have cried, "You think you have a problem! Listen to this!" then Estella would tell about her own little problem and slam down the phone.

That's probably why, she thought, softly shutting the study door, Rob never lets me answer the office phone.

* * *

"The thing about the meeting in Albuquerque," explained Selena, almost as soon as Estella climbed into the truck, "is that you get a better group of people, really. They're professionals, you know, doctors, lawyers, accountants, even an author. The guy who wrote *ESP and Your Pet* goes to this meeting. They're my kind of people."

Estella shot her cousin a curious look. Since when was Selena a professional? She still worked in her ex-husband's law office as a secretary. Did marrying a lawyer catapult her into the professional class? And what happened to that status when she and Jimmy divorced? Estella didn't want to get her arguing, though, so she changed the subject. "I've always liked those hills over there, red like apples with the caves bitten out of them."

The ride to Albuquerque could be soothing, she thought, if you didn't have to drive there every day. Joshua trees, yucca, barrel cacti, and scrub rushed past Estella's window along with the telephone poles, one after another, like a roughly textured chain.

"Yeah, they're nice," she agreed, staring straight ahead. "It's just that the people at the T or C meeting, well, they aren't very knowledgeable about the disease. They aren't very compassionate."

"That reminds me," Estella snapped her fingers. "I heard Jimmy got a DUI."

"That's a laugh," said Selena, forcing a chortle.

"What do you mean?"

"I mean, some people will do anything to make trouble for him. They're jealous is all it is. They can't stand that he's a professional with some means and a good family. They'll do anything to bring him down a peg."

"But Driving Under the Influence?" argued Estella. "Wouldn't the police have to be able to prove that with blood tests and stuff?"

"Everyone knows Jimmy doesn't drink. I'm the one. I have alcoholism. Why doesn't anyone understand?" Selena cried.

"Because you don't drink," suggested Estella, "because you never drank, because you just say you're an alcoholic without ever drinking."

"You don't know," Selena insisted. "How would you know? You only see me a few times a year. I don't want to argue with you. That's not why I asked you to come with me. Grant me this, though, I *could be* an alcoholic, and you might never know it. Can you grant me this?"

Estella shrugged and turned her head in time to see a roadrunner—its head-feathers fanned like a fright wig—peek from behind a tumbleweed.

* * *

At the meeting, Selena busied herself shaking hands with anyone in her path, saying, firmly, "Hi, I'm Selena. I'm an alcoholic." Which was what the others replied to her, using their own names, of course. When a lumpy-looking little man—wearing a suit that called to mind a couch left out in the rain—approached Estella to give this greeting, she pulled her hand away, saying, "Leave me alone. Just leave me alone."

The meeting was held in the basement of a church. Flocculent curls of cigarette smoke gagged Estella. She had to seek a seat by the air-conditioning duct so she wouldn't be sick from the eye-searing clouds. Selena took a seat in front.

People assembled in the folding chairs set out to face the stage, where the flag—yellowed and dusty—drooped near a lectern. Estella watched with detached interest as some protocol was observed. A long-limbed man with a cadaverous face climbed on stage, opened a binder and read a prayer that was so familiar that Estella noticed people moving their lips with the words. The man made a few inaudible announcements and returned to his seat. A woman, stepped to the lectern and told an elaborate story in a whispery voice that Estella could barely hear. The gist of it seemed to be that the woman was looking forward to handing out Halloween candy sober this year. Everyone clapped, including Estella who did not want to make herself conspicuous, as the woman descended to her seat.

There seemed to be a call for new speakers, and Selena jumped forward as if a powerful spring released under her seat. Estella sat up, curious to find out what someone who did not drink would have to say about the drunken experiences which led to her sobriety. Since she had taken a seat far from Selena's, it was easy for Estella to pretend she did not know her cousin, and she could watch this public display with mild interest. Of course, she had no trouble hearing Selena, the former drill-squad leader.

"Hi," she began, "I'm Selena, and I'm an alcoholic."

"Hi, Selena," the audience replied in unison, Estella blending in her voice.

"I've been an alcoholic for as long as I can remember," continued Selena, sadly.

Why, you big liar, thought Estella, glancing around at the trusting faces turned toward the stage. What would Selena say next? She felt pretty certain Selena would tell about the night on the *llano* when the drinking and the mescaline made the others wild enough to bury raw meat and then eat it, insane enough to conjure devils from the campfire to run over with their trucks, mad enough to draw pistols in inebriated attempts to shoot the stars out of the sky. Yes, that was the obvious choice for a good drunk story.

"The turning point in my drinking life came one night when I abused the trust of my family and my date's family and the relatives of an innocent dead woman. It was a time I helped steal a hearse from the funeral home to use for selling Christmas trees to get more money for more alcohol and drugs. Because of my actions, an old woman is buried with a small Douglas fir alongside her in the coffin..."

Estella's jaw unhinged. She sucked back a gasp. She wanted to lunge for the stage, take her cousin's neck in her hands and throttle it. Selena had no right. No right to tell a story that didn't belong to her, a story that should have been buried in that sealed casket with the old woman's pine-scented bones.

* * *

Selena had to beg Estella to get in the truck for the ride back to Truth or Consequences. Estella was ready to call a cab or hitch a ride with one of the former drunks to the shuttle station at the airport. Selena prevailed only when Estella realized she had brought very little cash with her, and fist-sized balls of hail began pelting down on them.

She climbed with reluctance and great distaste into the cab beside Selena, promising herself she would not speak a word the whole way. Selena didn't seem to notice her cousin's silence as she kept up a steady stream of talk about being an alcoholic and how alcoholism was an allergy and an addiction, a brain disease, really.

Nearly a half-hour later, as they approached Las Lunas just outside of Truth or Consequences, Estella had to break her silence to ask, "Why, Selena, why did you do that to me? Why did you bring me out here to tell my story—the worst story of my life—to a bunch of ex-drunks like that? Why would you do this thing? I trusted you when I told you that."

"Just because a thing happened to you doesn't mean it couldn't have happened to me," said Selena blithely as she flicked on the turn signal. "There's a cafe. Want a cocoa?"

"Knock it off! You stole my story. You know it."

Selena pulled into the cafe parking lot and turned to face her cousin. "I didn't steal your story. I only borrowed it. Here," she said, handing an imaginary bundle to Estella, "now it's back. It's your story. I swear I won't use it again if you stop asking me about it. Ask me anything else, but don't ask me about that anymore."

"Okay, I'll ask you something else," said Estella, bitterly. "How come you never wore Grandma's cameo on television for the Watergate hearings? The only thing she ever asked of you, and you wouldn't do it. Do you know that Carmen had to lie to her? She had to conspire with Tía Selsa to take Grandma out for a hair appointment and an ice cream so that she could say you had been wearing it on TV while she was gone. Why couldn't you wear the thing, Selena, just once?"

Selena stared down at her hands in her lap. She mumbled unhappily.

"What?" demanded Estella. "What did you say?"

"Jimmy didn't like it. I didn't wear it because Jimmy didn't like it."

* * *

Rob had placed a copy of *Bartlett's Quotations* and the New Testament on Estella's desk at home. Estella strummed the red-trimmed pages of the Bible dejectedly. She kept thinking of that cornflower-blue shift and of Selena and how she tried to eat her husband's sins to pull the disgrace of others onto herself. Estella flashed on a scene she had seen once in a documentary of a mother bird frantically flapping a single wing, feigning injury to draw a predator away from the nest. She shook her head to free the image and placed her fingers on the keyboard. There was really only one thing Estella could think to say about the power of love, and she couldn't put that in Rob's sermon.

Ivor's People

Ivor blew his nose between his thumb and index finger onto the unswept floor of the airport. Volcanic ash billowing in from Montserrat cast a haze like a dingy mantilla over all of Antigua. The fine gray dust collected in the cab driver's nostrils to be sneezed and snorted out with growing frequency in the late afternoon breeze. He believed they were coming from a lay-over in Puerto Rico, his people. The plane was delayed, but they would soon be arriving from San Juan. Ivor prepared the words he would use.

Walter told him they were Americans from the South, and that was all he needed to hear. Hastily, he cleared his small bundle from the cabin, swept the ants from the kitchen linoleum and sloshed a jigger of disinfectant into the rust colored toilet basin. The ball of his shirts and shorts nested in the hull of the spare tire; he would stay with his blind aunt or—with luck—with a sympathetic woman in St. John's. He didn't know which; he didn't care. He hoped the Americans would stay a week or a month, two months, a year. For sixty dollars U.S. a night, he would sleep forever on the narrow, poking sofa in his aunt's parlor. He would sleep standing on his head for that money.

That was the only hard part—the money. Foolish Walter had reserved the cabin for the Americans at only thirty dollars a night. Can you believe that? Thirty dollars a night to stay in Antigua. This stung Ivor's pride. He cleared his throat righteously and hocked into an ash can. He would fix that first thing.

"Ivor," called Jeannie, the information girl. "Ivor, your plane is come." Ivor had shown Jeannie the envelope flap on which Walter had written the Americans' names. Ivor made a great show of being unable to decipher Walter's block printing as though it were an illegible scrawl. Jeannie had merely rolled her eyes and told Ivor the Americans were called Singer, Aaron and Elaine Singer.

The first burst of tourists through the glass panel door was led by a tired-looking bearded man. He was followed by a woman wearing a baseball cap and sunglasses. At first glance, Ivor had the idea the woman had just had surgery; she moved so slowly and so gingerly, as though she might break. He fervently hoped these were not his Americans. He judged them to be too weary, too thin and, surely, too poor to be much worth his while. He looked beyond these two to the usual cluster of returning islanders, business people returning from New York through San Juan to Antigua. Ivor recognized many of them from his sporadic school days. Ordinarily they would not even nod to him on their way to the parking lot. And today Ivor did not stop to chat them up as he liked to do in idle moments. He reminded himself that he, too, was a businessman with clients to attend to.

He pushed his glance past these islanders to the gaggle of wealthy Puerto Riqueños—honeymooners, vacationers—jabbering away in their sing-song voices. Come on, come on then, thought Ivor, let the others in.

After the Puerto Ricans, a small group of American businessmen wearing great cowboy hats filed through the entrance. They were so stout and tall that they could only squeeze one at a time through the doorway. Ivor could see from their chalk-striped suits and calf-leather cases they were certainly as wealthy as he hoped his people would be, but somehow he did not feel equal to handling these comers.

"Ivor," repeated Jeannie, "your people are come." She tipped her head to indicate the bearded man and the weak-looking woman, the first couple to disembark from the plane and wander into the airport.

Ivor smoothed his hair and hurried to shake the man's

hand before he could get away. Already, Ivor could see Mellie, the driver of the Fantasy Wagon, eying the American couple covetously.

"How you do?" asked Ivor, hurriedly thrusting the envelope scrap at the young man as though it were a certificate of legitimacy, a ticket of entry. "You are Singer?"

"Yes?" said the man.

"I am Ivor, Ivor Gore. I drive the taxi to the place. It's my place, actually," he blurted nervously.

"Your place?" asked Singer, raising his eyebrows.

"Actually, I manage Sunshine Cabins," amended Ivor. "Actually, I manage the business."

"Do you work for Walter then?" asked Singer softly. Singer was the kind of man who projected a nonspecific gentleness; a vague kindness radiated from his softly contoured features and warm green eyes. He was the sort of person most people like immediately but forget soon after meeting. At a closer look, Ivor was well-pleased by Singer's sensitive and thoughtful look. Not a businessman, he concluded with relief. And the woman, Ivor scarcely glanced her way again. She was very quiet under her cap and sunglasses. She edged out of the conversation, stepping away from Ivor and Singer to watch the luggage ride around and around on the conveyor belt.

"Not exactly work for Walter," explained Ivor. "I manage the property. I show you around, collect the money, make sure everything is A-okay."

"I see."

"And, you see, the thing is, well, when Walter made the reservation, well, how much he tell you?"

"Thirty dollars a night."

"See, that's the thing. That's the mistake, see. It's thirty dollars a night you rent for a week, two weeks. But how long you here?"

"Three and a half days. Four nights," calculated Singer.

"See, there it is. That's the thing." Glimpsing the Singer

woman haul a scarred valise from the rubber belt, Ivor hastily and realistically reduced his rate. "If it's less than a week, it's fifty a night. Walter, he give you the weekly rate."

"Where is Walter?"

"Walter, he is out of town. I run things now."

"Well," breathed Singer, giving himself over to what Ivor perceived to be consideration of this new rate. "I think I'll pay the rate I agreed to pay over the phone. That's what we've budgeted for, and that's what we'll pay."

* * *

Singer's gentle and pensive demeanor masked a profound obstinacy. Elaine returned, dragging the bag, to observe Singer in action. His intractability, his absolute stubbornness fascinated her. In most things, Singer could be flexible, open and generous. But, when he decided to stand his ground, it was impossible to move him. *El Jibarito*, she called him affectionately, the little hillbilly. She learned the word in Puerto Rico, when they took a day-trip into the country and encountered a few rustics hiking to the market. But Singer was really more the hillbilly goat—impossible to pull on a lead. She smiled, imagining herself tugging uselessly at Singer's neat little beard. Elaine was curious what effect Singer's imperturbability would have on the island taxi driver.

"It's a mistake," Ivor repeated. "You see, that's the weekly rate Walter give you on the phone, and you're not staying a week." It was clear the cab driver believed that if he explained his point enough times, Singer would yield.

"I think we'll pay the thirty dollars we agreed to pay." Singer smiled in a friendly way, but he firmly latched his merry gaze on the taxi driver's obsidian eyes.

"Walter, he made a big, big mistake," persisted Ivor, breaking the stare.

"There's our other bag," Elaine interrupted to put a skip in the taxi man's record. "Oh, no, that's not it."

"This is Elaine," Singer introduced her, still smiling as though he were introducing two people he hoped would become friends.

"Hello," she said, but she would not extend her hand to shake Ivor's. She had watched him blowing his nose on his fingers through the glass door.

Finally, their bags pushed through the plastic curtain-flaps on the conveyor gate. Singer pulled both off the conveyor, and Ivor grabbed one while Elaine dragged the valise. Ivor gave a two-finger to Jeannie, who rolled her eyes again, and he led his people out to the taxi van.

The drive out of the airport was fairly smooth, although it felt strange for Elaine to be riding on what felt like the wrong side of the road. And she jumped every time Ivor tapped the horn to greet other vehicles or pedestrians coming from the opposite direction. The car horn on this island, she noted, seemed more an instrument of sociability than warning. Ivor seemed to know an alarming number of people.

He tooted every time an islander appeared by car or on foot on the hard-scrabble horizon. Soon after the airport the road became jarringly rugged with worn swatches, creases, cracks, crater-sized potholes, and bumps. Elaine and Singer were bounced against one another and the car doors, while Ivor anticipated and rode the lurches like a surfer negotiating a choppy, but familiar, sea.

The landscape lay flat, inert on either side of the road, biscuit-colored stretches interrupted sporadically by tufts of harsh-looking brush that bristled with spiny gray quills.

"Scrub," said Singer pointing instructively.

"Shrub, don't you mean?" Elaine asked.

"No, scrub. They call it scrub."

"Looks like shrub." And so it did—low-lying and menacing, untended shrubbery. Now and again, a tree flashed past. These were extraordinary trees—ordinary in appearance up to the leaf level where the branches twisted back on themselves and grew like contorted appendages downward, dripping fringed leaves and scarlet blossoms—bead-shaped and clustered like berries. These trees looked like strangely mutated cousins of the crimson blooming flamboyan they had seen in the pigeon park next to the Governor's mansion in Puerto Rico.

The sun sank, purpling the blossoms and blackening the leaves. Fields appeared and cows and goats wandered the unfenced meadows. The goats formed groups that seemed organized and purposeful, while the cows meandered indecisively and separately. The cattle seemed confused, as though they were a little surprised to find themselves on this Caribbean island.

"Ever hit a cow?" Singer asked Ivor.

"What?"

"Ever hit a cow with the van?"

Ivor hesitated. "Yes."

"What came out worse? The car or the cow?"

"Both come out bad. Bad for the cow. Bad for the car." He hit a pothole hard.

"Ever hit a goat?" asked Singer.

"No, goat, he too smart."

"Does the road get better?"

"No, man, never."

After several more miles, Ivor pointed out some interesting spots. "That's the way to St. John's, where they keep the market," he said, spitting out the open window to indicate the direction. "Up there on that hill, see there? They're trying to put up a hotel." He pointed to a shadowy, roofless structure near a hilltop. "And that's the road to Half Moon Bay, over there." He tooted at a bus full of islanders passing on the other side and lifted two fingers in salute.

"Do you know everybody on the island?" asked Singer.

"Most everybody."

* * *

The cabin—Sunshine Cabins, as advertised in the economy travel guide, though there was only one—was a crumbling yellow structure in a small, dust-blown, fenced yard. Thirty dollars a night, Elaine could see at a glance, was exorbitant for this hovel.

Ivor led them through the tiny rooms, pointing out the ancient and rusted rotating fans, the dented and filth-clouded ice box, and the gas stove that hissed ominously. Water rushed incessantly in the toilet, and flying beetles pipped against the lamps. The lights were just bright enough to attract insects but too dim to read by, though Ivor quickly replaced the two bulbs that flickered most.

"Normally," Ivor began again, "this place goes for sixty dollars U.S. a night if you only stay a few nights. Fifty if you stay four. But I will call it even if you pay forty a night for three nights in advance."

"No," said Singer shaking his head. He pulled a twenty and a ten dollar bill out of his pocket. "We are paying the thirty we agreed, one night at a time, and that's all."

"On this island, nowhere can you stay for thirty a night."

Elaine had taken off her sunglasses so as not to bump herself walking through the shadowy little rooms. She put a hand to her face and gingerly touched her cheek to see if it felt real. Often her skin didn't feel like flesh these days. It felt numb, rubbery, orchidaceous, she thought, thinking of the waxy blooms she and Singer had spotted peeking from hairy clumps of moss in El Yunque, in the rain forest.

Singer had finished arguing with the taxi driver. He pulled a bag onto the bed and unzipped a compartment to remove the shaving kit and a newspaper.

"Look, look," Ivor persisted, "I got mosquito spray here for you, sun block and books." He held up a couple of worn crossword puzzle magazines. "You got books here to read."

The taxi driver fanned the pages enticingly. Elaine could see all of the puzzles had been scribbled in. She wanted to laugh.

"I got tissue," cried Ivor in triumph. "I even got some tissue for your lady." He proffered a travel-size box of tissue to Elaine. "Here, miss. Don't cry."

"Elaine?" called Singer. "Are you okay?"

Elaine shook her head and took a tissue, the last one, which fell apart as she plucked it from the box.

* * *

"Well, my people are come," Ivor bragged to his brother at the chip stand just outside St. John. "My pigeons are come." He laughed.

"Skinny pigeons, them pigeons," scoffed his brother. "Jeannie say."

"Nah, they rich," protested Ivor.

"How you know they rich, Mr. Businessman?"

Ivor searched his mind for some evidence that his people had money. Their luggage was shabby, their clothing worn, and neither of them wore as much jewelry as a watch. And, come to think of it, they hadn't even paid for the taxi ride from the airport. "From the States," he said finally. "They come from the U.S."

"Yeah, they rich, rich like me." Ivor's brother plucked at his raggy shirt. "Skinny like me, too." He rapped on the wooden stick that replaced his missing leg.

"Fool," spat Ivor disgustedly. He turned to leave the stand.

"Hey, buy me chips, Mr. Businessman!" his brother called after him. "Buy me paw paw!"

* * *

In the bathroom, Elaine put a towel over the shaving kit to unzip the bag silently. She pulled a plastic orange vial from a compartment carefully so the contents wouldn't rattle.

"You shouldn't take so many of those," called Singer from the bedroom.

"They help," she said, liberally shaking out capsules. She twisted the faucet, but eschewed the orange stream from the tap and swallowed the sticky pills dry.

"I wouldn't drink that water," said Singer.

"I didn't."

"Are you upset? Come on, honey. Come read the paper with me."

"We shouldn't have come," Elaine said. "It's a mistake."

"Come on, sit with me." Singer patted the bed beside him. "It isn't even like he's gone, Elaine. He would be visiting his father this time of year anyway."

"You can say that. You can say that. He isn't your son. But I know he's not coming back this time."

"Of course, he'll come back. He'll be back for Christmas, and next summer we'll take a trip with him, maybe camping or something."

"He doesn't like camping. When he was in Boy Scouts, he hated sleeping out—the bugs, the dirt." Elaine remembered how her middle son always detested dirt and disarray. When he played outdoors, he would frequently run inside, crying and holding his small brown hands aloft for Elaine to wipe as though the few grains of soil were as dangerous as a flesh-eating disease.

"Well, we'll take him somewhere else then. You haven't lost him, honey."

"But I did lose him. He doesn't live with us anymore. First I lost my baby, I lost Sanders, now I lost—"

"Hush, hush," said Singer, drawing Elaine into his arms.

"I know this is hard because Sanders died, but that was over four years ago, and this isn't the same, honey. This isn't the same at all. Teddy wanted to move in with his father."

"But why? Why? That's what I don't understand." Elaine pulled free and rose to walk to the window. The transparent husks of several desiccated moths lined the ledge outside the glass. Elaine traced them with her finger.

"He was unhappy, Elaine. You know that. That stunt with the belt. He could have hurt himself." Singer stood and leaned over the bed. Elaine could see his reflection; he appeared to be twisting the bedspread.

"What if he hurts himself over there? Who's going to stop him next time?"

"Maybe he won't be unhappy there. Maybe he'll get along with the kids out there, make friends. Maybe he'll like it there. He seemed to think he would."

"What are you doing?"

"There's a spring poking out. I'm coiling it back, so it doesn't pinch like the devil in the middle of the night."

* * *

As soon as Ivor parted the bead curtains at the Ha-Ha Club, Sheila, the bartender, told him his uncle wanted him. And before Ivor could take a step backwards to slip out into the night again, he heard his uncle wheezing, "Ivor, Ivor my son."

"Uncle, you in here?" asked Ivor, disingenuously peering through the cool, cramped, but otherwise deserted bar as though it were too vast and busy to discern at first glance his father's mountainous brother occupying a good third of the bar and two bar stools. The older man's grayish skin folded and creased around his bull-neck like an elephant's hide, and his bald head shone under the dim bulb dangling from a cord in the ceiling.

"They tell me you have business at the cottage. People staying. Americans."

Ivor rolled his eyes. "They some raggedy Americans. Poor and skinny as stick bugs."

"Still you got people," winked his uncle, twisting his bulk to signal Sheila. "Buy me a drink, boy, and tell me about our business."

* * *

In the morning, Elaine shook Singer awake. "We can't stay here," she told him. "We have to leave."

"The island?"

"We can't stay. I thought it would be okay, but it's impossible."

"Our plane isn't until Friday," said Singer, yawning. "Did you sleep?"

"No, there are bugs all over this place. Didn't you feel them. Look at your arms; they're all bitten up."

The pale undersides of Singer's arms were splotched with tiny pink weals. "I didn't feel anything," he marveled.

"There's no hot water, either. I heard you ask Walter on the phone about the hot water. You said there was hot water." Elaine tried hard to keep her voice from rising.

"We can go somewhere else," promised Singer. "If you don't like this, we'll go somewhere else. Let's go into St. John's today and find another place."

"Look," said Elaine, racing to the closet, "look. Ivor left a shirt." She unfurled a freshly-laundered blue shirt on a hanger. A patch with Ivor's name stitched in red over the breast pocket. "It's nice. I like this blue. I think I'm going to wear it," she told Singer. "Do you think he would mind?"

Singer shrugged and scratched at the bites on his arms.

* * *

"I saw your people," Jeannie told Ivor when she met him in the grocery. "They walking in the road. The woman wearing the shirt of your uniform. Why you don't drive them in the taxi, Ivor? Why you make them walk?"

"Where you see them? Where?"

"Walking for the bus stop in front of the boat dock."

Ivor quickly paid for his cigarettes and ran out to the taxi, cursing his people under his breath. Goddamn them, stupid, stupid Americans! Didn't they know to take the taxi? What had he done to make them insult him this way?

He reached the bus stop just as the Americans climbed on board. He followed the bus for awhile, but he stopped when he couldn't think what he would do if he caught up. He would look too foolish telling the couple to come off the bus and get into the taxi. He remembered the man's smiling eyes. What if they refused?

* * *

The bus, nearly empty when Elaine and Singer boarded, quickly filled with islanders. An ancient Chinese man in a black suit slowly climbed on board after a few stops to slide between Singer and the window, where he promptly curled against Singer's shoulder and fell asleep. The fare collector, a teenage boy, sat next to Elaine. He kept hopping up to gather coins in a canvas sack from passengers as they boarded, distressing Elaine. She worried that someone else might try to take his place, and she protected it with her baseball cap while he was gone.

Mothers with flocks of small children, young women dressed in bright dresses and heels for work, men and boys piled into the bus until there was no room for anyone to sit, and Elaine was certain the bus would no longer stop for people waiting at the side of the road. But it kept stopping, and more people packed in. Pull down seats appeared in every possible space, and when they filled, more people boarded the bus to stand, sit on the floorboard or in other people's laps. A man wearing only pajama bottoms climbed on at one point and hung halfway out the door, clutching at a seat strap. But Elaine was especially fascinated by one girl with large fleshy ear lobes which flapped and rippled with the breeze from an opened window. She could not stop staring at these amazingly mobile lobes.

The bus driver had a cassette deck in front and only one song on the tape that he played over and over as the bus lurched and leaped toward St. John. The only words Elaine could make out from the staticky speakers were:

Think about every night and day.
If I had wings I could fly.
I believe I can fly.

Over and over the refrain repeated itself until Elaine thought she might have to scream to release the song from her brain.

Soon she could feel vibration from Singer's ribs. He began singing the song with the tape, softly at first, then without inhibition. Elaine shot a glance at the Chinese man. She hoped Singer wouldn't disturb him. Breathing deeply and slowly, the old man obviously enjoyed the profound oblivion of natural sleep which so often evaded her.

Elaine looked at the boy beside her. As he fingered his cloth sack full of coins, he seemed unaware of the singing. Really, he was too young to have to work, she thought. He's not much older than ... Elaine noticed his fingernails were rather longish, filed to points and painted a shade of electric blue.

The girl with the movable ear lobes seemed to yawn and cry out at the same time, startling Elaine, who then realized the girl, too, was singing along with the tape. Some children and their mothers joined in, and a rich and triumphant chorus blended with the scratchy sounds of the tape. Then the bus hit a hard bump.

Reflexively, Elaine reached back with her forearm to protect the boy.

"Don't touch me, lady," he said coldly.

* * *

"Ivor! Ivor!" the one-legged man called, hobbling to catch the taxi driver before he pulled out of the parking lot at the dockyard. Ivor had finally gotten a fare to the airport: a Puerto Rican couple, newlyweds, crisp and bright in their new holiday clothes. They readily handed Ivor twenty dollars U.S. for the one-way trip.

"What you want?" asked Ivor, rolling down the window.

"Your people, Ki-Ki say they in St. John's, ask about rooms."

"Them, they stay with me," said Ivor, confidently. "Ki-ki drunk." He rolled the window back up and drove out of the parking lot. The entire ride to the airport, he did not honk at acquaintances nor point out interesting sights to the couple. He thought about those people, his people, and he shook his head from time to time.

* * *

In St. John's, the dense heat seemed to pound between Elaine's temples. In a storefront window she could see her face flamed red beneath her baseball cap, and her forearms had the raw-looking sheen of severe sunburn. They had been walking for hours. Singer steadily leading her from hotel to hotel, patiently checking rates, examining rooms, running hot water and testing mattresses.

Street hawkers crowded the wooden storefront walkways, frequently forcing Elaine and Singer into the busy streets, where cars screeched and honked at them. Over-ripe fruit and fish odors fouled the nearly unbreathable heat. T-shirt and souvenir vendors piteously begged the couple to examine their wares. Once Elaine wandered to a t-shirt stall, fingering a dark-blue shirt her son might like. Then she remembered he was gone, he would not be coming back, and she dropped it as though stung by an electric current. She stumbled away, deaf to the vendor's pleas, then insults. After that, she had the feeling that everyone there in that village, every islander she passed in St. John's hated her and hated Singer. She could see the sidelong glances and hear the mocking laughter echo from every direction. They despised her; she knew it. They wished she had never existed.

They detested Singer, too, she could tell. But that didn't matter. He didn't pay attention, and Elaine knew he didn't care. He was like that. Things didn't affect him. He probably sensed the hostility at some level, but it was of no account to him. Singer just kept walking through the streets purposefully, climbing steps to look at rooms and pleasantly asking questions of various contemptuous clerks. How ridiculous their hatred seemed in the face of his bland courtesy.

"Well," said Singer, finally. He had taken off his Panama hat to fan his face. Perspiration mashed his brown curls to his temples and forehead. "How about this steel-drum band? This Pepper Garden?" he asked. He had stopped to read a bill posted in a shop window. "That's just up the hill near the dockyard. We could take the bus back and hike that hill. I'd kind of like to hear this band. How about you?"

"What about a room, Singer? You said we'd get a room."

"I think I know a place," he said. "It's expensive, but there's really nothing here near the dock that costs much less. And this place is so noisy. I don't think you'd like that."

"Let's get the place first. Then we can do whatever you want."

* * *

At the airport, Jeannie told Ivor his people had been seen hitchhiking up the big hill to hear Pepper Garden play.

"Hitchhiking?"

"Yeah, your famous Americans catch a ride in Damon's truck."

"Those people, they not my people," scoffed Ivor.

"The woman," said Jeannie, "she wear your shirt."

Ivor sank deep into a plastic seat in the waiting area. He drew his legs up and wrapped his arms around them. He buried his head in his chest and closed his eyes.

"Hey, Ivor!" Jeannie called. "Hey, Ivor, they's no sleeping in the terminal."

* * *

Elaine wondered if she had been wrong. The man driving the pickup seemed to bear Singer and her no malice. He had not hesitated to stop to load them into the flatbed with several other people and a fly-spotted cur. Again, Elaine found herself seated near a teenage boy, near his dusty legs, really. He sat on the wheel-well, and she hunched cross-legged on the floor of the truck bed. Singer was next to her, talking amiably to the islanders sharing the truck-bed.

Singer had the habit of gesturing with his hat when he made a point or indicated a direction. He was telling the others where they had been that day. Elaine noticed the dog's low growl, like the rumble of a distant earthquake, every time Singer swiped at the air with his hat.

"Singer, don't do that," she warned him. "Don't wave your hat. Upsets the dog."

"Does it?" asked Singer, giving his hat an experimental flip. The dog snarled and lunged. The boy on Elaine's left caught the dog's ruff and forced him down. "You're right." Singer put his hat in his lap. He continued talking to the others. In a few moments, he forgot and began waving the hat again. The dog grumbled fiercely.

"Singer, put the hat down."

"Oh, right." He replaced the hat. In a little while, he was fanning it, and the dog shot forward, snapping and howling. Another man caught him this time and wrestled him back. "The hat," grinned Singer. "I keep forgetting."

"This dog," said the boy near Elaine, "he don't like things like that hat. Things, he don't like things in his face, and strangers."

"Is he your dog?" asked Elaine.

"No," the boy smiled, shaking his head, as though Elaine was absurd for suggesting he'd own such a dog. "No way."

"Whose dog is he?"

"That dog, he's nobody's dog. Just likes a ride up the hill. So we bring him. And later we bring him back."

In front of the restaurant at the top of the hill, the dog jumped from the gate and trotted stiffly to disappear in a nearby ravine. While Singer was thanking the truck driver, the dog reappeared and leapt back into the pickup.

"You going to stay to hear the band?" Singer asked Damon, the driver, companionably.

"No, not this time."

"They're a good band?"

"Oh, good, real good."

"Can you stay long enough to have a beer with me?" Elaine heard Singer ask as she stepped behind him to climb down a few chalky rocks.

"Well, sounds good." The man rubbed his hands together. "Your wife, she okay out there? Those yellow rocks, they crumble."

"Elaine!" called Singer without turning around. "You okay out there?"

"Yes!"

"She's okay," Singer shrugged, and they went inside for their beer.

* * *

Ivor got to the cabin as Ashley from the Paradise Cove Resort was putting the couple's worn-looking luggage into the resort's van. "Hey," cried Ivor. "Hey! Hey!" He grabbed a strap of the garment bag Ashley was loading and tried to wrench the piece of luggage free.

"What are you doing?" asked Ashley, who had been schooled in the States and spoke with deliberate precision. He yielded the bag, and Ivor fell on his backside lurching it free. "Have you lost your mind?"

"The Singer, they my people," Ivor protested, clutching the bag to his chest. "They stay here. You steal my people."

"They don't want to stay. They don't like it here," scoffed Ashley, his eyeglasses glinting. "They asked my father for a room this afternoon."

"They stay here."

"They rented a suite."

"They my clients."

"Air-conditioned, a view of the sea."

"These people, they make the reservation with Walter. They stay here."

"One hundred and fifty-five dollars U.S. a night," said Ashley. "And they're renting a boat tomorrow." Ashley took the garment bag from Ivor and tossed it into the van. He tooted his horn, raised two fingers and drove off in a cloud of dust.

Inside the house, Ivor found a scrap of paper and a fifty-dollar bill the couple left behind for the lodging and the cab ride. He recognized his name, I - V - O - R, printed in one corner and uselessly traced the letters under that with his finger tip.

* * *

After the steel-drum band played, Singer and Elaine decided to take a worn path that trailed down the hill. On one side of the path, the sun sinking over the bay made glitter of the particles of volcanic ash and motes that swirled in the late-afternoon sky. On the other, the facade of an abandoned armory blazed ocherous, while a small herd of dun-colored goats trickled down from the broad, rubied steps to the hillside below.

"Goats," said Elaine. "Goats again."

"Goats," nodded Singer. They rounded a bend, finding themselves on a narrow street.

"Ever notice how appropriate goats seem?" she asked. "Wherever you see them, they're never out of place." The street led to a row of shack-like houses similar to Ivor's Sunshine Cabin. Glaringly bright garments—shirts, shorts, shifts—fluttered from clotheslines in the small backyards.

"Well, goats certainly work well here," said Singer.

A man rushed out of his house to shoo the goats that had followed Singer and Elaine down the hill from a garden patch in his front yard. He cursed them and picked up a handful of stones to toss at them. The goats wagged their tails and brayed blithely. Elaine was about to remark on how foolish goats made people seem, when the one-legged man quickly limped over to them.

"Hey, man," he gasped. He was out of breath from rushing up the hill. "Hey, how you do?"

"Hello," said Elaine warily.

"Nice day," the one-legged man smiled.

Singer nodded.

"You like this island? This island, it's a friendly place. I see you people, and I have to come over. I want to be friends."

Singer and Elaine stopped walking to stare at the man expectantly.

"And friends, they help one to the other, right? They give help, right?"

"I don't have any money to give you," Singer said.

"Bus fare," the one-legged man blurted. "You must have one dollar U.S., man. That's nothing to you."

Singer shook his head and raised his eyebrows. Elaine felt her pulse quicken.

"You don't have to be like this, man. You don't have to be so bloody hostile, man. I just want to be friends. I try to be friendly with people."

"I don't have any money to give you," Singer repeated.

Lorraine M. López

The one-legged man thrust his arms out and shoved Singer in the chest. "You people make me sick."

Elaine shuddered. Singer was small and thin, but he was strong. She had no doubt he could beat a one-legged man fairly easily in a fight. She was worried for the islander, who seemed so upset he looked as if he might weep.

"It's okay," she told the one-legged man. She dug into her bag and pulled out a bill. "Here, here's five dollars. Take it." She held it out to him, but Singer's glare held him fast for a moment. "Come on. Take it."

The one-legged man snatched the bill and hobbled off down the street, yelling: "Bloody hostile!"

"I wish you hadn't done that," said Singer quietly. "I already told him no."

* * *

Ivor found his brother drinking a bottle of juice at the main fruitstand in St. John's. He slapped the bottle out of his brother's hand and sent it crashing against the plywood counter. "You! You!" He lunged and grabbed for his brother's neck. Ivor's brother slid off his stool. Ivor dove after him, slapping and kicking whatever he could reach.

The standkeeper and others in the street rushed to separate the brothers. Ivor's uncle was called from his house a few doors down where he was having a bath. He came running in his bathrobe. Two tufts of shaving cream or soap suds sprouted from his large ears.

"What's this?" the old man demanded, clutching his dripping robe close around his belly. "What's this about?"

"Him," spat Ivor bitterly. "He come after my people, begging and pushing, they say. Now, they go Paradise Cove. He ruin my business."

The one-legged man, sitting in the dirt between two bar stools, narrowed his eyes at his brother. He shook his head, but he said nothing.

* * *

"Well?" asked Singer, parting long floral drapes to reveal the sea, glittering under the moon. "Do you like this room?"

Elaine wound her hair in a towel and nodded. "This is a beautiful place, Singer. Thank you." Steam from the shower gave the well-proportioned room a fragrant and gauzy warmth. Thick cherrywood furniture bore soft cushions printed with the same splashes of pink, gray and white flowers as decorated the drapes.

"It costs a lot, but I was thinking there's no point in coming all the way here and suffering. So we'll pay the extra, and we'll stop suffering."

"I don't know if—"

"Elaine, come here." Singer pulled her towards him. He reached for the towel on her head and gently rubbed her hair dry. "I want us to try. In this room, we can try at least. Tomorrow, we get a boat, and we can rent some snorkels and flippers. We can watch the fish under the water. You like that. Remember Belize?"

Elaine nodded. Her son had found a starfish adhering to a boulder at the mouth of an underwater cave. He had pulled her arm. Look, look, his mask had bubbled. He kept the shells he had found in Belize on a shelf in his bookcase, where they still sat, furred with dust, untouched.

* * *

In the morning, Elaine woke to Singer pulling on her arm. "Wake up, honey. Wake up. The boat will be here in a few minutes."

"Can't it wait? I was really sleeping," she told Singer. "I think I was even having a dream."

Singer consulted his watch. "No, we've got to hurry. It's almost ten."

"Did I really sleep that long?" Elaine yawned.

Singer threw her bathing suit, some shorts and a shirt on the bed. She dressed quickly and stuffed her hair under her baseball cap. They clattered down the polished steps to the garden, where other guests were having breakfast. In a few minutes, a morbid-looking man steered a motor boat into the landing beyond the courtyard. Frowning, he put out his hand to help Elaine into the rocky little craft. Why, he'd rather handle a snake, thought Elaine, than touch me. She could see his plum-colored lips pursed in distaste as he guided her into the boat.

"This your boat?" asked Singer, climbing into the boat unassisted.

"No."

"But it must be pretty nice to steer it around the island." Singer smiled.

"Put on your life jacket, sir. You, too, ma'am."

Elaine pulled on the padded orange jacket, carefully fastening the canvas straps. Singer hastily threw his life jacket over his shoulders.

The boat sputtered away from the landing, pitching with each transparent turquoise push of the waves.

"You do much fishing?" Singer asked. The guttural motor roared when the craft reached the open sea, drowning his words.

The boatman cut the engine again when they approached a small bay, cut like a sickle at the base of tall jagged cliffs. He leapt out of the boat and tugged it close to the sand so that Singer and Elaine could step out and wade.

"I will be back at half past one," he told them, again taking Elaine's hand to help her out of the boat.

"Okay, we'll be here," Singer replied, tossing the borrowed masks and flippers onto the sand.

On an impulse, Elaine clung to the boatman's hard calloused hand. "I'm sorry," she blurted.

"For what?" asked the boatman, wrenching his hand free.

"I mean, thank you," she said, lifting her sunglasses to peer into the man's yellow-rimmed eyes. "Thank you for bringing us here."

"You be careful," he told Singer as he climbed back into the boat. "You be careful, they's pirates, real pirates, cut your throat for a cigarette lighter." He sputtered off before Singer could reply.

"Nice fellow," Singer told Elaine, who had waded ashore and was spreading the towels on a smooth patch of sand.

The water felt warm, so Singer and Elaine pulled on their masks and flippers and waded back out into the sea. Underwater, she could see the bay was filled with fish. Hundreds and hundreds of transparent gray-tinged fish shimmered and darted collectively, massing together like clouds. She reached to tug Singer's arm. Look, look, her face mask burbled.

When they were tired from swimming, Singer and Elaine waded out of the water. Singer unwrapped a package of sandwiches he had purchased from the hotel restaurant that morning. Then he produced a new deck of cards. "Gin?" he asked, stripping the plastic wrap from the box. "Penny a point." He shuffled and dealt the cards, and they ate the sandwiches while they played.

Then Singer took out the camera and snapped some pictures of the cliffs, of the sea, of Elaine in her swimsuit. She took the camera from him and shot him posing as a muscle man on top of a flat black rock. Laughing, Singer replaced the lens cap and returned the camera to its case. He slipped the camera and his wallet in a plastic bag left over from the sandwiches. He began digging a hole in the sand under his towel.

"What are you doing, Singer?" asked Elaine, watching him dig.

"Digging a hole."

"How come?"

"Hear that?" Singer placed the plastic bag containing the camera and his wallet deep in the hole he had dug and covered them up with sand. He smoothed the mound and replaced his towel over it.

"I don't hear anything." But, as soon as the words were out, Elaine heard the purring of a motorboat in the distance.

"Water carries sound," said Singer. "We hear the boat before we can see it."

"Is that man coming back for us so soon?" she asked.

Singer shook his head.

A small boat appeared like a blotch on the horizon, growing larger and louder as it approached. Two islanders— young men—steered the boat into the bay, cutting the engine to float toward the sand.

"Hey," called one man.

"Hey," said Singer.

"Nice day!" the other shouted.

"Yeah," Singer agreed.

"Gotta light?" asked the man, who climbed out of the boat first and waded toward the beach, pulling the boat on a stout rope.

"Sorry," Singer apologized. "Don't smoke."

"Nice, but very, very hot today," said the man in the boat. He also stepped out and waded through the shallow water. "Do you have any drinks?"

"Water," offered Elaine, holding out the canteen. The two men ignored her.

They appeared to be surveying the picnic site with intense interest. Elaine felt embarrassed proffering the canteen. She set it on her towel. She felt a chill on her shoulders and reached to put on the shirt she had brought— Ivor's shirt, the blue short-sleeved uniform shirt.

One of the men saw the shirt and motioned to his partner. "Ahh," he said, "you know Ivor."

"Sunshine Cabins." Singer nodded.

"He's good man, Ivor is," the islander told them. "A businessman."

Giggling erupted from a pile of rocks at the base of the

cliffs. Two small, very brown boys, tagging each other, raced from the foot path leading down from the cliffs. Soon after, a woman followed them wearing her hair wound up in a paisley turban. She wore a cotton housedress and cracked black flats. Laughing and shrieking, the boys scrambled into the water. The woman kicked off her shoes and followed the boys out into the sea, hiking her dress to her hips as she waded in deeper and deeper.

"Kids," said Singer. "You got kids?"

"I got four girls." The islander held out four fingers. "They's no peace in my house. And this man here, he got twins, babies."

The other man nodded sheepishly.

"Let's go," he said suddenly. "Come on. Time to go."

The two men pushed off their boat, climbed in and gave Elaine and Singer a two-fingered salute. "Regards to Ivor," one man called, before yanking the rip cord to start the engine. Elaine and Singer waved at them until the boat vanished in the horizon.

* * *

On the last day, Elaine and Singer stood in the dockyard parking lot looking for a ride to the airport. The one-legged man shook his brother awake from his nap behind the post office. "Your people waiting for you."

Ivor hurried to the parking lot, climbed in the van and tooted his horn at the couple. "Hey, I can give you a ride."

Singer hesitated.

"Hey, look, no bad feeling. Come on, I need the work."

Singer and Elaine piled their luggage in the van and climbed in.

Ivor turned to face them before driving off. "It cost twenty dollar U.S., up front," he said, holding out his hand. Singer paid him, and the van pulled out of the parking lot.

"You like the island?" asked Ivor.

"Yes," said Singer. "It's a nice island."

"You come back some time?"

"Sure," promised Elaine.

"Ahh!" Ivor flashed a smile in the rear view. "Now, everybody, they say that. But they never come back. Look, I'll show you the place they're trying to put a hotel," said Ivor, tooting his horn at a young girl raising two fingers in salute from her bicycle. "And then I'll show where is the road to Half Moon Bay."

To Control a Rabid Rodent

Jonathan Escamilla never meant to shoot Mr. Hudanish in the head with his new deer rifle. He barely knew Mr. Hudanish well enough to nod hello, and he certainly had no idea Mr. Hudanish would take the notion to stretch out on his firm carpet of St. Augustine to sunbathe early that summer day.

Jonathan had just been given the rifle for his thirteenth birthday the first week in June, and deer season would not open until October. For three weeks, Jonathan had polished and oiled the unused gun and resigned himself to wait out the interminable summer until his father would pile up the truck with the cooler rattling full of diet sodas (for Jonathan was a hefty boy) and cans of Miller's Genuine Draft Light (his father was hefty, too), the sleeping bags trussed like mutilated torsos, tackle boxes, canisters of insect repellent and sunburn spray, the Coleman kerosene lamp, fishing poles, and the guns.

It was not as though Jonathan were an impatient sort, greedy for adventure. He was a good boy; everyone said so. An altar boy, first baseman for the Land of Enchantment Savings and Loan Mavericks and president of Bosque Farms Four-H. Jonathan was a good boy, and he knew how to wait until deer season to bring out his new rifle.

Still, the new gun—gleaming with unnecessary care and leaning lover-like in a corner of his bedroom—was the first image to pop into his head when he noticed the rabid prairie dog, sputtering and running circles in the backyard. Sighting a prairie dog in town was, in itself, very peculiar. It was not to Jonathan's mind as unusual as seeing someone naked in

179

church, but the prairie dogs usually confined themselves to the *llano* and the new Camino Real golf course that was nearly started.

And the sight of this odd earth-colored rodent slavering froth sent an icy quiver up Jonathan's spine, as the animal wended a bizarre figure-eight, looping around the new chili in the garden and the clothesline posts stabbed into the pitiful summer lawn. Once it smacked headlong into the chain link fence, shook itself and resumed its mindless race around the Escamilla yard.

Jonathan thundered up the stairs to his bedroom, two at a time.

* * *

"Jonathan! Jonathan!" cried his mother, who really didn't like vibrations in the house. She still remembered the earthquake in Truth or Consequences during her senior year of high school that felled her chemistry teacher in a dead faint and spilled all the students out into the P.E. field to stare in baffled betrayal at the moody sky.

Next, she supposed Jonathan had burst another blood vessel in his septum. It had been a summer of prolific nosebleeds for her son. "Jonathan, is it another nosebleed?" she called upstairs after him.

"Prairie dog," he murmured, rushing back down past her on the staircase cradling the new gun in his long brown arms. "Rabies, I think."

"Oh, dear," she gasped, recoiling from the sight of the gun. A town girl—Inocencia Trembly Escamilla's parents had owned and operated Trembly's Jewels on Main Street since before she was born—Inocencia maintained a profound terror of guns and snakes and changeable weather conditions. Like her parents in their winter years fumbling about the musty shop and shouting themselves hoarse to be heard over the shrieking drill, Inocencia's hearing had dulled to the point that she could no longer hear water plop in the sink.

"But is it necessary to shoot the babies?" she asked. Prairie dogs were no doubt a nuisance, Inocencia conceded, but did their gentle offspring pose such an immediate and terrible threat?

Jonathan had already slammed out the screened porch, and there was no mistaking the next sickening reports of sound before the long silence.

Then Jonathan clomped back up the splintery porch steps and slammed back into the house. Would she never train him? Sasquatch, she called him, the Big Foot, stomping with his heavy steps that rattled the little porcelain devils she collected in her china closet.

Jonathan sank into the plastic sheathing covering the divan, sighing louder than the air escaping under his thighs.

"Did you kill the babies?" his mother asked, popping open the glass door to peek in at her red painted devils and to make sure they hadn't been nicked.

"No, ma'am," Jonathan managed to raise his voice to be heard and sounded quite dull like a machine.

"What, in heaven, were you shooting at, young man?" The peach-lacquered faces grinned impishly at Inocencia, as she fondled them for traces of blemish. "May I ask that?"

"I shot the gun."

"I heard that, my goodness!"

"I fired the gun, but, ma'am, something's not right with the cross hairs. Something's not right with the lens."

"That's a brand new gun, Mister. Your daddy got it for you, just fresh for your birthday."

"I know that, ma'am. I know it. That's why I just can't understand..."

"If there's a problem with the gun, son, you must tell Daddy so he can write the catalog people. You must tell him right away." One of the tiny ceramic demons had a whitish filament in the prongs of its trident. She swiped it clean on her apron and set it neatly on the shelf.

Jonathan could hear the siren whining off Hermilio Salazar Boulevard long before she did. He watched her propping the little fetishes correctly in the case. He didn't want to interrupt this single-minded and pleasurable pursuit of hers, but the siren persisted.

"Ma'am, I'm afraid I may have shot Mr. Hudanish, the next-door neighbor," Jonathan blurted.

"What did he want?" She turned to her son in exasperation. She really did not like to be distracted while she toyed with her devils.

"I think I've killed him. I think I shot him dead!"

"There, there, Johnathan." Inocencia immediately abandoned the bric-a-brac to stroke her son's wrist. "It doesn't matter what he's said." And by that time, the siren's wail had penetrated her hearing like persistent crying into a pillow. "We know the truth, don't we. We know the truth, after all. Anyways, it can wait until your father gets home. Everything can wait 'til Daddy gets home."

But the sheriff would not wait for Pedro Escamilla to finish delivering truckloads of frozen french fries to fast-food restaurants in Las Lunas, Peralta, and Tomé before manacling Jonathan and speeding him to the station house to be processed and fingerprinted.

At the house, Sheriff Block's questions had been succinct and impersonal. He seemed profoundly more interested in dislodging a wedge of beef from his back teeth with a strand of thread than getting to the bottom of the shooting. "Are you the kid that shot the Hudanish fellow?"

"Yes," Jonathan sighed, "I shot Mr. Hudanish."

"Write this down somewheres willya, Jaime?" The sheriff glanced vaguely at his deputy, who dutifully pulled out a spiral tablet and began scribbling. "Okay, son, you wanna lawyer or something? What's the story here?"

"I want my husband here," piped in Mrs. Escamilla. "I

don't think you ought to be questioning my boy without his father here."

"Are you coming, Mom?" pleaded Jonathan over his shoulder. "Please!"

"I'm coming with you," she promised. "I'll leave a note for your dad. Well, you better write it, deputy, and explain." Inocencia hated leaving the house without her husband. The shopping, the repair work on the car, the banking, the visiting with friends—all of it—was better managed with Pedro, who could hear precisely what people said when they blurred words into her ears like feathers tossed into an electric fan.

* * *

All of his life, Jonathan would remember his huge relief upon seeing his father bustle into the station with Miguel, their *curandero* tenant. His father clasped him forcefully to his chest, but Jonathan managed to peek over the broad man's shoulders at the dour little homeopathic doctor in his sleeveless undershirt. Old Miguel clutched a cardboard box that advertised Lux Soap.

"My son," Pedro Escamilla choked, "my son is...an altar boy!"

"Yes, yes, we know all that stuff from your wife." The sheriff blew his nose into a paper towel. "These allergies, you know."

"I told them Jonathan would never do such a thing, honey. I told them quite clearly, but they don't seem to want to listen to me."

"Miguel," the boy whispered. "Miguel."

"An altar boy, a good boy, this an' that an' the other. Regular little politician," Block chuckled. "Gonna run for sheriff, huh? Gonna take my job away?"

"So, I got a question," put in the laconic deputy, suddenly energized by the memory that he needed a promotion to move out of his parent's house and buy a mobile home with his fiancee Lúpe. "So, what's this good kid, this altar boy, doing shooting the neighbor dead? Bam, like that? I mean, like, what's the motive?"

"My son ain't no murderer."

"Isn't, honey, isn't."

"Miguel, what's in the box?"

"Shh." The old man put an etiolated finger to his tan lips.

"Lemme see, they sez you was shootin' some kinda—what's this word, Jaime?—golfer?"

"Gopher. That's the modern word for prairie dog," added the deputy with a touch of pride.

"Gophers!" cried Inocencia. "They were running all over the house!"

"Ma'am, please, be quiet."

"My son was trying to shoot a rabid prairie dog, that's all." Jonathan's father tried to explain the incident as Jonathan had in a lucid and simple way. "He knew it was dangerous, and he knew he had to destroy it."

"Ain't no prairie dogs in town since they dynamited for the highway."

"Only prairie dogs," the deputy pointed out, "is in the *llano* or the Rio Communities with that Camino Real golf course they're about to start diggin'."

"What did you have against those people? The Hudanish? They weren't Catholic, were they, Jaime? Was it the altar boy angle?" the sheriff pondered.

"I don't even know the Hudanish! They just moved next door a couple of years ago!" Jonathan yelled. "I never wanted to kill a Hudanish!"

"Explosive temper," observed the deputy.

"Gotta mean temper, kid," Block agreed.

"I don't even know the Hudanish," Jonathan insisted.

"That's not true son," his mother recollected. "You went over there once to ask if you could cut the grass—" She clasped a hand over her mouth. Jonathan's ears burned, recalling for the first time since the shooting how Mr.

Hudanish had angrily yanked his shoulder and led him around to the backyard to show him a lawn more perfect than paint, shouting the whole while: "Snot-nose! You think I'd let a punk like you spoil my grass!"

"Hush up, Mom," Jonathan pleaded.

"Kinda disrespectful for an altar boy," noticed the sheriff.

"Sheriff, can I talk with you outside?" the deputy asked. He could hardly wait to see Lúpe's eyes sparkling over her beer when he'd tell her the good news at the Railroad Club that evening. "I think I can crack this thing."

The sheriff rolled his eyes, but followed his assistant out into the parking lot. "Make it quick. It's hotter than shit out here."

"I think there's more to the lawn-cutting story than meets the eye here, sir. I think we gotta motive with this grass thing. Did you see how the perpetrator's family reacted. Holy cow, it was like they was stung by a wasp!"

"Hmmn, so you think there's more to the grass-clipping thing."

"'Zactly, I mean, like they practically, you know, exploded from the inside when the woman mentioned that, you know what I mean."

"Hmmn, so you got this theory the boy got this grudge from the grass-cutting incident?"

"Yessir!"

"An' how do you propose to find out this information?"

"Well," said the deputy, thinking it over. "I guess we'll have to ask some questions. Like question the people?"

"Hmmn, so you think we should ask them some questions."

"Yessir!'

"Hmmn, so I gotta question for you. How come we're out here in this Goddamn blazing sun, if you think we should be inside askin' more questions? Just what do you think we were doin' in there?"

The two men silently trudged back into the station house.

All members of the Escamilla family regarded the officers quizzically, but none had the temerity to inquire about their short caucus. Miguel, though, seemed amused in a detached way by the returning lawmen.

"Ain't no gopher in or around the premises," the deputy opened his little spiral notebook, trying a different tack. "No gopher bodies, neither."

"I got the creature," rasped Miguel, holding the box high above his hairless, walnut-ridged head. "I got the animal, the prairie dog with the rabies right here in this box."

"Who is this old guy?"

"Give me your full name, age and occupation," demanded the deputy. "Then, I take your statement."

"I am Miguel, I am older than the wind that bites into the Sandia Mountains, and I am a full-time *curandero*. I have been dead many times, but I decided to be alive today."

"What kind of nonsense is that?" asked the sheriff. "And what is this koo-ran-day-ro business anyway?"

"The *curandero*," explained the deputy, relieved to be useful in some way, "is the name for a male witch, I guess you could say."

"More like a witch doctor," Pedro Escamilla amended.

"Witch, witch doctor," shrugged the deputy, as if there were very little distinction.

"There's a big difference," argued Pedro. "It's not like he puts spells or anything."

"I do spells," Miguel corrected. "I do spells, hexes and once in a while put pins in a voodoo doll—very reasonable rates. But mostly, I do cures for any problem you got. I use herbs, teas, a little magic and sometimes Anacin. I would have a pretty nice little business, too, officers, if they," he indicated the Escamilla's with a push of his chin, "would only let me put a sign up."

"Absolutely not!" Inocencia had been a part of this old bone of contention for so long she did not even need to hear it to know what the old man was complaining about. "We are a civilized household!"

"Now, my cousin's a *curandero* in Tomé, and he just got himself a new Chevy. Me, I have to walk everywheres because I ain't got no sign."

"No signs!" cried Inocencia.

"If you let me put the sign, I could earn enough to move out," Miguel reasoned.

Inocencia turned her back.

"You let the boy put the lawn-mowing sign."

"Stop this bullshit!" thundered the sheriff.

"Every other *curandero* in the state's got a sign, I betcha."

"Come on, old guy—"

"I found this," the old man resigned himself, offering up his box. "I found this prairie dog on my porch after the gun spoke. I found him beggin' on my porch." Miguel unflapped the carton's lips to reveal a still, but breathing, sandy-colored rodent. "He was beggin' me to hypnotize him. He had the hydrophobia, you know, the rabies disease, and he knew it. But, still, he had some hope that I could hypnotize him."

"You hypnotize him?" the deputy was intrigued. This might have implications for his girlfriend, Lúpe.

"Yes, I always hypnotize the sick animals, and I try to cure them." He caressed the coat of the sleeping prairie dog.

"You cure rabies?" the sheriff asked skeptically.

"Oh, no, he will die in his sleep. It is a brain fever. He will die in a dream." Miguel smiled self-consciously.

"This the animal you tried to kill?" The sheriff bored his sharpest stare into young Jonathan.

"Yessir," Jonathan said. "I recognize this prairie dog as the prairie dog...I attempted to shoot." Jonathan, despite his initial panic, began to derive a curious comfort from station-house protocol.

The deputy poked an exploratory pencil at the animal's muzzle.

"Don't touch him! He's only hypnotized. He can wake

up and kill you." Miguel carefully replaced the flaps covering the box. "I will bury him in my garden tomorrow."

The dramatic sight of the diseased rodent satisfied the two lawmen in a strange way insofar as determining Jonathan's innocence. They released the boy—free, and unfettered by probation even—to his parents.

* * *

"Don't 'but, Mom' me, sir," Inocencia snapped at her son that night. She rose to switch the television set off. "You shot that poor man next door, after all, and it's just plain rude not to go on over there and apologize." Inocencia was the kind of woman who sent thank-you notes for thank-you notes. "I spent all afternoon chilling that pineapple Jello mold for you to take over there and you're not backing out now."

"*Da-ad*!" Jonathan implored his father desperately.

"You heard your mother, son." The older man swallowed his irritation at being interrupted in his enjoyment of an educational program on the wild dogs of Africa. "Do what she says."

"They're our neighbors, for goodness sake!" Inocencia threw up her hands. Do you want them to think...that, that... we're the kind of people who just shoot folks without dropping by to say sorry?"

Jonathan shrugged. He didn't think sorry would do it. Somehow he didn't think a gelatin mold would compensate either, and he was more than a little sensitive to the notion that they—based on his rough encounter with the deceased— might be eye-for-an-eye types, only satisfied by shooting him in return for their father's death. "It was an accident."

"All the more reason to get over there and beg their pardon. What do you say when you bump someone in the street accidentally, huh?" she demanded. Here, again, Jonathan felt the comparison grossly inadequate. "You apologize for things you didn't do on purpose that hurt other people, and you do it right away before they forget!" Her voice took on that familiar hysterical pitch that seemed to strip the nerve endings behind Jonathan's teeth. "So get up, out of that chair, comb your hair, and take my Jello salad over right this minute, young man! And I mean right this minute, before those miniature marshmallows pucker up like raisins!"

"You heard your mother, son," said his father.

If Jonathan were the kind of boy who cursed, he might have said: "Goddamn you! You're crazy!" and stormed straight up to his room. If he were sarcastic, he would have asked why they had a death wish for their only child. But, Jonathan really was a good boy, who never did anything to displease his parents, outside of slaying Mr. Hudanish, the neighbor.

So, he gathered up the Jello mold from the kitchen counter and held it—cold and hard in its aqua plastic shell—against his breast as he stepped out onto the back porch to make his way across the yard to the Hudanish house. He hoped vainly that Tupperware—in addition to keeping fresh foods from spoiling—was also bulletproof.

* * *

The Hudanish gate slapped shut on Jonathan's buttocks with a spanking sound that made him lurch in surprise, nearly forfeiting his mother's salad to the neat pansy bed. Inside the tall fence, the Hudanish yard startled him—though he'd seen it once before—even more than the tightly coiled spring on the gate.

In the dead of August, when most people fought to keep tumbleweeds from their dry dirt lawns, the Hudanishes kept an emerald carpet of closely cropped and very dense...grass! Jonathan rubbed his eyes. Mr. Hudanish had flowers, even, delicate lacy blooms along the walk and thick beds of geranium, pansy, marigolds—even rose bushes.

Jonathan felt certain as he picked his way carefully along the stone path that the people who tended these plants in this garden would not like to find a stalk of grass bruised. And they were not likely—in his mind—to be all that nice about his killing Mr. Hudanish, albeit accidentally.

He brushed his knuckles lightly against the doorframe, hoping he would not be heard and could retreat honorably— gelatin salad in hand—to tell his parents, "I knocked, but no one answered. I guess they moved to Kansas, or something."

"Coming!" Jonathan heard a voice sing out from the dark, quiet house. "I'm coming." The back door yawned wide, and the screened door framed the thin face of a young man. The fly-spotted mesh gave the man a cinematic look as though he were being gazed at through a gauze-covered lens; he was wearing women's makeup. "Well," he smiled, puckishly, "where are you hiding it?"

"Hiding what?" Jonathan had never heard a grown man talk in such a high-pitched, lilting voice.

"The pizza, silly!"

"What pizza?"

"You didn't bring the pizza?" The young man seemed terribly disappointed.

"I brought a Jello salad," Jonathan proffered the plastic bowl.

"I don't think I ordered a salad." The man narrowed his black-smudged eyes suspiciously. "Who are you?"

"Jonathan Escamilla." The words escaped like criminals from prison.

"A cousin? What?" The young man rotated his hand to indicate Jonathan should give a little more information.

"I'm Jonathan Escamilla from next door."

"Next door?"

"I'm the one that...you know..." Jonathan felt every ounce of water in his body draining through his armpits in a violently itchy way. "I'm the one that shot Mr. Hudanish."

"That was you!"

"Yes, I'm very sorry. You see, it was an accident. I really didn't mean to."

"So you're the kid that killed Dad," the Hudanish scion scratched his chin regarding Jonathan more speculatively.

"I brought you this Jello salad my mom fixed," Jonathan offered the bowl again.

"*A Jello salad!*" the man laughed. "That's priceless!" He pulled open the screen door to admit his neighbor. "So you are Jonathan." He took Jonathan's hand in his and shook it warmly. "Do you know I've kind of been expecting you?"

Jonathan stepped uncertainly into the kitchen. The young Hudanish may or may not have been wearing mascara and face powder, but he was definitely draped in some kind of kimono dress with salmon-colored water lilies printed on it. Jonathan wanted to dump the salad on the counter and run out of the kitchen like a cucaracha when the lights go on.

"Ronnie, who is it?" another voice called from the recesses of the house.

"It's Jonathan Escamilla!" Ronnie answered.

"Does he have the pizza?"

"He brought a Jello salad!"

"Isn't he the pizza boy?"

"No, he's the champagne boy!" Ronnie shrieked. "Come on out here, Franklin! You'll never believe this!"

"I'm half-dressed!"

"No, really, you've got to get out here. This is the kid that killed Dad!" Ronnie reached to pull open the refrigerator door. He brought out a great dark green bottle. "Am I glad I remembered to bring this. I bought it in New York. Do you know how long I've been saving this? Do you have any idea?"

Jonathan—stunned dumb by this reception—shook his head.

"This is real champagne, Jonathan, from France. I doubt if there's another bottle like it in all Truth or Consequences." Ronnie wiped the bottle with a dishtowel. "Do you like champagne, Jonathan?" He fished in the cupboards near the sink.

Jonathan shrugged.

"You don't even give me time to comb my hair," another young man appeared in the doorway and Jonathan was relieved to note he wore jeans, albeit without a shirt. "I'm Franklin," he smiled at Jonathan, extending his hand. "I know, I know it's a dreadful name. It's the kind of name you give a kid you don't like very much."

"I'm Jonathan," he murmured, clasping the warm fleshy hand.

"Jonathan? How perfectly droll."

"Puh-leeze don't start with that name thing," begged Ronnie, belting his kimono more firmly. "Franklin's a fiend for names." He knelt to peer into a cabinet under the sink. "Where in blazes are those glasses I bought?"

"What's your middle name?" demanded Franklin.

"Wayne."

"Jonathan Wayne," he enunciated carefully. "Jonathan Wayne, your car is ready, sir," Franklin intoned, bowing graciously.

"John Wayne, you ninny," cried Ronnie. "He's John Wayne!"

"Yes! Perfect!"

"Who's dere?" an old woman's voice—thin and accented in a German way to Jonathan's ear—called out from the recesses of the house.

Though Jonathan relaxed somewhat with the increasing awareness that the Hudanish boy bore him no ill will for his accidentally killing his father, the frail sound of the woman's voice shocked him like an electrical charge.

"It's Jonathan, Mom," Ronnie called out, "from next door."

"Haf you got company, den?"

"Come on out, Mom. Come and meet the kid that shot Dad."

A diminutive woman, with a great skein of yellowed gray hair spun about the top of her ovoid head like a smaller egg balanced atop a larger egg, shambled into the kitchen. "It izz a big sin to kill a juman being." She wagged a swollen finger at Jonathan. "Vee must be more careful vit life. All uf us."

"I - I - I'm terribly sorry, ma'am. I apologize for shooting Mr. Hudanish. Really I do. I am really, really sorry to everyone and I mean it."

"Ta-da!" crowed Ronnie, proudly bearing four crystal flutes from under the sink. "Franklin, you uncork while I rinse these out."

"Can you see my face, boy?" the old woman demanded, suddenly and desperately, thrusting her chin toward the kitchen light. Jonathan winced inwardly at the bald lumps of purplish scar tissue and the intricate amber detailing of old bruises and welts. "Do you know where my nose choost to be?" The topography of her bumpy face comprising of endless fissures, craters and broken tributary blood vessels drove Jonathan even further toward the door until he was uncomfortably aware of the knob molding into the base of his spine.

"Can you take some bubbly?" asked Ronnie, filling a glass with foam and putting it in Jonathan's thick hand. "We are about to toast you. So you don't even have to drink any, really. Just hold the glass up like this." And Ronnie struck a pose that reminded Jonathan of the Statue of Liberty.

"Ven you kilt my husband, ven you kilt Mr. Hudanish," the old woman tried to explain, taking Jonathan's hands into her own. "Ven you dit dat, I vas born again. A new baby!" Her lopsided smile—paralyzed on the right side and twitching timorously on the left—pricked Jonathan's conscience. He had only meant to control a rabid rodent. "An' after seven years—seven years I don't see him, I write letters, I call from the pay phone—after seven years, you have given me back my son!" Mrs. Hudanish cried, as she raised her glass to be filled.

* * *

"He only just died," Miguel murmured, grasping Jonathan under his armpits and dragging him toward his *cuartito* at the end of the yard. "That little prairie dog just died a few moments ago."

"Gopher," corrected Jonathan. "This is the modern world." Jonathan had the sensation that this—the modern world, the modern sky, the modern earth—had somehow in the course of the evening tipped wrongways. He had been flying with his back pinned to the grass as he looked down on the moon deep in a well of darkness when Miguel found him in the Hudanish backyard. Jonathan had to mind his steps to avoid squashing stars with his big feet. "It was a gopher," he insisted.

"No, he was a prairie dog. Gophers are different. They got different jaws and different ideas, too."

"So, he just died? Just like that?"

"Yes, just like that." Miguel grew weary of dragging the boy. "Are you going to walk now, or what?"

"I can walk. I can walk." Jonathan wrenched free from the *curandero*'s grasp and stumbled a few steps. "I was just thinking and I thought...I thought...what if everything was upside down like pineapple cake?"

"It's true."

"And the stars and the falling stars and the clouds and the moon are at my feet?"

"Yes," the old man nodded. "Everything you say is true, boy. All of it."

Mother-in-Law's Tongue

Aaron told Elaine that the man who had come to cut their grass had asked for some toilet paper to take out in the woods. Aaron wrinkled his nose, curling his upper lip. Elaine wondered why he was telling her about this, why he simply didn't let the man indoors to use their bathroom. After all they had two, and since Elaine had just finished her shower, neither one was being used.

"Why not let him in to use the bathroom?" she asked. Aaron hesitated, frowning. Elaine could see he wanted her to make the decision. In his fastidiousness, he abhorred the idea of letting a man who *would go* in the woods inside to use their bathroom. "Why shouldn't he use our bathroom?" demanded Elaine.

"He said something about eating bad chicken last night."

"I'll tell him to come in if you don't," threatened Elaine, but it was an empty threat. She was wearing only a smallish bath towel knotted at her breasts and another one turbaned over her wet hair.

"No, no, I'll go tell him." Aaron sighed, before slipping out of the bedroom, closing the door quietly behind him.

Elaine pulled two dresses from the closet and spread them on the bed. She was determined not to be the kind of funeral-goer who belabors dressing and grooming. Besides it would be inconsiderate to let her daughter Tina catch her trying out different outfits or overhear her grumbling about having to wear hose on a Saturday. She would just wear the dress or skirt that needed no ironing and that was long enough to evade the issue of nylons altogether. Early August in North Georgia was certainly warm enough for sandals and bare legs. Elaine finally selected the soot-colored cotton dress instead of the navy linen, which needed ironing. The cotton, though it looked slightly rumpled, would surely smooth out with body heat.

After a moment, she sensed more than heard the yard-man's heavy footfalls as he made his way to the front bathroom, a thin wall away from her closet. When she rehung the other dress, Elaine could hear his muffled grunting. She quickly shut the closet door. They had never hired a man to cut the grass before, and for some indefinable reason, the idea of paying a grown man to mow embarrassed Elaine. When he came to the door to ask for the job, she had hidden in the hall closet, listening to his slow baritone blending with Aaron's nasal drawl. After the mowing began, curiosity drove her to peek at him from a window which was so low that it neatly framed his chest, large belly and knees. He appeared to be pushing the mower with his great hanging stomach, his hands idly resting on the top handle. His flannel long-sleeved shirt and work gloves covered his skin from her view. Not that it mattered. She had stared for a moment, oddly relieved that she could see neither his face nor his shoes.

As she pulled on the cotton dress, she heard the toilet flush—a feeble half-flush. The front toilet could be tem-peramental. It required patience. The handle had to be held down for a few extra seconds for full flush. Now it would be necessary to wait for the tank to refill before a thorough flushing could be achieved. From the sound of the door yawning open, Elaine could tell the yard man wasn't one to wait.

When his heavy footsteps receded and the mower resumed sputtering, Elaine took a tissue from the box on her dresser, covered her nose with it and hurried to the bathroom. She pulled a book of matches from under the sink, lit several and dropped them—hissing—into the bowl, her eyes averted. Then she wrapped her fingers in toilet paper, flushed properly and shut the lid.

"Generations," she told Aaron, whom she met in the hallway as she was lighting and waving around several more matches. "Not just years, but solid generations of poor dietary habits."

"You were the one who wanted to let him in." Aaron shrugged. "He'd have been just as happy to go in the woods. That would have been my preference too."

Elaine knew well that Aaron disliked any kind of disturbance or intrusion in the house, so she changed the subject before he could elaborate on his preference. "When are you going to dress?"

"Now, I suppose. Should I wear a suit?"

"I wouldn't think so," said Elaine, remembering the junked cars and broken down appliances scattered in the yard of Terrell's mother's house and the slack-faced, toothless woman herself, rocking in a chair that was not a rocker, muttering about the fee the sheriff's deputies had charged for impounding her car, which Terrell had been driving the day he died. "Probably just some dress slacks and a nice shirt." She chose the soot dress for its plain, inexpensive appearance as much as for the fact that it needed no ironing and required no stockings. Elaine had a closetful of tasteful, costly dresses—most of them black for some reason, but she hadn't wanted to outdress the other mourners, to draw attention to herself in that way.

Elaine's daughter Tina emerged from her room in a diaphanous black sheath trailing over patent leather heels that were so high they caused her to lurch forward a bit like a blackbird on a precarious perch. She had swept her dark hair upwards in an intricacy of teasing, twisting and spraying that, along with her heavily made-up but red-rimmed swollen eyes, made her look much older than her twenty years, something of a superannuated prom date. And she had doused herself liberally with a scent that Elaine found particularly noxious. The sour-saccharine watermelon fragrance wafted after Tina like an invisible airborne veil that stung Elaine's eyes and made her nose run.

"Do you think I look okay?" Tina asked, quietly.

"You look nice, honey," said Elaine right before she sneezed.

"I don't want to look nice. I don't even want to go."

"I know." Elaine sneezed again. "I know you don't."

"I think I'll take my car. You'll probably want to come home before I do. I'll want to stay around afterwards, be with people."

"Will someone go with you? Those boys he lived with, maybe?" suggested Elaine. She was secretly relieved that she would not have to endure the forty-minute trip inhaling artificially sweetened watermelon fumes, but she didn't like to think of her daughter driving out into the country alone.

Tina shook her head. "I want to go alone. You remember how to get there?"

"It's that church just before you turn for his mother's house, isn't it?"

* * *

A week ago, Tina had gotten up from bed, asking if her boyfriend Terrell had called. When Elaine told her he hadn't, she leapt for the door and drove off, unwashed, before even brushing her hair. Half an hour later, the phone rang, and Tina was on the line, alternately sobbing and shouting incoherently.

"I can't understand you," Elaine had said. "Slow down. What's going on?"

"Terrell's ex-girlfriend was at his apartment," she finally managed to get out.

Oh, no, thought Elaine, here it comes. Terrell was a black man six years older than Tina, and from what Elaine could glean, he had something of a complicated life—unresolved relationships with former girlfriends, illegal aliens for roommates, a bit of a gambling problem, even a heart condition, and a five-year-old son that his grandmother looked after. Elaine was convinced it was only a matter of time before the tragedy named Terrell inexorably unfolded in her daughter's life. "Come home, honey," she had said to Tina on the phone that morning. "Just come on home."

"No, wait!" Tina had shouted. "Listen. She told me that Terrell's dead. That he died last night. Then she slammed the door in my face."

Tina had called from a pay phone, so Elaine told her to stay put. She would drive out, meet Tina. Together they would drive to the little town called Stephens Community, where Terrell's family lived, and find out what had happened.

All the way to Stephens, Elaine talked and talked, explaining to Tina that it might all be a mistake, a cruel joke on the part of the vengeful former girlfriend, or that Terrell might only be ill, not really dead. Tina sat, staring out the windshield, dully repeating from time to time. "I knew this would happen. It was just too good to be true. I knew I would end up losing him. It was too good to be true."

As they turned off the highway onto the country road leading to Terrell's mother's house, Elaine noticed a graveyard and a small gray church between two cow pastures. Then a monster car with huge airplane tires—something between a jeep and a tank—overtook them, nearly forcing their little car off the road.

"Honk, Mama, honk!" Tina became agitated, noticing the passing vehicle. "That's Terrell's cousin. Honk!" Tina reached over her mother and punched at the horn, producing a few feeble bleats. The larger car swung a broad U-turn. The way the gravel sputtered out from under the oversized tires made Elaine fear the driver had turned to exact vengeance. But the car's occupants soon recognized Tina, who had rolled down her window and was leaning half out of the car, when Elaine pulled to a stop alongside the other car—faced in the opposite direction.

Four men stepped out. Elaine could see that each of them was carrying a brown bottle of beer and was crying. Their unshaven cheeks were wet with tears. Elaine thought she could recognize from her daughter's description the three brothers who were Terrell's roommates—their flat Mayan faces pitted with blemish scars and their long straight black ponytails snaking all the way down their backs. The fourth, an African American, she took to be Terrell's cousin. He was the biggest of the four, and he had the same thick calves she had noticed on Terrell the time he pounded on the door in the middle of the night drunk and demanding to see Tina. Elaine had flicked on the carport light and noticed at once the extraordinary bulk in his lower legs—a family trait, she guessed, seeing the man she took to be his cousin.

"Terrell's dead," this man told Tina. "Some guy shot him, killed him dead."

Tina's wild hair flew from side to side as she shook her head, screaming, "No, No, No-o-o-o!" Her face reddened and her mouth burst open with a terrible shriek as she crumpled back into the car. Then she bellowed long hiccoughing howls that threatened to rend the small white car in two, shattering through to the cloudless deep blue Georgia sky. Elaine feared the earth, even the universe was not big enough to hold her daughter's grief.

She pulled Tina close, patting down her rough unbrushed hair, smelling her sour milky breath as it gasped out spasmodically. She cradled her daughter's head and shoulders and rocked her the way she had done when Tina was a baby, saying, "I'm sorry, I'm sorry, honey, I'm so sorry." Elaine could think of nothing—not one thing—that she could do or say to make this any better for Tina.

After a while, Elaine asked the men, standing helplessly around the car while her daughter wailed, "Who did this?" No one seemed to hear; no one answered.

Instead, they told her to follow them to the house.

And so she had, thinking along the way how she would

throw her arms around Terrell's mother when they met. She would hold her tight and try to pull some of the grief from this woman, whose son's death made her own inability to comfort her daughter seem insignificant. But when they got to the house—an oversized shanty, really, with the junk-strewn yard, cardboard wedged in paneless window frames, the ripped screen door—and Elaine stepped into the house to meet the woman, she did not even shake her hand.

For one thing, the woman sat on her own hands, rocking and rocking in a dinette chair, muttering, "Goddamn sheriff's deputies, goddamn them, charge me fifty dollars to get that car out. Fifty dollars! Who's got fifty dollars?"

The airless front room was filled with women, young and old. No one wept but Tina. And no one introduced anyone. Through the screen door, Elaine could hear the man she took to be Terrell's cousin cursing and threatening revenge. "Somebody's gonna die tonight. Some mother-fucker's gonna die for this."

The room itself was hideous. Mismatched, threadbare couches slumped along the fingerprint-smudged walls. Leaning in the corner was a vinyl wet bar, charred mysteriously on one side, that held an array of dingy porcelain figurines—poodles, angels, and ballerinas. Discolored sheets were strung as curtains in the doorway to the rest of the house and over the windows. Not wanting to stare about, Elaine fixed her eyes on the pocked and dust-furred linoleum at her feet, listening in dismay while Tina announced that she was pregnant. It was still early enough for Tina to change her mind about this, and Elaine had been hoping, hoping hard, that she would.

"And I'm going to have his baby," she said, sobbing. "I'm pregnant."

The younger women's eyes widened, but they made no comment.

"Fifty dollars a lot a money." grumbled Terrell's mother.

"They call me up and say, fifty dollars. Who told them to take that car? That's what I want to know."

A diminutive elderly woman fought her way through the doorway sheet. Tina rose to embrace her, but the old lady shook her off. "Terrell ain't here," she croaked, shaking a warning finger. "You ain't gonna see that boy anymore. He's gone. Terrell's gone. Ain't never coming back here."

"Fifty dollars is just too damn much money."

A black teenage girl turned to Elaine and explained, "She's upset about her car."

"Does she know about her son?" whispered Elaine.

"You mean my cousin Terrell. Oh, yeah. She knows all about that."

Then everyone was talking at once. The teenage girl told Elaine that she would graduate from high school next year and had plans to go to the technical training school in town to become an EMT. When Elaine asked what that was, the girl said, "emergency medical technician," and Elaine told her it sounded like interesting work. The girl nodded, smiling, and went on to tell about the classes she would take.

After an hour, Elaine and Tina rose to leave. No one said goodbye, but Terrell's grandmother again promised they wouldn't be seeing Terrell anymore.

On the way home, Elaine asked Tina if Terrell's mother had lost any other children.

"No, how come?"

"Just wondering. Does she have other sons then?"

"No, he was her only son. He was the oldest. Why do you ask?"

"It's just that she didn't seem that upset. The car thing seemed to bother her more. Did you find out what happened?"

"It's so stupid," Tina's voice broke, and she began crying anew. "It's the stupidest thing. This guy he went to school with, this Brian was going around for like weeks, saying how he was gonna kill somebody, how he had a gun and he was gonna blow somebody's—" her voice caught. "He just kept bragging about it and bragging about it. Then on Friday night, a bunch of these guys went out into the woods. They go out there all the time to drink and throw dice and stuff like that. Well, they ran out of beer, so Brian said he would take Terrell in his truck to get more. And everyone says they were getting along. They were laughing and kidding around when they left, but then they didn't come back. They didn't come back at all.

"This Brian took Terrell deeper in the woods and shot him, I guess. They said he shot him three times, then he dragged him—" Tina broke down again, weeping. "I keep seeing him dragging Terrell, dragging him to hide his body."

Hearing this, Elaine's tears splashed onto her sunglasses. She, too, could see the young men in the darkness, in the deep woods, laughing and talking. Then the flash of gunfire. She wondered if Terrell had known he would die? Had he been afraid? "How do they know all this?" she asked Tina instead.

"Brian confessed. He went home to his mother's house and told her he killed Terrell. He told her how it happened, and she was the one to call the police."

"So this Brian's in jail now?"

"Since last night."

"But that's so crazy. It doesn't make any sense."

"It's stupid. A stupid way to die," said Tina, as though she blamed Terrell as much as anyone.

* * *

Stephens Community was a good thirty miles from town, maybe more. Tina wanted to be early for the funeral to talk with Terrell's sisters who had called during the week and had been kind to her on the phone. She left soon after she applied a final slash of ruby lipstick to her lips. Tina's fancy dress, exaggerated makeup, and piled-up hair both saddened Elaine and made her feel tired.

"I'm ready," said Aaron, stepping into the front room. "Where's Tina?"

"She's gone to the funeral alone. She might want to stay longer."

"You know, this morning they called her from that chicken restaurant where she works. She ought to call them and start thinking about going back."

"But it's only been a week," protested Elaine.

"She can't sit around forever watching television. She needs to earn some money, so she can move out on her own. She can't have a baby here. That would be too much. Just too much."

Elaine sighed. "Terrell's not even buried. Can't you have a little patience?"

"I do. I do. I'm sorry. I'm just worried we're the ones who are going to end up raising that baby, and that's not going to do anyone any good," he said, softly.

"I know," said Elaine, thinking of the baby. The past week she found herself thinking more and more of the baby, her grandchild. At first, she'd agreed with Aaron; they couldn't have the baby, Tina's baby, in their house. "So disturbing," Aaron had said many times, shaking his head. Once he even rose from the dinner table—muttering about the inconvenience, the impossibility—while he absently closed every window in the front rooms, as though shutting out imaginary fetuses that threatened to flutter indoors like moths drawn to the light.

"I know a baby would be too much," Elaine prevaricated.

"You know, but does Tina know?"

"I don't know what Tina knows."

"You've got to tell her."

"This isn't the time, Aaron. For Godsake, we're barely up to the funeral."

"I suppose you're right," Aaron admitted. "Well, let's go

then. We ought to pick up some flowers. Do you really think I look okay? Maybe I ought to put on my navy blue suit."

A smallish, spare man, Aaron managed to look neat no matter what he wore. In a plaid short-sleeve shirt and dark brown pants, he looked as cool and orderly as an accountant on a day off.

"You look perfect," said Elaine. She wished she looked so tidy, so composed. In the front room mirror, she could see the soot-colored dress had not smoothed out. It even looked dusty where the dull nap was beginning to rise from the fabric. She'd had no time to put on make up, and her hair had not even begun to dry, giving her the appearance of someone more prepared to hang out washing than to go to the funeral of her grandchild's father.

At the flower shop, they initially had chosen a sheaf of red and white carnations to bring to the funeral. The florist had several funeral displays, but Elaine found them ostentatious, even tacky, with their large shiny sashes and sentimental sayings woven into the wiring: *At Rest With The Angels, Eternal Peace, Beloved Friend.* Aaron simply said they were too expensive. Then Elaine noticed a lovely sansevieria plant—so understated with its striated spiky leaves, so appropriate for the discreet young man her daughter had described to her. Terrell was so private that he made Tina leave his apartment and sit out in her car when he had to use the bathroom.

"Ah, Mother-in-Law's Tongue," said the florist, startling Elaine as he came up behind her, wiping his water-reddened hands on a towel. "That's the common name for it. Don't touch the tip," he warned, "it'll jab you."

"Really, honey," pleaded Aaron. "What do they want with a plant?"

But Elaine had to have the plant. The florist wrapped the pot in green cellophane and tied a dark blue ribbon around that. Elaine felt pleased at the elegant sight it created.

At the church, a thick disorderly line of people wound

its way from the cow-pasture fence, where latecomers were forced to park, to the whitewashed vestibule doors. Elaine was glad for her damp hair and stocking-less legs when she stepped out of the air-conditioned car into the stultifying heat. The baked red clay burned the soles of her feet through her thin sandals. A loosely strung cloud-cover cupped humidity over the churchyard, making it feel as though all of Stephens Community were trapped in a suffocatingly steamy plastic bag.

"Do me a favor, will you?" asked Aaron. "If I die in the summer, don't bury me at mid-day in Georgia."

Elaine took his hand and squeezed his long, cool fingers, guiltily. In the car, she had been thinking it would have been easier for her to bear Aaron's death than for her young daughter to lose her mate. She'd started out reflecting that her years and experience provided her with more resources to deal with loss, but then her thoughts had wandered to the changes she and Tina would make in the house if Aaron were gone.

"Oh, I won't," she said, truthfully. She had made up her mind already to cremate him.

Aaron and Elaine met Tina as their end of the line entered the church. Elaine could see at once that her daughter, in her tall hairdo and fancy gown, had dressed more appropriately for the funeral than she had. Men wore double-breasted navy and charcoal suits, while the women were dressed in jet beaded bodices and black chiffon skirts, form-fitting lamé and silver-spangled shifts with fringe. Elaine, flushed with self-consciousness, tried vainly to brush the lint from her skirt. She shot a look at Aaron, who, if he noticed he was underdressed, gave no indication. Instead his little egg-shaped head was tilted back and his glasses glinted with the light, in the attitude of an anthropologist surveying a scene with keen but detached interest.

"Where should we sit?" asked Elaine. The church was nearly filled but for a few seats on one side in front. Elaine didn't know whether or not, as mother and stepfather of the deceased's pregnant girlfriend, they merited those seats.

"Up there, I guess," whispered Tina, resolving the question. An usher appeared at her elbow and led them to the empty seats. Elaine traded shy smiles with the other people already seated in the row, while Tina stared straight at the closed gun-metal gray coffin covered with a spray of blue flowers arranged like a cross at the end of the middle aisle. Thank heavens it's closed, thought Elaine, casting discreet looks about the small church. She spotted Terrell's mother in a tight, shimmery black gown that gave her the look of a dissolute mermaid. She tried to catch her eye, give a sympathetic nod, but it didn't seem the woman recognized Elaine at all.

A pigtailed girl in black taffeta walked up and down the aisles, handing mourners paper fans affixed to wooden sticks the size of tongue depressors. The fans had the name of the funeral home printed on one side and a picture of an auburn-haired and green-eyed Jesus kneeling at a rock in a sheep pasture on the other. Jesus wore a confused expression on his gently-featured face, as if he couldn't figure exactly why he had to kneel before a rock among all these sheep.

Another young girl handed out a folded piece of white paper which, when Elaine unfolded it, turned out to be the program, listing the various speakers and hymns scheduled for the service. Elaine, never a churchgoer in her adult life, was astonished that it had come to this—churches preparing agendas for services. Opposite the agenda was a picture of Terrell, leaning and stroking a pale Labrador retriever. Poor Terrell, smiling so kindly at the dog in the photo and now sealed in the coffin up front. Elaine noticed he had died a month before his birthday, which was also her birthday. She was curious why Tina had never mentioned this. He would have been 26. She wondered what had become of the dog.

The service began with the raspy-voiced minister delivering a rambling and convoluted eulogy which heaped praise and admiration on the departed, while decrying the violent circumstances of his death. Elaine had learned over the past week—during the course of Tina's obsessive remin-iscences—that Terrell had made his living selling crack cocaine, and she couldn't help wondering just how well the preacher had really known the young man. When the minister ended with a prayer, the choir—a gaggle of elderly women in the loft—sang a painfully off-tune hymn. Elaine glanced at Aaron, who loved all types of music. He raised his eyebrows, as though privy to yet another anthropological revelation.

Throughout the service various people succumbed to loud, inconsolable weeping, sometimes shouting in their grief. "He's gone! Terrell! God forgive him!" Terrell's mother screamed the loudest and had to be carried out at one point. His cousin, with the oversized calves, had stood shouting his grief before collapsing into a faint. He also had to be taken out. Elaine, a lapsed Catholic, was alarmed by this carrying-on. She could not remember more than numbness during the services for her youngest son, but recalled that at her own deeply beloved mother's funeral, she had allowed tears only to well in her eyes, not to trickle down her cheeks and streak her mascara.

To Elaine's dismay, two middle-aged women began lifting the floral arrangements from about the coffin, an-nouncing in turn who had provided what piece and reading the florist cards aloud. Elaine was grateful they had neglected to write out a small card. She felt chagrin that the plant, which had looked so handsome and dignified at the shop, was clearly the paltriest floral gift in sight. The two ladies hefted great daisy crosses and rose-covered hearts, enormous plants in pots—she shot another look at Aaron—and sashed wreaths. "With sympathy and love, the Evans Family," one or the other read. "We will miss you always, Myrtle and Lloyd Davis." And on and on. Finally, one woman reached for the little plant. "No card!" she cried. "Who gave this?" Elaine looked about the church with an arched eyebrow, as if searching out the ungenerous soul. She almost carried it off, but when the woman asked again, Aaron slowly raised his hand. "What was your message for the family?"

Aaron shrugged, but Elaine cleared her throat to say, "That we're very sorry. He was..." she cast about for the right words. What could she say about the boy her daughter had loved? About the young man she had planned to have over for dinner once Aaron had the air-conditioner fixed? That he seemed shy, but polite? That she was sorry she had spoken to him harshly once, telling him never to come to her house drunk again? ("This is not Aaron's house, this is not Tina's house, this is my house, and you do not do this here," she had said. And he had called her "ma'am" and he swore he would never do it again.) That he had kept his word? "He was a very nice person." Her voice inflected involuntarily, making this sound like more of a possibility than a certainty.

The woman holding aloft the pot gave a disgusted look and set it aside, lifting a tremendous display of bronze mums in its place. After all the flowers were admired, another hymn started up, and the ushers rose to lift the coffin's lid. Oh, no, thought Elaine, clutching Tina's elbow. As the lid was raised, Tina buried her face in the hollow of her mother's collar bone and shuddered, weeping. Ushers directed the rows of mourners up to the front to view the body in turn. Starting on one side of the church they proceeded directing people in a horseshoe configuration, so that Elaine realized their row would be last. Terrell's mother, revived and returned to her seat, was among the first to view her son. She wobbled on tiny heels before wailing once more and falling backwards into the arms of the ushers, who again dragged her outside. Next Terrell's grandmother, in black jersey, clutched her handbag to her chest and perched on tiptoes to peer into the coffin. Elaine heard her croaking, "I ain't gonna see you no more, Terrell. You won't be coming around no more." Elaine saw a woman lift a small boy in a suit up to the coffin. "Say good-bye to your daddy," the woman said. "Come on, now, you gotta say good-bye." The boy stared silently a moment before screwing up his small face and screaming in terror. More and more people filed past. Elaine recognized no one else, until the weeping Mayans made their way to the front. Tina clung to her mother, darkening the front of her dress with her tears.

"We don't have to go up front," Elaine told her.

But Tina drew herself away and stood. They filed out with the others in their row and followed them to the center front. Aaron and Elaine preceded Tina. Aaron gave a cursory glance into the satin-lined box, but Elaine stood and gaped. This was not Terrell! Not at all. This was a papier-maché replica, a horrible fake. The skin was lumpy, badly patched. It looked worse than wax. It reminded her of topographical maps she had made in elementary school with flour and salt and covered over with cracking tempera paints. And that expression! She was sure he never looked this smarmy, like the cat who swallowed the canary, like he knew a secret he wouldn't share. Terrell would have been mortified to see himself looking like this. Elaine had heard that the Georgia Bureau of Investigation kept the body an entire week. But how could these morticians do such a thing? Of the dozen funerals she had attended, this was the worst job of embalming she had ever seen.

She tried to catch Tina about the waist and steer her away from the sight, but Tina sidestepped her. She put both hands on the coffin's sides and leaned in to whisper at the crudely prepared corpse. Elaine could barely hear her daughter's words. "You ass," Tina hissed. "You stupid, stupid ass." Then she reached in and lightly fingered the white carnation in the lapel of his suit. "What's going to happen to me?" she asked softly, before turning to Elaine. "I shouldn't have loved him, Momma. In the end, he was just another fool, wasn't he?"

Elaine shrugged without saying a word. She was only beginning to understand her gratitude to this young man she barely knew, this young man who had leapt in and out of her daughter's life—seizing the future from them all—this fellow to whom Elaine had no connection, but was now inexorably linked by the warm knot of tissue in her daughter's womb. She would never say that she was glad he had died, glad he was gone, taking his dangerous ways from her girl, that she was thankful he had left her a place in her daughter's life, left her a grandchild in his wake. She would listen to Tina rant, but she would never blend her voice in complaint. Elaine glanced a last time into the satin-lined casket, peering at Terrell's eyelids—chalky and crumpled like crêpe paper.

Turning, Elaine gently led her daughter out of the church. She circled Tina's shoulders with one arm, feeling only slightly absurd, as though she were leading a wounded comrade from battle. Stepping across the threshold into a blaze of sunlight, Elaine reached to hook Aaron's elbow with her free arm. But he had fallen too far back, lingering in the cool shadowy church, pinching the skin between his eyebrows with one hand and slowly shaking his head. No doubt he also had his hard words for Terrell, the disturbances he had caused. Again Elaine would listen, never speaking sharply against the father of her grandchild. She had given Terrell her word.

Walking Circles

Clearly the woman did not want to walk. She lumbered several paces behind Elaine and her hugely pregnant daughter Tina as they trod the thin carpet winding through the Labor and Delivery wing of the hospital. Mother and daughter marched the corridors with brisk purpose, arm in arm, up and down, back and forth, like comrades, like guards conducting an odd but relentless watch on these peaceful, somnolent premises. But the other woman lagged. The slack flap of her slippers—graying with lint—grew fainter and fainter with each corner they turned. Impelled by a herding instinct she would be hard pressed to explain, Elaine cast frequent glances over her shoulder to mark the distance between them and the woman. When the woman vanished from sight just before the neonatal nursery, Elaine caught her daughter's elbow more firmly.

"We ought to stop," she said, slowing her pace.

"Why?" asked Tina. Elaine's daughter was slightly winded. Her smooth pink cheeks billowed and contracted as she caught her breath, and her dark eyes glimmered from the exertion. She used the break in stride to rewind her mass of dark curls in a knot at the base of her skull. "Walking makes me feel better. I don't want to stop."

"But we've lost Laura."

"Linda, her name's Linda."

"Linda? Are you sure? I thought she said 'Laura.'"

"It's her teeth, Momma. Half the time you can't tell what she's saying."

"Linda, then. We've lost her." She craned her neck to search around the corner they had just turned. Elaine felt ashamed that though she had been to the woman's house after her son, Tina's boyfriend, had been shot, though she had been to the funeral, and even now as they waited together at the hospital for Tina to bear their first grandchild, she hadn't really known the other grandmother's name. "She was keeping up, but I don't see her now."

"Good," said Tina. She swiped a damp lock of hair from her brow. "She's too slow. She's holding us back. And did you see those slippers. God, it's embarrassing. I'm glad she's fallen behind. I don't care if she is Terrell's mother. I don't want people to think she's with us."

"What people? There's no one here but us," Elaine pointed out. At two a.m. the hospital's halls were completely empty. The few nurses at the front desk seemed preoccupied with their work and barely glanced at the marching women, let alone their footwear. Even the newborns, bound in pink or blue receiving blankets and nested in their clear plastic bassinets, slept with their puffy little eyes squeezed tight.

"Still," Tina pouted, "I don't know why she has to walk with us. I didn't ask her, did you? I don't even want her here."

"Shush, she'll hear you."

"I thought you said we lost her."

"She could be coming, though."

"She won't; she's probably sitting her big butt down in one of those rockers by the front desk. I don't know why she just doesn't go home."

"She wants to be here, honey. This is important to her," Elaine tried to explain. "And she's probably tired—"

"From what?" demanded Tina. "Gambling? That's all she does all day. She doesn't have a job. She just goes to that electronic gambling place on Lexington every day, the whole day long. We *worked* all day. The only thing she did was sit on a stool, smoking and putting quarters in a slot."

"Well, that could be tiring, too." Elaine was astonished to learn there was an electronic gambling place in town. Illegal, no doubt. Nevertheless, Elaine wondered whether what she did all day long—reading poetry and fiction manu-scripts for a literary journal—could be called work. So often it seemed like eavesdropping on other people's daydreams. It would be much more stressful to risk coins at computerized black jack or five-card draw.

"And did you see what she was wearing?"

"Those slippers?"

"Not just the slippers, but the shirt and that cap. They were Terrell's. She always wears his clothes."

"But that's sad!" She had noticed the bold logo shirt and skater pants stretched taut on the large woman's frame and wondered why a woman her own age would dress this way. Now she understood. Elaine knew what it was to lose a child, and though it would not occur to her to don her dead son's clothing—Sanders, her youngest, had been only four when he died—this habit seemed as pathetic as her keeping her son's pillowcase unwashed all these years to inhale from time to time the salty traces of his scent, to gently finger the few fine black hairs trapped in the weave, to call memories back to her. "She must miss him terribly."

"No, Mom, she doesn't wear that stuff for his memory or out of grief or anything like that. She wears them because they're expensive, brand names, you know. She never wears anything of his that doesn't have a label on it."

"Oh," said Elaine, frowning. "Still, I better go back to look for her."

"I want to keep walking. The contractions don't hurt as much while I'm walking. I can't see why I should have to stop and be in pain just because she's worn out from gam-bling."

"I'll catch up with you the next time you come around," Elaine promised.

Elaine doubled back, adopting a slower pace as she did not have to keep up with Tina and rummaging her thoughts for some idea of what to say to the woman, to Linda, when she did find her. Elaine read the bright wall posters advocating breast feeding and infant inoculation, the directions for sounding the fire alarm, and the nameplates on doors to private rooms. Some families decorated their doors with pink or blue balloons, cardboard storks, and large floppy ribbons. Elaine had not thought to bring such adornment, though this was exactly the kind of thing Tina would want, even expect. She hoped there would be time the next day to find ribbon and a colorful stork somewhere. Perhaps the gift shop sold such decorations.

Elaine enjoyed reading the names that couples and single mothers had given their infants. Mr. and Mrs. Kwan Park called their new son Christopher Brendan. Another couple named their baby girl Xylophonia Shadderica Wright. Both blue and pink balloons were affixed to one door. Hermaphrodite? she wondered. But, reading the nameplate, she found twins had been born to these parents—Amrita and Vinai Deepali. The last door she read gave her pause. Only the mother's name was given—no father, no baby. "Gretchen Ellsner" by itself had been penciled into the cream-colored card.

When Elaine taught middle school, she had known an eighth-grader named Gretchen Ellsner. She had not been one of Elaine's students. Elaine taught the "regular classes," which consisted mainly of black and Latino students. No, this Gretchen Ellsner had been a white girl, so she would have been with the "gifted" group, composed of middle-class children of varying learning abilities, but all with one thing in common: pushy parents. To Elaine's thinking, all this was just another way around desegregation in the New South.

Though not legitimately gifted, the Gretchen Ellsner she remembered had been self-motivated. Elaine recalled the poems, stories, and drawings the girl had submitted to the literary magazine that Elaine, as faculty sponsor, had moderated. The work was not exceptional, but Elaine recalled the sense she had gotten of knowing the girl, knowing this Gretchen Ellsner and her comfortable world of friends and shopping at the mall and violin lessons and even a pet pot-belly pig named Hamlet.

This had been about the time Elaine was having so much trouble with Tina—the running away, the high school truancy, the thirty-year-old boyfriend with blue-green tattoos crawling obscenely from his elbows to his wrists. Tina had even managed to get herself arrested for biting a red-haired policeman, a rookie who'd had the temerity to ask her what she was doing in a phone booth downtown at three in the morning.

During that time, Elaine would look at girls like Gretchen longingly. At graduation, the Ellsner girl had trotted to the front of the stage several times for awards in music, Spanish, citizenship, band, and physical fitness. And after the ceremony, Elaine spied Gretchen flinging her thin arms around her mother and father, her wheat-colored hair flying like a veil as she drew them into the circle of her thin arms with quiet, natural grace.

* * *

Elaine picked up her pace. If she did not hurry now, Tina would catch up with her in a short while as she rounded this part of the floor. True to Tina's prediction, Elaine found the other woman, Linda, rocking in one of the rockers and fanning herself with a pamphlet on preventing sudden infant death syndrome. Elaine thought she might finally have the chance to tell the woman how sorry she was that her son had been killed, that she knew what a terrible, terrible thing it was to lose a son. But any words she could think of to frame her commiseration seemed weak, false, a gross understatement deserving of this strange woman's harshest scorn.

As Elaine drew closer, she caught strong whiffs of cigarette smoke, heavily applied scent, and something else, what was it? Yes, alcohol. She could smell hard liquor every time the woman swished the fan in front of her face. Elaine noticed the nurses at the station, just across the hall from the rockers, moving stiffly now and peering over their files from time to time at the large woman rocking and fanning herself.

"There you are," said Elaine, not sure what else to say.

"Tired," the woman replied, but it sounded like "toad," the way she pronounced it. After considering a few moments, Elaine decided it had to be "tired."

"Yes, it's tiring," she agreed, though she had no idea what the "it" she mentioned was, but as she uttered them, her words seemed true. Everything was tiring—raising children, cooking dinners, washing load after load of laundry. Now that Sanders had been gone all these years and Teddy, her middle son, had moved to the west coast, and Tina was usually at work, the house was often empty but for her and her husband Aaron, and that somehow was tiring too.

Most tiring of all was this waiting for her grandchild to be born. She and Tina had been walking since after midnight, walking and walking and practicing the breathing while Elaine dutifully jotted down times between contractions. Just thinking about it all made her eyes sting with self-pity because who would be the one to help Tina take care of the new baby when it arrived, to get up in the night, to hold it when it cried, to love it with all of her power to love, and then, and then perhaps she would lose that baby like she had lost Sanders, and Teddy too, like she was always losing Tina.

* * *

She wanted to sink into one of the rockers alongside Linda and rock some of this overwhelming tiredness away. But a glance at the nurses' station kept Elaine on her feet. What if these rockers were meant only for the new mothers? The nurses were already behaving as though they were affronted, and Elaine didn't like to break the hospital's rules.

"It is tiring," repeated Elaine. Why didn't the woman speak? Why did she let these awkward silences grow between them? It was so quiet Elaine could hear another nurse walk toward the desk, her pantyhose rasping together at the knees, and the dull squeak of her rubber-soled shoes.

"The Ellsner baby turn yet?" she heard the approaching nurse whisper.

"Still breech," another nurse whispered back.

Elaine tried to smile. Linda gave her a startled look and Elaine wondered if she had grimaced instead of grinning. Elaine could hear her own stomach rumble. "You know, we have a word for what we are."

"Huh?" The woman's shiny dark brow rippled; her eyes crinkled in puzzlement. Nice eyes, Elaine noticed. Very little, white-rimmed, deep, almost velvety black eyes, and what little showed was bluish white like skimmed milk—in spite of the cigarettes, the liquor. Perhaps the woman's features, her cheekbones and nose, were really quite fine under all that heaviness. Try as she might, Elaine could not conjure up Terrell, and the snapshots she'd seen only made his image more enigmatic to her. It might not be so bad if the baby looked like this woman.

"My parents spoke Spanish. There's a word in Spanish for what we are. I don't think there's one in English, but in Spanish it's *comadres*. We're *comadres*." In truth, Elaine, a sixth-generation Mexican American, never really understood how *comadrazgo* worked, but she wanted to make some connection, establish a bond between herself and the strange dark woman in the rocker.

"Huh?"

"There's two kinds of *comadres*. There's the godparent kind, but there's another kind, the kind we are—both mothers of the parents of our grandchild; we are *comadres*. We have a special relationship through responsibilities toward our grandchild. You know what I mean?"

"One thing I can't understand," mumbled the woman, rocking and fanning.

"What's that?"

"What all you just said."

* * *

"No baby tonight," said Toni, the Nigerian midwife. The woman's slightly accented speech was so soothing that Elaine wanted to just close her eyes and let it wash over her like warm bath water. "See here." Toni pulled a trail of graph paper from the fetal monitor at the side of the bed in Tina's room. "See how the blue line is flat. The contractions have stopped."

"Did the walking make them stop?" Tina wanted to know.

"No, not at all. If it was true labor, the real thing, the walking would accelerate the contractions. But this is not true labor. You must go home tonight. Get your rest. It will not be long, but it will not be tonight."

"But I wanted to have the baby tonight," protested Tina, her voice rising. Elaine tensed. Her daughter was not one to cry easily in public, but she was not shy about raging anywhere, anytime.

"We can go get some breakfast," Elaine offered hastily. "I bet we can find some place open, even this early. How'd you like an omelet with cheese and some potatoes."

"But I've got my bag here. I'm ready to stay and have the baby. I don't want to wait any more!" Tina's eyes flashed. "I've been waiting and waiting. It's too much!"

Elaine remembered the time Tina had overturned the dining room table with dinner served on it. She had risen from her seat and heaved the table over on its side, crashing china and glassware, and spattering food and iced tea onto the carpet and wainscotting. How many times, bellowed Tina, how many times did she have to tell people she didn't like tuna casserole?

The midwife grabbed Tina's forearm, looked into her eyes, and said firmly, "Listen to me. You are not having the baby tonight. You go home, and you rest. You understand me?"

Tina nodded, silently, and Toni gathered up the chart, ripped the graph paper from the machine and took off her gloves. Elaine stepped around the curtain to give Tina time to dress.

Outside of the curtained-off section of the room, Linda had found another chair near the door. She sat in that, swaying from side to side with her arms folded over her massive breasts.

"They're sending Tina home," Elaine told her.

"Huh?"

"You may as well go home. They're sending us home. She's not going to have the baby tonight."

"For reals?"

"Of course," Elaine said more sharply than she liked. What reason would she have to lie to the woman, to send her away if the baby was about to be born?

Terrell's mother sighed heavily and hefted herself out of the chair. Her slippers scuffed the linoleum as she slowly lumbered out of the room. No goodbyes, no pleasant wishes for the next day. The woman just walked away.

Elaine stared after her, baffled. It was hard for her to understand when people displayed antipathy or even indifference toward her. She decided this woman, this Linda, must have a mental illness, an emotional deficit of some kind that immunized her against friendliness.

* * *

"Why, of course, she's mental," Tina confirmed as they ate breakfast at a pancake house just before dawn. "Don't you notice the way she talks?"

"But I thought that was her teeth, her lack of teeth, I mean."

"There's that, but if you really listen, you notice that what she says has nothing to do with anything a lot of the time. It's just not connected."

221

"But that's sad," sighed Elaine.

"Everything is sad to you," said Tina. She speared a sausage with her fork and wagged it at Elaine. "I think you just like feeling sorry for people."

"What do you mean?"

Tina shrugged. "You just seem to like giving sympathy."

"I don't like giving sympathy. But I am sorry for her. She just lost her son."

"She acts like it's no big deal. I'm the one who really misses Terrell. I'm the only one who really knew him. She didn't know a thing about him. He didn't even like her. He was always complaining about how she kept bugging him for money."

"Still he was her son," pointed out Elaine. "She must miss him horribly. I remember how it felt when—"

"Don't, Mom, please don't start."

"I'm just saying... Well, forget it." Elaine found a water-spot on her knife and wiped it away with a napkin. "Did they ever charge that boy who shot him?"

Tina shook her head. "He's out now."

"Out? For murder?"

"Out on bail. They haven't had the trial yet."

"He got bail?" Hearing this, Elaine felt depressingly naive.

"Now they're saying it was self-defense. He didn't just murder him in the woods like everyone thought. Now they're saying Terrell and him were fighting."

"Fighting? Over what?"

"Another girl. Oh, Mom, I don't want to talk about all this." Tina pushed her plate away. Her face crumpled, and the color drained from her cheeks.

"Who told you all this?"

"She did. Linda called me a few days ago. She told me the whole thing."

* * *

In the morning, Tina decided she would go to work. But after a few calls to the clothing shop from the phone in the front room, where Elaine could hear her daughter's voice alternately pleading and threatening, Tina raced to her room and slammed the door. Aaron raised his fine eyebrows over the morning newspaper, and Elaine trailed Tina to her room. She knocked hesitantly at the door.

"What is it? What's wrong? Are you going to work? What happened? Did someone say something to upset you?"

"LEAVE ME ALONE!" Tina roared. And Elaine jumped, retreating a few steps, but she could still hear Tina's muffled, "Why can't everyone leave me alone?"

"Do you need anything?" Elaine tried again.

But Tina didn't answer. Instead she stormed out, buttoning her uniform blouse—an extra-extra large, specially ordered to cover her growing abdomen. Then she stuffed her mass of black hair under the company baseball cap and stomped out of the house. Revving her car and screeching in reverse out of the drive, Tina didn't seem to notice her mother watching her from the window or return her wave. "Oh, dear," said Elaine.

Aaron turned a page in the paper, refolded it, and grunted.

"You stop it," snapped Elaine, glaring at her husband's calm face—his well-groomed beard, his neat blond curls and his glasses as they twinkled in the morning sun streaming through the window.

"What? What am I doing?" He lowered the paper.

"You know what you're doing, sitting there 'hmmphing' like you knew this would happen, like you knew it all along."

"I didn't do anything. I didn't even say anything."

"That's right. You can't be bothered. All you have to do is act like you're never surprised, like you couldn't care less and I'm the stupid one, I'm the fool—" Elaine interrupted herself fearing her voice would break.

Aaron gazed at her with mild concern, the same expression he wore when the sink backed up or wasps nested in the barbecue. These things act up, his face told her. I am sorry that it happens, but it does. "What do you want me to do?" he asked quietly. "What do you want me to do? She's pregnant, she's hormonal—"

"And she's my daughter, my problem."

"I didn't say that. Tell me what you want me to do and I'll do it."

"I just want to know what's going on. Somebody said something to her. I know it. Someone at that shop must have upset her."

"Ah, the cult," said Aaron. Many times, they discussed the strange involvement of Tina's co-workers in her life, in her personal business. Aaron compared their influence and meddling to that of a cult, but Elaine called them "the coven." A trio of women—witches all—boiling up innuendo, imagined slights, and petty accusations in the great cauldron of gossip they swirled between marking prices and ringing up sales on the computerized cash register.

"Maybe I should call over there? Make sure she got there okay. Did you see how she tore out of here? I'm worried she'll get in a wreck. Maybe I'll just call over there." Elaine headed for the phone.

"I wouldn't," Aaron called after her. "She'll think you're interfering."

Despite this, Elaine picked up the phone and dialed the shop. After a few rings, Maya, the most noxious of the trio, answered, audibly snapping a wad of gum. After shouting the store greeting and listening briefly to a request to speak to Tina, Maya brusquely put Elaine on hold. The inane recording advertising the store's hours and special values blared in Elaine's ear for several moments until Maya came back on the line. Elaine pictured the trio of women sequestering her daughter in the back storage room—the two older blondes and young Maya, an African American girl—and brainwashing Tina against her mother. She could almost hear the three of them cackling about Elaine waiting on hold.

"She doesn't want to talk to you?" blurted Maya when she finally returned.

"What? Why not?"

"She says she doesn't want to talk to you and to tell you she doesn't want to have you at the birth," said Maya in her loud flippant voice.

"What? But I'm the coach. We took the classes together. I know the breathing, the exercises—"

"Both Desireé and Sandy had babies," Maya informed Elaine, popping her gum vigorously. "They'll help her with that stuff. Tina doesn't want you there."

"I see," said Elaine after a pause. "Well, tell her to give me a call when she's ready to talk, will you?" Numbly she replaced the phone in its cradle.

"What did she say?" called Aaron from the kitchen. He stood to stack the newspaper neatly and clear away his coffee cup.

"I didn't talk to Tina. Maya told me I can't come to the birth. She said Tina doesn't want me there." Elaine still couldn't believe it. "Maybe I should drive out there and see what's going on. Maybe they've tricked her in some way. Think I should go out there?"

"I think that would be a waste of time." Aaron stood in the doorway, rummaging in his pants pocket. "I think it would be just what they want, having another person jump at their will. And I think when the time comes Tina is going to call you regardless of what the cult says."

"What if she doesn't? What if—"

"Look at this." Aaron waved a slip of newsprint he'd pulled out. "Tomato plants. Buy two get one free."

"What about Tina? What should we do?"

"We should go to this nursery. Let's pick out some tomato

plants, some green peppers and marigold seeds. It's a beautiful day. Let's plant the garden. Tina will call when she needs something. She always does."

At once, Elaine saw the futility of driving to the shop where her daughter worked. She foresaw the coven's glee at provoking this desperate act and her daughter's stony refusal in the face of apologies and pleas. Aaron was right; Tina would call when she needed her. Elaine hated to think that this call might not come until after the baby was born, that she might miss her grandchild's birth, something she had anticipated for so long—and something she had dreaded—ushering her child through hours of agony with only feeble exhortations to breathe correctly to offer in solace. It was an exceptionally fine day—sunlight flooded the backyard and from the kitchen window she could see a pair of cardinals teasing, tagging one another—animate red slashes, silk scarves fluttering against the deep green field of lawn that was so perfect it seemed painted.

"Damn it. I better get the hose," murmured Aaron as he noticed the cavorting birds. "Those two will rip each other to shreds."

"You're kidding. They're just playing together."

"They'll kill each other, honey. Those are very territorial birds," said Aaron, heading for the back door. But before he could reach the garden hose, Elaine watched the faster of the two birds swoop and tear the other's breast open. The wounded bird dropped, twitching and spurting blood on the grass until Aaron mercifully smashed its head with a brick.

* * *

After the last tomato plant had been tamped into the soft earth, Elaine heard the muffled ringing of the phone inside the house. She threw her spade, tore off her gloves and ran, nearly trampling the cat in her haste to answer it.

"Momma, I'm at the hospital. Hurry up and get here!" Tina cried. "The baby's coming!"

Elaine brushed the soil from her jeans and lunged for her purse. "The baby!" she shouted at Aaron, as she bustled out the door. "She's going to have the baby."

They had decided long ago that Aaron would not attend the birth. Tina had not asked her stepfather to be present, and Aaron, although interested in many things, was not anxious to see "placentas and whatnot" slithering out of anyone's body. He would wait at the house for Elaine to call before he drove to the hospital to see the new baby. "Be careful," he warned as Elaine backed out of the drive.

* * *

Of course, the entire coven—Desireé, Sandy and Maya—crowded the small Labor and Delivery Room, along with Terrell's mother and her three teenage daughters—all lean, tall, very dark, and giggling as they shared a pizza from a large white box. Tina, sitting upright in a hospital bed at the center of the room, seemed distant, unfazed by the large number of spectators. The midwife had to jostle elbows and part shoulders—as Elaine had—to approach the bed.

"There are too many people in this room," said Toni. "Some of you must leave. I have to examine the patient. There are simply too many people here."

At this, Tina seemed to focus, and she grabbed her mother's hand with a fearsome grip. "Make them leave, Momma. I don't want them here. They're making me sick."

"Who?" asked Elaine cautiously.

"Make them all leave for the examination, but you stay, please, Momma. You stay with me."

Elaine wondered how she would get this group's attention. Except for Linda, they were all chatting and laughing among themselves; they had not seemed to notice or care about the midwife's announcement. Elaine considered clapping or standing on a chair to let out a whistle, but she rejected those notions as silly and instead circled the small room, murmuring, "Let's leave for the exam, shall we? Let's step out for a moment. C'mon, let's go." Soon she was leading the group through the door, but she managed to fall behind while herding them out, remaining inside and shutting the door after the last one.

As soon as she sighed and turned to her daughter, Elaine noticed she had missed one of the visitors—Terrell's mother Linda, who stood like a monument, her arms folded over her chest again, at the foot of Tina's bed.

"Momma," hissed Tina, trying to whisper.

Elaine quickly rounded the bed to her daughter's side.

"Momma, get rid of her," she managed to truly whisper. Toni powdered and snapped on surgical gloves. "That smell —the cigarette smoke—it's making me sick. And she just keeps staring, she doesn't talk, she doesn't smile."

Elaine feared Linda might have heard Tina, and she stole a guilty glance at her, but the woman stood as immobile and inscrutable as ever. It was as though she had been installed like a heavy piece of hospital equipment.

"Um," began Elaine, unsure how to throw the other grandmother out of the room politely, "ah, Tina would like you to wait outside while she's examined. I'm sure you can come back in after the examination."

"No, she can't," piped Tina from her bed.

"Or you can wait in the outer waiting room. I noticed they have a TV. We'll call you if anything happens," Elaine promised.

The woman turned her deep black eyes on Elaine, staring long and hard. Elaine gulped, wondering if she should try guiding the woman by the elbow. But after a few seconds, Linda drew her eyes away and slowly strode out of the room, her gray slippers slapping with sullen dignity.

"Now lie back," the midwife told Tina. "Put your feet in

the stirrups. This might bring on a contraction. Just be prepared."

"Don't let her back in, Momma. I can't take it, the staring, the not talking. She's creepy. Eeyoww-ww!"

"Remember your breathing. Don't lose control now," warned Toni.

"Let it out," Elaine instructed, "let your breath out slowly, like you're cooling tea."

* * *

After the examination, Tina asked her mother to readmit Desireé, Sandy and Maya to the Labor and Delivery Room, but she again begged Elaine to make Terrell's mother go away, said she couldn't have the baby with that woman silently staring, just staring at her. She claimed it made her labor pains worse. As Elaine trudged out to the main waiting room, she wondered how to keep the other grandmother from the delivery room tactfully. Elaine no sooner stepped into the waiting room than Maya jumped up from one of the green vinyl chairs before the television and rushed to her side as though accosting her.

"You got to do something about that mother of Terrell's— her and her daughters." Maya had a breathless, excitable voice. "They are really getting on Desireé's nerves. She told them they had no business being here. Desireé said they didn't give Tina the time of day, never once so much as brought over a plate of food the whole time she was pregnant, and now they're crowding up the delivery room. Desireé goes, 'you all better leave on accounta there's not room enough for you.' And the woman goes, 'I got more right to be here than you,' she goes, 'I'm kin.'"

"Well, she is," put in Elaine.

"She never so much as brought over a plate of food during the whole pregnancy," Maya repeated, shaking her head. Her brown eyes bulged with indignation in her pretty brown face. "What kind of kin is that? We gave the shower; we had a cake for Tina and gave her all those baby accessories."

Desireé and Sandy sidled up to join in the whispered conference. Though they were not related and, in fact, behaved as though they were insulted when asked if they were, they looked like sisters. Both were blondes with lank hair and fair, almost transparent-looking skin that threatened to crack, fissure, and fade early, and both had the same glassy blue eyes, a color that Elaine had only seen in the faces of plastic dolls. Desireé, the shop's owner, already revealed a nest of wrinkles around each blue eye when she smiled as she did at that moment, handing Elaine a yellow gift bag decorated with pastel bunnies and chicks.

"Got you a little something," she drawled, coyly. Tina had once told Elaine that Desireé had wanted to be a country western singer at one time, but wound up an alcoholic instead. She only sobered up a few years ago, when she met her current husband, a wealthy man who bought the clothing shop for her.

"What is this?" asked Elaine, suspiciously.

"It's not much. Just a little something for Granny. Go on, open it up."

"Thank you. I'll open it later. I'm afraid I didn't bring you anything."

"Aw, you don't have to bring me nothing, honey. That's plain silly!"

Elaine decided to take this moment of truce to ask why her daughter had not wanted her at her grandchild's birth.

"Why, let me tell you something," began Desireé by way of explanation. "They's once this woman we had working with us, always talked trash on her husband—how he treated her, what all he said to her. And then one day her husband got awful sick, and she starts crying and carrying on. We all just had to laugh at her. You see what I mean?"

"Tina kept going on about how you tried to get her to

have an abortion," charged Sandy, the younger blonde. She looked to be several months pregnant herself, and she seemed very weary—drawn and gaunt in the face. "You were even gonna pay for it, huh?"

"You was gonna destroy her last link to her love who had died so young and so tragically," put in Desireé. "We, on the other hand, we tried to help your girl. We told her it was okay to go through with this, that she had friends to back her, to help her out. Together we can do this." Her voice rose, swelling at the end of this speech as though she were reciting an anthem or making a pledge on public television.

"I see," said Elaine.

"Now you gotta do something about that Linda person, Terrell's mother. She's upsetting Tina, and I almost had to haul back and clock her one myself. I will, too, if she doesn't go away."

"There's too many people in the room for me to set up the video camera," Sandy complained, hugging her large belly protectively.

Elaine figured she had been away from Tina longer than she should have been. She abruptly excused herself and rushed back to Tina's room without throwing anyone out or inviting anyone back. She about jogged around the hospital's serpentine corridors to get back to her daughter's side. Rounding a corner near the nurses' lounge, Elaine nearly collided with a pregnant girl in a surgical gown. She righted herself by catching the wall and clutching the girl's soft shoulder, snagging a skein of soft pale hair in her fingers.

"Are you all right?" asked the girl, freeing her hair.

"Gretchen?" asked Elaine. "Gretchen Ellsner?"

"I'm Gretchen Ellsner. Do I know you?"

"You probably don't remember me. I moderated the literary magazine at the middle school. You wrote stories and poems—the potbelly pig, remember?"

"Hamlet?"

"Yes, Hamlet. How is Hamlet?"

"My parents gave him to some people," said Gretchen, wearing a blank look on her face. "These friends of theirs have this farm. Well, he's happier there. I can't keep him where I'm staying now."

"How are your folks?" Elaine asked.

"I really don't know," shrugged Gretchen. "They don't talk to me any more."

"I'm sorry to hear that."

"It's okay. I'm used to it by now."

"Look, I've got to go. My daughter's waiting for me. But I'm glad I saw you."

"Yeah," said Gretchen. "Good seeing you." She waved and went on her way.

* * *

"Momma, what took you so long? Where were you? I must have had like a dozen contractions. I'm ready to have the baby by now."

"You had only two contractions," corrected Toni. "The baby won't be here before dark. She's only five centimeters dilated."

"But that's good, isn't it?" asked Elaine.

"Well, women can stay at five centimeters for hours, even days."

Tina twisted the cotton sheet and moaned. "Don't say that."

"Listen, honey," began Elaine. "I was just out in the waiting room. And it seems like even if Terrell's mom and her daughters leave, there's still a lot of people left. Are you sure you want them all here? I mean do you really want Maya, Desireé and what's her name? Sandy?"

"Really? If you really want to know, the answer is no. But I can't ask them to leave. Look over on that shelf."

Elaine cast her eyes on a shelf at the window sill loaded with opened gift boxes and shopping bags. "They gave you all that? You can still ask them to leave or at least wait in the waiting room. I'm sure they'd understand." But Elaine was not that sure at all that they would understand.

"No, Momma, I can't. Desireé's promised to make my car payment next month. Sandy's making the videotape, and Maya, she thinks she's my best friend. She's getting me a certificate to join the gym. They bought all these decorations to put on the door. It's like they paid for tickets to be here. I can't throw them out."

"I can."

"I don't want you to, Momma, that would be bad for business. But make Terrell's mother leave. If I've never asked you anything, I'm really asking you this. Don't let them back in. Do whatever you have to."

Tina was very far from never asking her mother for anything over the years, and as usual Elaine could not deny her. She would ask the woman to leave.

She returned reluctantly to the waiting room, and Maya once again sprang at her. "Can we go back in now?"

Elaine nodded, and the three women gathered their handbags and rose to head for Labor and Delivery. Terrell's mother also pulled herself up with a groan and followed Tina's coworkers, her daughters in tow.

"Wait a minute," Elaine stopped her. "Mrs.—uh—Linda, listen for a moment, please. Tina feels uncomfortable with you in the room. She doesn't know you as well as she'd like to, and she's embarrassed about giving birth in front of you and your girls here. I know you'll understand how she feels, and you can wait out here. I promise I'll tell you as soon as the baby is born."

"What are you saying?" asked the large woman, her face twisting into a scowl.

"Tina would be more comfortable if—"

"You kicking me out? Me and my girls?" She plunged a thick finger into Elaine's chest, causing her to stumble back a step. "I got all the right you got to be here. You hear me?

That is my grandchild. I got a right." Anger had sharpened her pronunciation notably. Elaine understood every word.

"You have to respect—"

"That's bullshit. You are bullshit with your Spanish words and making nice like you're all glad to be a grandmother with me. You are just bullshit." The woman swept around Elaine and strode majestically toward Tina's room as her long, slender daughters trailed, casting resentful glances back at Elaine.

The other woman was certainly stronger, but she wasn't faster. Elaine raced back to Tina's room, using another corridor. The coast was clear at the desk in front of Tina's room; she'd beaten Linda back. Elaine leaned over the counter and called one of the nurses, a pudgy girl, her snub nose peppered with freckles. "I need some help. There's a woman, she's coming this way, and she's trying to get into my daughter's room. My daughter's having a baby, and she doesn't want her there. Do you understand? Is there any way to keep her from going in my daughter's room?"

"Is she a relation?" asked the pudgy nurse in a little girl's voice.

"She's the other grandmother. She's the mother of the baby's father, but he's passed away. She's not close to my daughter. I asked her to leave, but she won't."

"Well, I can call security. What does she look like?"

"She's very big. You might have to call two security people. She's wearing old gray slippers, and she's got three daughters with her. There she is now!" Elaine felt her heart pump with fear, seeing Linda round the corner and stride up the hall.

"That black lady?"

"That's her. Can you do something?"

"There's already a whole bunch of people in that room," said the nurse. "Does your daughter want them in there?"

"I suppose. They work with her."

"So you want me to have security keep all the black people out?"

"It isn't that, for Godsake! My daughter's friend Maya is black. The midwife is black; she has to be in there. I'm not trying to keep the black people out. Some black people can come in, just not that woman, just not now."

"I can keep her out," promised the nurse, lifting a phone from its cradle. "And I'll give security a call in case I need help."

Linda was only a few steps away when Elaine slipped back into Tina's room, shutting the other woman out. She felt sick at heart—like a thief, like a coward.

* * *

Toni's prediction had been accurate; Tina stayed at five centimeters for the next four hours, after which the contractions became more frequent and more intense as she moved through true labor. All four women remained the entire time, offering Tina ice chips and lollipops, taking turns operating the video camera, shooting photos with Molly's camera, rubbing Tina's back and wiping her face with a damp washcloth. When Tina was at her worst, cursing, screaming to be released from the pain, Elaine wept, and someone snapped her picture.

When it grew dark outside, as Toni had predicted, the baby—a girl—was born. The infant emerged hot and tight like a loaf of bread and smelling of warm blood and salt. Her eyes sealed shut with the waxy stuff of birth, the baby croaked irritably as Toni placed her on Tina's bare stomach. The midwife then handed Elaine a pair of blunt-nosed scissors and told her to cut the blue-veined and snaky umbilicus, which she did quickly and neatly. The pudgy nurse with freckles took the baby into a corner of the room for cleaning and weighing.

Elaine followed her to the baby examination area. "What

happened to that woman I told you about?" Elaine asked quietly. "Is she still in the waiting room, because I ought to tell her the baby's born."

"Oh, her. She's gone."

"Where'd she go?"

"Don't know. Security took her."

"Took her where?"

"Removed her from the premises. Warned her not to come back. That's what you wanted, right?"

"I just wanted her to wait in the outer waiting room."

"Well, she made such a fuss, they had to cuff her and lead her out, right in front of those girls too. Some people..." the baby-doll voice lamented.

Wordlessly Elaine watched the nurse swab the baby. As the young woman toweled the rust-colored blood and wax from the baby's face, Elaine recognized the fathomless dark eyes and the hint of fine features under the swelling of birth. This was so clearly Linda's grandchild that Elaine felt she could keep the promise she had just made to herself. Relieved and dismayed there was no hint of her son who had died as a child, nothing of Sanders in this budding face, Elaine vowed she would not give herself away this time. She would not lose herself in this child as she had lost herself in her own children. She would not love this one too hard; she would take Aaron's advice and be careful, very, very careful, keep herself safe this once.

The nurse slipped a duck patterned gown over the baby, pulled the drawstring and wrapped her in a receiving blanket. "Here," she said, thrusting the little packet she had trussed at Elaine. "Here, you want to hold her?"

Elaine cradled the baby to her breast. The baby stared up at her with Linda's eyes, but the expression was not Linda's. It was oddly familiar; it was a look of benediction, forgiveness, a look of pity, even. Elaine touched the infant's head with her lips—already it was too late for promises to keep herself safe. That time had passed in an instant, without her knowing it, and she had lost her chance. She felt like someone who only noticed she had stumbled off a cliff after she had been tumbling for some time in the abyss.

Elaine glanced up to see that the coven had made a semi-circle around one side of Tina's bed. Someone, Maya maybe, called out a question to Elaine. They seemed to be beckoning her to join them, but Elaine wouldn't listen, didn't want to move. She considered how they kept drawing and redrawing circles, putting people in and out, and how she had been a part of that, turning Terrell's mother away as she had. Elaine thought of the Ellsner girl estranged from her parents, and she couldn't understand the impulse to draw people in only to shut them out, and she hoped she never would. She would go to look for that gambling place on Lexington the same night, she'd find the other grandmother, buy her a strong drink and have one too.

Elaine held the baby close and swayed slightly on the balls of her feet, rocking her. She might even stop in to see the Ellsner girl. Glancing at Tina in the bed, Elaine was beginning to see how it was more important for a daughter to get the right mother than for a mother to have the kind of daughter she wanted. She remembered how she had pained her own direct and forthright mother with her vagueness, her chronic uncertainty. Yet Elaine's mother had loved her despite these weaknesses; she had drawn her in and never put her out. Elaine wondered what the right grandmother would count for in this baby's life and if she would have the chance to be that.

Staring deep into the infant's calm eyes, she pretended she could not see the women gesturing from the side of Tina's bed, could not hear them calling. Soon they would place Tina on the outside; Elaine was certain of that. And Tina would make her own circle with the baby. This thing that Elaine feared could overwhelm and ruin her daughter might be the one thing that could save her. Elaine could see that now, as she saw how tenuous her place in Tina's circle would continue to be, how she would keep being drawn in and out. She would lose this baby again and again. But for now, all she wanted was to hold on—just for a moment—before bringing the baby to the others by the bed. They were saying her name now, calling her. She could hear them clearly, even though they still seemed very far away.

Lorraine López has worked as an educator for over a dozen years. She has taught middle school, high school, and at the college level. She completed her undergraduate degree at California State University, Northridge, and earned her Master of Arts and doctoral degrees at the University of Georgia. Her stories have appeared in numerous publications, including *New Letters*, *The Crab Orchard Review*, *The U.S. Latino Review*, and *The Watershed Anthology*. She is Co-Founder and Education Programs Director for the Institute for Violence Prevention in Athens, Georgia, and she teaches English at Brenau University in Gainesville, Georgia.

CURBSTONE PRESS, INC.

is a non-profit publishing house dedicated to literature that reflects a
commitment to social change, with an emphasis on contemporary writing
from Latino, Latin American and Vietnamese cultures. Curbstone presents
writers who give voice to the unheard in a language that goes beyond
denunciation to celebrate, honor and teach. Curbstone builds bridges
between its writers and the public – from inner-city to rural areas, colleges
to community centers, children to adults. Curbstone seeks out the highest
aesthetic expression of the dedication to human rights and intercultural
understanding: poetry, testimonies, novels, stories,
and children's books.

This mission requires more than just producing books. It requires ensuring
that as many people as possible learn about these books and read them. To
achieve this, a large portion of Curbstone's schedule is dedicated to
arranging tours and programs for its authors, working with public school
and university teachers to enrich curricula, reaching out to underserved
audiences by donating books and conducting readings and community
programs, and promoting discussion in the media. It is only through these
combined efforts that literature can truly make a difference.

Curbstone Press, like all non-profit presses, depends on the support of
individuals, foundations, and government agencies to bring you, the reader,
works of literary merit and social significance which might not find a place
in profit-driven publishing channels, and to bring the authors and their
books into communities across the country. Our sincere thanks to the many
individuals, foundations, and government agencies who support this
endeavor: J. Walton Bissell Foundation, Connecticut Commission on the
Arts, Connecticut Humanities Council, Daphne Seybolt Culpeper
Foundation, Fisher Foundation, Greater Hartford Arts Council, Hartford
Courant Foundation, J. M. Kaplan Fund, Eric Mathieu King Fund, John D.
and Catherine T. MacArthur Foundation, National Endowment for the Arts,
Open Society Institute, Puffin Foundation, and the Woodrow Wilson
National Fellowship Foundation.

Please help to support Curbstone's efforts to present the diverse voices and
views that make our culture richer. Tax-deductible donations can be made by
check or credit card to:
Curbstone Press, 321 Jackson Street, Willimantic, CT 06226
phone: (860) 423-5110   fax: (860) 423-9242
www.curbstone.org

IF YOU WOULD LIKE TO BE A MAJOR SPONSOR OF A
CURBSTONE BOOK, PLEASE CONTACT US.